Across the Kala Pani

Shevlyn Mottai

Published in 2022 by Penguin Random House South Africa (Pty) Ltd
Company Reg. No. 1953/000441/07
The Estuaries No. 4, Oxbow Crescent, Century Avenue, Century City, 7441, South Africa
PO Box 1144, Cape Town, 8000, South Africa
www.penguinrandomhouse.co.za

© 2022 Shevlyn Mottai

All rights reserved.
No part of this book may be reproduced or transmitted in any form
or by any means, mechanical or electronic, including photocopying
and recording, or be stored in any information storage or retrieval system,
without written permission from the publisher.

First edition, first printing 2022
Reprinted 2023

3 5 7 9 8 6 4 2

ISBN 978-1-4859-0486-1 (Print)

ISBN 978-1-77638-032-9 (ePub)

Cover images: portrait of a young Indian woman (detail): photographer unknown, 1870s,
courtesy of the Jane and Howard Ricketts Collection;
ship image: Robert W Buller News, Service postcard, 1907
Quotations on the opening pages of the five parts of this book were
sourced from the University of KwaZulu-Natal, Special Collections,
Gandhi-Luthuli Documentation Centre.

Cover design by publicide
Text design by Chérie Collins
Set in 12 on 16 pt Adobe Garamond Pro

Printed and bound by Novus Print, a Novus Holdings company

This novel is dedicated to the Indian women of indenture –
those who took a leap of faith against tremendous odds.
Your sacrifices were not in vain.
With your wings, we soar.

Author's note

In August 1834, Britain passed the Slavery Abolition Act, outlawing the owning, buying and selling of humans as property throughout its colonies around the world. As a result, these colonies suddenly found themselves in dire need of cheap, easily acquired labour.

'Indentured labour', a system of bonded labour in which workers signed a contract in their own countries to work abroad, usually for a period of five years, was introduced. Between 1834 and the end of the First World War in 1917, more than two million Indian indentured labourers were recruited to work on sugar-cane, cotton and tea plantations in colonies including Fiji, Mauritius, Ceylon, Trinidad, Guyana, Malaysia, Uganda, Kenya and South Africa. Many of those who signed up were fleeing poverty and starvation, and/or were deceived or coerced by unscrupulous recruiters.

Indians were first sent to what was then the Colony of Natal in 1860. These indentured workers (known derogatively as 'coolies') were meant to receive wages and, eventually, a small plot of land, or a return passage to India once their contract was over. In reality, in the 1900s, heavy taxes were imposed on those who wanted to go back home to India, effectively putting a return passage out of their reach.

In addition, some of the indentured chose to stay at the end of their contract, as, by crossing the 'black water', they had broken caste and would probably not be accepted back into Indian society and would bring shame on their families. Many women had left India because they had already been ostracised by their communities because they were unmarried or widowed or were from lower castes; they were even less likely to be accepted back.

The first journeys from India to South Africa took twelve weeks, and conditions on the ships were inhumane, similar to those on slave ships, with diseases like dysentery, cholera and measles rampant. The conditions on the plantations were equally harsh, with long working hours in all weather conditions, and low wages. Children were expected to work alongside their parents from the time they were five years old, and whippings for the slightest infraction were common.

Many workers tried to escape this unforgiving life but were almost inevitably recaptured and imprisoned; sometimes their initial five-year contract was doubled to ten years for attempted desertion.

In June 1909 my great-grandfather Sappani Mottai, then twenty-seven years old, a one-year-old female child listed as Padvattal Mottai and a twenty-year-old woman named Munichi Ramasami left Madras on the ship *Umzinto*. Stories about their arrival and subsequent life in South Africa were passed down through the generations, but very little was known about the woman Sappani had arrived with, apart from the fact that she had not been his wife in India.

A note on the terminology

The terms 'kaffir' (also spelt 'kafir'), 'native' and 'coolie' were used freely in official documentation and newspapers in the time and place in which this novel is set – India and South Africa at the turn of the twentieth century. Although historically accurate, these terms are very offensive. I have used them to support the narrative as well as to stay true to the context of the novel.

Place names are used as they were at the time in which this novel is set.

Southern India

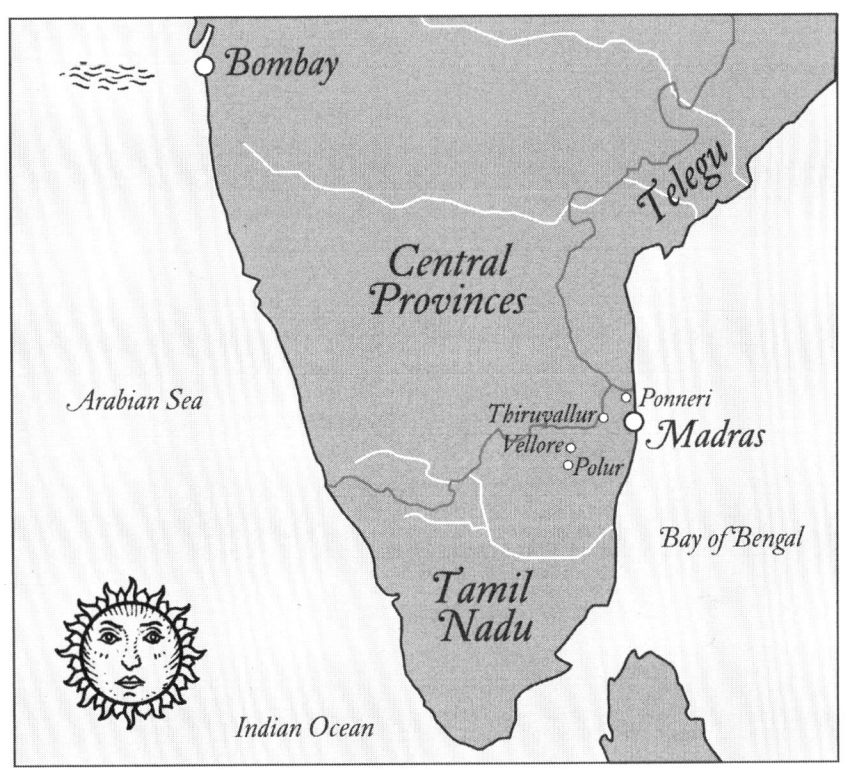

East Coast of South Africa

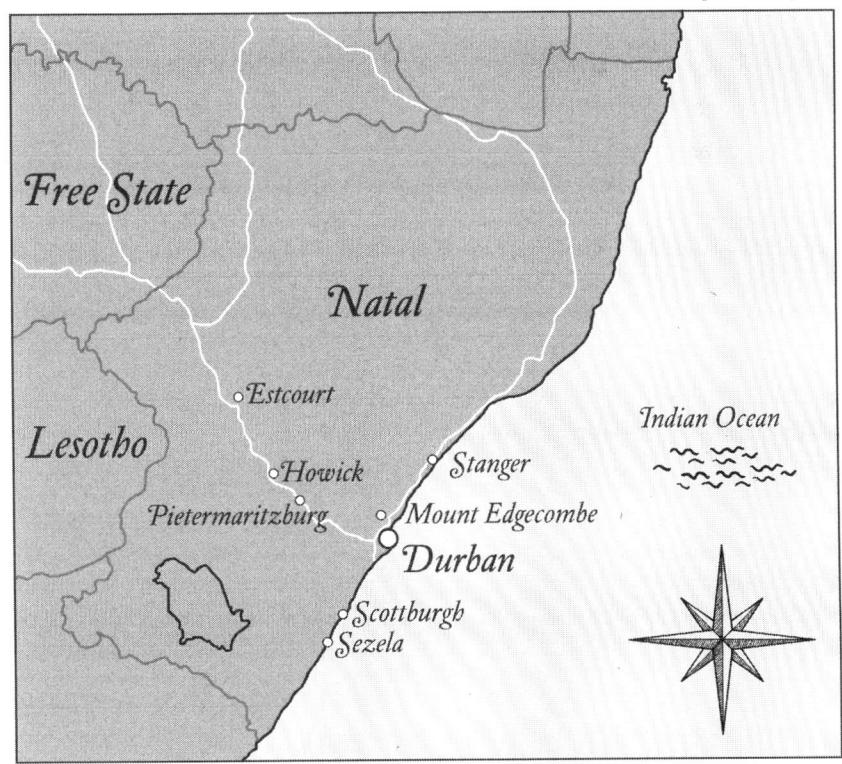

Contents

Part I: Recruitment   13

Part II: Crossing   61

Part III: Arrival   109

Part IV: Tribulation   159

Part V: Home   223

PART I

RECRUITMENT

By 1830 the Industrial Revolution which had changed the material prosperity of Britain had left India economically poor. The slump in the cotton industry was accompanied by wide-scale unemployment, which caused many to seek work among the large peasant population of village India. But even the land was not secure, subject as it was to recurrent droughts accompanied by starvation on a huge scale.

– Indians Overseas: A Guide to Source Materials in the India Office Records for the Study of Indian Emigration, 1830–1950

I
Coolie camp, Madras
April 1909

Sappani stared vacantly at the snaking lines of Indians as they filed through the gates of the coolie camp. All were cloaked in a dusty film of mud and poverty, but their optimistically raised voices revealed their relief and hope – a sharp contrast to what Sappani himself was feeling.

A few days ago, he had stood in those very same lines, with the very same hopes. Now he was a different man – a helpless man, with nothing and no idea how to move beyond this moment.

Seyan, his son, barely a year old, was asleep in his arms, his mouth open, his head lolling back. Sappani paced past the hospital shed – just a few rooms with a thatched roof – and back across the dusty courtyard. His eyes were fixed on the entrance, on every movement there.

Four days ago his wife Neela had been carried into the hospital shed, and the news since then had not been good.

The two-week journey on foot from the village of Polur in North Arcot on the Palar River in southeastern India, to Madras, this eastern port city on the Coromandel Coast of the Bay of Bengal, had been difficult for Neela. Along with other recruits from their village, they had joined the arkatis, whose job it was to get as many Indians as possible to sign up for indentured labour in the British colonies. Only when they stopped and in the subdepots – small camps along the roadside – would Neela have a chance to rest.

'Let's go back, Neela. Maybe when you are better we can try again.' He thought about how he had begged her.

Sappani could still hear an echo of her voice, soft but determined. 'There's nothing left here in India for us, nothing for Seyan.' She had said it so often that the doubt that Sappani felt would grow silent for a time.

During the day, to give Neela some respite, Sappani sometimes would leave his wife resting in a subdepot and take the baby with him into a nearby village. There, they would watch the villagers collect water or firewood and go about their lives.

Sometimes, though, he would stay in the subdepot, and watch and listen as the British-paid arkatis delivered their well-rehearsed speeches and promises to the crowds. 'In South Africa, gold coins grow like chillies on trees and there's work for every man and woman. Natal is booming,' they said.

The gathered men and women always had the same questions. What work could they do? What would they earn? Could they take their families with them? And how soon could they return to home?

The men and women who joined were mostly pariahs, the lowest in the caste system. Usually, their jobs were menial: they worked on the lands owned by the superior Brahmin caste, swept roads and removed dead animal carcasses.

For the weavers, who for centuries had supplied their own countrymen with high-quality printed cotton fabrics, and whose exquisite floral chintzes, khassas and bandannas had been in high demand among the elite in England and Europe, the invention of the steam engine had been a death knell: not only did Britain impose punitive import duties on incoming Indian textiles, but exports of British goods to India increased, and cheap, machine-made cottons from Manchester flooded Indian markets. The weavers simply could not compete.

Those who planted and harvested their own food, tending modest patches of land that sustained extended families, and sometimes even having enough over to sell or trade, now too felt the pangs of starvation. The dry season had gone on for too long and food crops that had once thrived lay limp and burnt in the surrounding fields.

Sappani's father had worked the land, and Sappani had done the same. A cane knife had first been placed in his tiny hands at the age of four, and he'd learnt quickly how to swing it. He'd been taught how to dig neat, endless furrows in hot fields and nurture the buds of the seedlings until they became stronger, from sun up to sun down, for as long as he could remember.

When the British government had introduced the land revenue system in order to milk as much money as possible from the peasants, families like the Mottais had found that they couldn't grow enough food to feed themselves and pay the required taxes. Sappani had offered his labour to other landowners but the work wasn't reliable and sometimes there would be forty men when only five were needed.

In the subdepots, once the women and children had gone to sleep, the men would talk among themselves. Perched on tree stumps and logs around the dwindling embers of a fire, they'd share their hopes and dreams. The poorest yearned for Natal, a place without castes, where everyone was mixed up together. Others spoke about steady work and the chance for their families to know what a full stomach felt like. They spoke about the other busy port, in Calcutta in northeast India, where thousands of Indians were also signing up and leaving for countries all over the world, to places that Sappani had not even heard of – Mauritius, Fiji, Guyana, Jamaica.

Sappani listened intently as the men shared stories they'd heard about life in Natal. Some told of a place of lushness and justice, where free men and women could raise their children in the sun, where the rain fell reliably and regularly to feed crops that sprang green and golden from the fertile soil, where just five years of hard work would earn for a committed indentured labourer a lifetime of contentment for himself and his family.

But others told of the rape of women and the natives who did not take well to the arrival of coolies, and of wages that were barely sufficient to keep a person alive, and which were docked for the slightest infraction, and of regular whippings.

'It's just a new way to have slaves,' an older man with a grey beard said, shaking his head dolefully.

'Mohandas Karamchand Gandhi – he's a lawyer, a very good one,' countered a young man with bright eyes. 'He is fighting for the settled Indians in Durban to vote, even, and making sure those bastards treat us well.'

'Let's hope, bhai, that he wins, then,' another man said and they all nodded in agreement.

Seyan stirred as he shifted in his father's arms. Sappani gently rocked the little boy until his thick eyelashes met, fluttered, then were still. His breathing fell into a steady rhythm again.

There was some commotion in the courtyard. Two guards were roughly carrying a man out the gate, his legs dragging behind him as if they belonged to someone else. From the shouting, it was clear that he had failed the doctor's examination and could not be allowed on the ship. Sappani watched as the man begged, then began to cry openly and angrily, his shoulders heaving as he kicked and spat like a cobra. A third guard threw his clothes after him and they slammed the gate shut. The man collapsed in the dust, weeping, clinging with his dirty hands to the fence around the camp.

A crowd had gathered, questions being asked and voices raised. Then word spread like a monsoon flood; the man's testicles were enlarged, a certain sign of venereal disease.

Every recruit had to be checked by the doctors and nurses for diseases like cholera, chickenpox, dysentery and sexually transmitted infections, as well as anything that may mean they weren't capable of hard work or, worse, might pass on infectious illnesses to the others. Only when they were checked and vaccinated were they permitted to join the coolie camp, as a prelude to being assigned a spot on an outbound ship. They would have to remain isolated in the camp until all available places on the ship were assigned to healthy Indians – the vessel wouldn't leave the docks in Madras until it was full. During that isolation and waiting period, nobody could leave the camp, so that no new illnesses would be brought in when they returned.

Sappani winced with the memory of his own inspection. The British officials in the coolie camp hadn't been slow to get the Indians to do exactly what they wanted them to do, flourishing sticks and threats with equal ease. Crude demonstrations showed that the Indians should remove their dhotis and cup their testicles for inspection. They had also checked Sappani's teeth, ears and hands – callouses were a good sign; they showed that a man was accustomed to hard labour.

Once they had passed their medical inspection, the Indians were to stay in the camp, behind the high fences, under the watchful eyes of the soldiers. These rules were in place not only to prevent them from getting any illnesses, but also to ensure that the Indians who'd signed up didn't give in to second thoughts before the ship was ready to depart.

Sappani had been given the all-clear and had been sent to complete the indenture contracts. The arkatis explained the conditions of the contract in the respective Indians' native languages, their words sliding easily off their tongues into desperate ears. The men shuffled forward and signed the papers. Those who were illiterate confirmed their indenture with inky thumbprints.

The white officials doing the paperwork were sweating and ill tempered. Cramped inside the tents, pink and irritable, they had great difficulty with the Indian names. Names were often misspelt, or shortened, or simply omitted. Family names that had been used for generations were butchered using pens instead of knives or swords.

If this was going to be the start of something new for his family, Sappani knew he had to get his name recorded correctly. He had taken special care as he wrote out his details: *Sappani Mottai, indenture number 140316, age 27*.

He'd felt a surge of pride that he could spell his name and make sure that it was written down accurately. His ability to read and write had been a gift from the persistent Christian missionaries who had come to India in a steady stream, and whose sole purpose had been to convert the heathens and turn them away from their idolatry. Most families in Sappani's village had sent their sons along to the mission schools when they were not needed in the fields. They listened to stories about Jesus and were taught to read using the Bible. Sappani was a quick learner and enjoyed sitting crosslegged under the neem trees, practising the English alphabet on his slate board.

His mind circled back to Neela. The doctor who'd inspected her hadn't been pleased with her condition. She was too thin and very weak. After more questions, the doctor had put it down to her being undernourished. He'd given her medication and instructed her to stay in the medical tent so that they could keep an eye on her.

At first, this news had been welcome: Sappani had thought that she would get better and they would be together. However, since then he hadn't been allowed to see her, and all he'd heard since was that she had been moved to quarantine as there was a risk of infection.

In the coolie camp the number of Indians rose and fell. More arrived and stayed, while some were turned away. A few, once the initial excitement of being recruited had died down, and the temptingly shimmering goal of a new life across the black water had tarnished somewhat, realised that leaving India was a mistake and escaped from the camp at the first opportunity.

The arkatis had been instructed by their British bosses that forty per cent of the indentured Indians had to be females, as there were far too many men in Natal; they needed more women. The indentured men wanted to have families and often preyed on the wives of other men; this led to violent attacks and a spread of venereal diseases among the Indians.

The authorities were all for the indentured men setting up families, as not only did this mean that any children would be born into indenture as well, but the Indians seemed to work harder when they had little mouths to feed. And there was a fiscal reason for wanting women, too:

for half the wages, they got workers whose smaller hands meant that they could pick the youngest leaves of the tea plants without doing any damage.

Single women who arrived at the coolie camp were often those who'd been shamed – widows, and those whose husbands no longer wanted them. They were mostly welcomed, but being locked away in the crowded camp while they waited for the ship to fill up, with the added indignity of the medical inspections, made many rethink their decision. Like shadows, they would slink away quietly at night, past the soldiers on patrol, never to be seen again.

Sappani found himself missing his old misery; at least then Neela had been nearby and Seyan had had his mother. Life in the village was familiar and that had been comforting. They'd barely been surviving on one paltry meal a day but at least they were together. Maybe this was punishment for thinking that he, as a pariah, could do better than a life of servitude.

The sun was sinking low and Sappani knew that soon the bell would ring to signal time to eat. If he wasn't quick, Seyan would have to go without the daily ration of dhal and rice. Shifting the sleeping child to his other shoulder, he approached the hospital shed.

'Can I see her, please? The boy needs his mother,' he said to the nurse, who knew by now who he was.

'She's sick, and she could make you sick as well, and you have a baby to think of too,' the nurse replied and turned her back to him as she continued to roll a pile of bandages.

Sappani stood there as if he hadn't understood a word she'd said. Perhaps realising that she'd been a bit harsh, the nurse added, 'This is the best place for her.' She walked in through the curtains.

Outside, Sappani waited until Seyan screamed to be fed.

The next day, Sappani resumed his position outside the hospital shed. The doctor emerged, his grave face confirming Sappani's fears. 'Your wife is not getting better,' he said flatly. 'We tried but now she has dysentery too. It may be too late.'

'But there must be something ...?' Sappani pleaded.

'She should have been brought here straight away. Others could also get sick,' the doctor chided. 'We could have quarantined her and kept this from spreading.'

Sappani stared at him, dejected. He knew that whatever he said would make no difference.

Chinmah, just fourteen years old and already showing the telltale bump of a baby on the way, had heard the women talking about Sappani. She had seen the father carrying his son, waiting in the courtyard for news of his wife. That afternoon, she offered to play with the child while Sappani took the chance to have a wash and check if there was news about Neela.

Rubbing her hands over her own swollen belly, she hoped that her husband Ramsamy would in time pay some attention to her condition, and the fact that they would soon have a baby of their own. So far, he hadn't shown any interest, or any emotion one way or another.

Her husband was almost twice her age. Her poverty-stricken parents had seen fit to marry her off to him, even though he was considered somewhat odd by the villagers. Chinmah's father, a toddy tapper, had had an accident a year before that had plunged the entire family into poverty. He'd been up a coconut tree when a snake had scared him, and he'd lost his grip and fallen to the ground. He was now an invalid, unable to move the lower half of his body.

Ramsamy, a skinny man who lived in their village, was aloof and spoke to nobody. His mother had become desperate after his younger brothers were married, and still Ramsamy showed no interest in finding a bride, even at the age of twenty-six.

Then the arkati recruiter had arrived in the village and told them about the promised land. Ramsamy had become obsessed, pleading with his mother to allow him to go. He'd return after five years, he promised, with plenty of money in his pocket.

His mother, who knew her son only too well, was unconvinced. As it was, his family couldn't rely on him to provide for them – he would often be seen near the river, wandering about in a dreamlike state. 'Who will take care of you there?' she asked him.

'I will find a wife there,' he said.

But his mother had a better idea: she would give him her blessing to leave, she said, if he agreed to be married first. Secretly, she'd thought that once he got married, he might give up the idea of emigrating and would settle down to life in the village.

The tiny dowry they'd offered for Chinmah – three chickens, three saris and a little money – couldn't be refused by people who had nothing. She'd been married to him a week later, seeing him for the first time as they circled the hawan, the fire prepared especially for the marriage rituals.

Later, with the sounds of the wedding guests still rising into the dark sky outside, Ramsamy had crawled on top of her, ignoring her screams. After that first night, Chinmah did not scream again. She realised that this nighttime assault was something that, as a wife, she had to accept.

The doctor announced that Neela's condition had worsened overnight.

Feeling useless and frustrated, Sappani left Seyan asleep on Chinmah's lap. He walked to the fence that ran around the camp. The street wallahs sold all manner of things and Sappani decided on a few sticky, plump gulab jamuns – some for Seyan and some for Chinmah who he thought would enjoy something sweet. He remembered how much Neela had enjoyed them when she was pregnant with Seyan.

He was on his way back when he saw the nurse scanning the yard, looking for someone. Terror gripping him, he increased his pace, but Chinmah appeared in front of him, the baby clutched to her chest and her mouth set in fierce determination.

'She is gone, bhai,' she said.

Seyan reached out for his father but Sappani didn't move his arms from his sides. The gulab jamuns fell from his numb hand. His knees quivered and he flailed briefly before he fell to the ground.

Chinmah tried to help him up as Seyan screamed for his father but Sappani had slipped into another world and began to wail and beat his chest. The baby cried louder and Chinmah struggled to keep her balance and hold the boy.

Other women and men helped Sappani to his feet and led him to a place where he could sit. He watched, slack-jawed, as flies with iridescent wings and metallic bodies covered the sticky gulab jamuns and began to gorge themselves.

The nurse approached Sappani and this time she was softer, kinder. 'We gave her treatment but she was too sick already. She held on for as long she could. I am sorry.'

'Was she in pain?' Sappani whispered, his mouth as dry as dust.

'No, she was not. She was at peace and pain-free until the end.'

The nurse turned and moved away.

Sappani tried to follow. 'I am sorry, you can't. The dysentery is very contagious so no one can view the body. We will do the cremation in the funeral ghat in the morning.'

In the yard it seemed like even the breeze had paused. There was an unnatural calm, the heat rising from the ground in lazy coils, with only the calling of the street wallahs and the occasional child's cry to be heard. A slow trickle of people gathered around Sappani, who had slipped from his seated position and lay once again in the dirt. Some watched in silence as he wept. Others, mostly women, lifted the edges of their pallu and wiped their tears away and moved on.

Sappani wept for Neela, from a place that he did not even know he had. His guilt held him in a vice: he was to blame for taking her away from the village; it had been his idea, and this seemed like a punishment for defying his circumstances. A waterfall of regret cascaded over his grief.

His anguish was powerful and all-consuming. As Neela's frail body grew stiff a few yards away, her husband's tears sprang from new wells.

Sappani lost track of how long he lay in the dust in exactly the same spot. His mind had no single coherent thought.

Meanwhile, Chinmah did her best to keep the child quiet, but he was inconsolable.

With the dawn came the dread of what this new day would bring. Sappani walked to the fence and looked out at the Indian Ocean, his fingers gripping the mesh tightly, as if it were the only thing holding him upright.

The sun glimmered like a newly lit fire above the Bay of Bengal and a dreamy orange glow touched the silken waves. It lulled his soul briefly, before bringing the realisation that Neela was going to be cremated on a funeral pyre today.

Sappani scanned the bay for rising smoke from the funeral ghats along the shoreline. He had to say goodbye to her.

Leaving the camp was a risk, but one he was willing to take. If he was caught he could be denied re-entry to the camp and sent on his way. But the soldiers who'd been on night patrol were usually sleepy at this time of the morning and less likely to notice movement among their charges. Sappani took advantage of a delivery of goods at the gates, slipping out under cover of the noise and confusion as boxes and bags of supplies were being hauled in.

Along the cut-out steps of the ghats on the river bank, the burning pits were already alight. The reflection of the flames danced on the murky water that washed in from the sea. Here, the water, thick with ash, was reduced to a grey sludge, as if the sea itself was refusing the offer of the dead. Columns of smoke the same grey as the water hung in the air. The acrid smell burnt Sappani's nostrils and the heat of the flames brought him out in a sweat.

He made enquiries about any bodies coming from the coolie camp and was told that the doms, a low caste whose job was to perform the last rites and cremate the dead, had yet to fetch them. Sappani waited, crouched on his haunches some distance away, watching the doms who, wearing only dhotis, tended to the dead.

The sun was directly overhead when one of the doms called for Sappani.

The body-burner removed the cloth covering a lifeless form on a bamboo bier. Sappani gasped and reached out to touch his dead wife, but his hand was quickly caught by the dom to prevent the forbidden contact. Tears streamed down Sappani's cheeks as he took in Neela's face: thinner, her cheeks sunken, her dark hair making her complexion look as if it was made of wax.

The doms hoisted the bier onto their shoulders and walked out into the sea until the water lapped around their waists. Briefly, they immersed Neela's body before carrying her back to the shore and laying the bier on the cut-out stairs to dry while they made some final checks on the funeral pyre itself.

Large piles of logs were arranged at the edge of the ghats. They were different prices, and Sappani knew that it would be the cheaper mango-wood logs that would have been secured by the authorities for Neela's pyre. He had nothing to offer the doms to buy the more expensive sandalwood logs, which burnt quicker.

Sappani pleaded with the doms, who finally relented and let him help them. They mumbled orders, telling Sappani how many logs he would need, and how to stack them to ensure that the body would burn fully so that moksha would be completed. One of the doms offered Sappani a pot of ghee, showing him how to liberally spread it over the logs beneath the bier to keep the fire burning.

The doms chanted in unison as they lowered the bier with Neela's body onto the raised platform of logs, her feet facing south, in the direction of the realm of Yama, the god of death. A dom handed Sappani a flaming kusha twig to set the body alight, so that Neela's soul could be offered up to Agni, the god of fire. Once the body was ablaze, the doms dragged heavier logs over it, so that the corpse would not sit upright when the heat caused the muscles to contract.

Raging now, the fire hissed and smouldered, fuelled by the ghee and fanned by the wind. It grew. Crackling and bursting, the flames received the offering, purifying the soul and freeing it from the body.

A cow edged closer and slowly settled next to the fire.

Sappani watched as its head lolled, its ears twitching occasionally. It ate a few marigolds that had been left behind by mourners carrying out last rites, tucked its hooves beneath its body, and closed its eyes in blissful sleep.

The smell of burning ghee now mingled with the sandalwood powder that the doms had scattered over the pyre to disguise the smell of burning hair. Her hair, her beautiful hair! Sappani choked at the thought and a fresh bludgeon of despair hit him. His pain left no room for anything else; like the fire, it was all-consuming.

Nearby, a group of holy men began their prayers at the water's edge. They sang bhajans, mournful songs about grief and loss, and the sound wrapped around Sappani like a blanket. Grey tendrils of incense and the rhythmic chanting from the holy men rose, dancing within the coils of smoke.

The doms sat on their haunches and idly poked at the pyre, as if cooking a meal over it. They lit and tended to other pyres, and Sappani waited through the day, watching the sun track across the sky, occasionally looking up to the camp, wondering if his absence had been noted. His hope was that the bureaucracy required to move him from the family section into the men's quarters would temporarily disguise his absence. Chinmah had insisted that she keep Seyan with her – the men's quarters was no place for a child, she'd said. Sappani was pleased that Seyan wasn't with him, and hoped that the child was in a deep sleep with dreams of his mother.

Later, the doms shared their meagre food with Sappani, then let him sleep, promising to wake him when it was time.

Sappani's grief was so sharp that he'd thought he would never sleep again, but instead his exhaustion dragged him into darkness, despite the fact that he was curled up directly on the filthy river bank. He woke the next morning with a dom poking him with a stick.

Placing both palms together and tipping his head, Sappani thanked the doms and took the clay urn containing Neela's ashes. He waded out into the bay with it held high above his head. The cool water lapped around his legs and then his waist. For a moment he thought about dipping his head below the waves and being done with it all but Neela's concern haunted him: 'What about Seyan?'

Without any ceremony, he turned the urn over and emptied his wife's ashes into the water. He watched them float on the surface for a while, hovering, uncertain. Then he turned and waded back to the shore.

Sappani watched the gates of the camp from a distance. A breeze skittered across the camp, stirring the stench of the depot, where the contents of the latrines flowed through an open sewer.

Sappani crept closer. It was time for the morning meal, and a few women were gathered near the gate, buying coconuts and betelnut from the street wallahs who carefully kept their distance, stretching their hands out to exchange their goods for rupees. Sappani stepped forward casually, thinking this was a good chance to slip in.

'Where do you think you are going, hah?' bellowed an Indian soldier. His uniform was clean and new, which meant that he was probably still taking his job seriously.

Sappani froze, his mind frantically trying to think of a response. He opened his mouth and closed it again.

'You pugla! You know you are not allowed outside the camp gates!' a young woman said, taking his arm. Clicking her tongue in irritation, she scolded him, 'You are lucky you have taken just one step. If you had crossed the road, you would have been in real trouble.' Rolling her eyes in exaggerated exasperation, she addressed the soldier. 'Sir, forgive my husband. He doesn't listen.'

Sappani stared at the woman. She looked to be about twenty years old, with large, luminous eyes and a light complexion. Her English was flawless.

Her outburst had created a scene and several people slowed down to watch. The soldier looked at the two of them, mildly amused, and turned to Sappani. 'Looks like you will get into more trouble with her than me.'

Holding him tightly by the elbow and frogmarching him away, the woman whispered, 'I'm Vottie. Just walk with me,' then, loudly, she added, 'I can't trust you to do anything on your own!'

Struck dumb, Sappani allowed the woman to lead him away, grumbling about how he was indeed the good-for-nothing her appah had warned her about.

Losing interest, the soldier instructed the crowd to move along, while Vottie steered Sappani around a corner of a tent, where she finally loosened her iron grip on his arm. 'I will let Chinmah know you are back,' she said. 'We were getting worried about you, for Seyan's sake.'

'Thank you,' was all Sappani could manage.

Over the next few days, Sappani felt restless. He had insisted on taking Seyan back with him to the men's quarters, but the men did not want the crying child there. Most nights, Sappani would pace the camp, the restless and often whimpering child in his arms.

Sappani could see that during the day, when Seyan was with Vottie and Chinmah, the little boy was settled and at ease. Chinmah, who seemed to be barely more than a child herself, had a wonderful connection with the baby, probably because she was soon going to be a mother.

With each passing day, Sappani doubted more and more that he could raise his child on his own. He thought about returning home, going back to his father and begging for forgiveness. As the only son, it had been his responsibility to look after his parents but he had made the decision to leave, promising to send them money as soon as he could. His father had especially not wanted Neela and Seyan to leave – he had doted on the boy.

Sappani recalled, with a painful knot in his stomach, how, on the morning of their departure, he had knelt and touched his father's feet with each hand, waiting for his blessing. But his father had stared blankly ahead and not said a word.

Sappani shook his head as if to dislodge the idea: he could not, anyway, return to his village without his wife, where it would be clear to everyone that her death was his fault. More than ever now, he needed to get on that ship, but his chances were much reduced without someone who would be a mother to Seyan. When they reached their destination, he would not be able to care for such a young child and work on a plantation too.

Sappani was sitting with his back against a small, crooked tree in the dusty centre of the camp when Babuji, one of the arkatis, came to sit alongside him. From neighbouring districts, they both spoke Tamil and English.

'When do you think we will go, then?' Sappani asked.

'I don't know,' the arkati said, sounding annoyed, and offered Sappani some of the paan he was rolling. Sappani declined. 'Every time I think maybe today I've done enough, they tell me the number of Indians is still not enough.'

Babuji's irritation was partly because, despite getting all the recruits safely to the Madras camp, he would only be paid for those who made it onto the ship.

During his nightly walks with Seyan, Sappani had seen Babuji bringing women into the camp. Their stories were as commonplace as rice: they had brought disgrace on their households so their families had disowned them – concubines, widows who had stood to inherit their husbands' land but who had been turned out by their families so that they could be rich instead, women with serious illnesses.

'I had no sleep last night. Too much of trouble,' Babuji continued self-indulgently. It was clear that Sappani did not know what he meant so he decided to elaborate. 'You know how we have to get as many ladies as possible? Some ran away last night. I had to go looking for them. Thatuvani mundas,' he spat.

Sappani nodded as if he understood the complexity of Babuji's job.

Babuji chewed his paan thoughtfully, then expertly ejected a bright red stream of juice through the gap in his front teeth. 'So very sad about your wife, bhai,' he said.

Sappani nodded, then decided to seize the moment. 'Babuji, I need your help. I need to find another wife; my son needs a mother.'

In Babuji's eyes, Sappani could see the glimmer of greed. 'What would be a good price for a new wife at such short notice?' the arkati mused aloud, extending a hand.

Sappani placed the last few shillings he had on Babuji's open palm, then he got up, dusted off his khurta and went in search of Seyan.

2

Thiruvallur, Vellore, South India
1906

It was just before Lutchmee's sixteenth birthday when her parents told her about her impending marriage to Vikram. Vikram, two years older, was from an important family, new landowners whose farm provided the village market with mangoes and nuts.

'He is a good match. At least you won't ever need mangoes in your house,' her mother had said playfully.

Vikram was a timid creature, small for his age, and with widely spaced teeth. His mother had constantly fussed over him, her only son, sometimes even yelling at the river's edge for him to come inside while all the other parents were happy to be rid of their children for a little while. His father had died only a year before and his mother seemed to hold onto him even tighter after that.

When Lutchmee's mother had approached Vikram's mother for a wedding date, Vikram's mother wouldn't agree. 'I need to see that she can give me grandchildren first. She has not bled yet,' she'd retorted, throwing her sari pallu over her shoulder as she shut the door.

Lutchmee waited eagerly for the bleeding to arrive, but when it did, she was confused. It seemed like a big deal was made for nothing. It was painful and messy and she did not enjoy trying to wash the bloodied rags in the river, away from prying eyes.

A message was sent to Vikram's mother and the marriage agreement was drafted by the priest. As part of the pre-wedding rituals, a meeting was arranged at Vikram's house and both families exchanged trays of bananas, betelnut and coconut as a symbol of the intention to join their families.

Excited to break away and begin a life of her own, Lutchmee did not mind that her mother-in-law made all the arrangements. It seemed acceptable for her mamiyar to even decide on how the bride should wear her hair. After all, it was a chance for Vikram's family to show off their wealth. Vikram's mother wanted everyone to gawk at the bride's wedding jewellery, gold valayals the colour of turmeric and matching earrings, and the Kanchipuram sari with gold thread that she had bought at great expense.

At dawn on the day of their wedding, priests performed the nelengu ceremony in their separate homes. As part of the cleansing rituals, brass bowls containing turmeric paste, kumkum and sandalwood oil were prepared by the married women and applied to the bride and groom's hair and skin. A bath in holy water to cleanse their bodies and souls followed, and they were then able to get ready for their wedding.

When Lutchmee was brought into the wedding mandap, there were titters of excitement. Lutchmee was tall for her age, with long, slender legs and graceful arms. Her red sari, which her parents had sold almost everything they owned to buy for her, and which was the nicest sari she'd ever worn, draped her body like a second skin. Her face was a perfect oval and her delicate features meant that she was anything but plain.

She found it difficult to keep her head down as a good bride should, and waited excitedly to be able to look up and take in the sights and sounds around her. When it was time to exchange the flower garlands, symbols to show the start of the married couple's life together, she felt hopeful that her new husband would like what he saw. But he seemed absent, and her smile faded quickly as she realised that he did not want to be playful and pretend that he was trying to evade his garland or that she was trying to evade hers, as most couples did. Disappointed, Lutchmee stood still, avoiding his gaze as he draped the garland over her head three times, and she did the same over his.

Vikram then looked to his mother and she gave him a slight nod, as if to say that he had accomplished something that he did not want to do.

As part of the rituals, Lutchmee's mother washed Vikram's feet with sandalwood and milk. She then used flower petals to rub them dry and knelt before him, accepting him into her family.

Then came the moment her new mamiyar had been waiting for: it was time for her to present the Kanchipuram sari to her daughter-in-law. There was a hush in the mandap as Mamiyar opened it up to show the richness of the silk and the glittering golden threads along the borders. She draped it extravagantly around Lutchmee's shoulders as the couple sat in front of the priest.

Vikram then applied pottu to Lutchmee's hair parting, as a sign that she was now married, before she was led off by the women to change into the sari she had been gifted. While the women draped the bride in the nine yards of luxurious fabric, Lutchmee found herself wanting to remain with the women, in the sari that her parents had bought her, instead of returning to the gathering.

Back in the mandap, the thaali was tied around her neck, and then guests showered the couple with atchadhai, flower petals and rice as a blessing. As Lutchmee knelt to touch her new mamiyar's feet, she looked up at her. The cold expression she saw there was puzzling: why was there not even a hint of happiness on the woman's face for this successful marriage of her only son?

Later that night, as the wedding party was gathered around the fire singing the bhajans, a log spluttered, showering glowing embers in all directions. There was a flurry of confusion and everyone scattered. A small fire started but was quickly put out. 'It's a sign,' Vikram's mother said loudly. 'My son has made a bad choice.' Bursting into tears, Lutchmee ran out.

She watched her new husband, but he pretended that he hadn't heard his mother, and insisted that they retire to bed as well.

All women go through this, Lutchmee reminded herself, trying to quell her feelings of uncertainty as she prepared for her first night alone with her new husband in the small room in his mother's house that would be theirs. She smoothed down her nightdress and brushed her hair until it took on a velvet sheen.

Vikram appeared at the door and seemed almost surprised to find his new wife in his bed.

It was over as quickly as it had started. Exhausted from his exertions, Vikram rolled over onto his side and began to snore.

Lutchmee got up to clean herself. Returning to bed, she placed her arm gently around her husband. She knew there was much she was going to have to do to please him and his mother, and if she could give him a child that would change everything. She wanted nothing more than to keep her husband happy, but she'd also realised it would be difficult to win her mamiyar's approval.

The next morning Lutchmee was awoken by Mamiyar standing at the foot of the bed. 'Get up, get up! I have been awake for hours and here you are still sleeping,' she scolded.

'I'm so sorry. We did not get to sleep till late,' Lutchmee lied.

Vikram stumbled out of the room and disappeared to wash. Mamiyar waited for him to leave, then tossed aside the bedcovers, searching for something. Exposed and uncertain, Lutchmee watched as Mamiyar found what she was looking for: smudges of dried blood.

Satisfied, she turned and left.

Mamiyar put Lutchmee in charge of the cooking, but it seemed this was only so that she could find fault. There was never enough salt in her curry, the rice was overcooked, and the roti was too hard and had to be thrown to the dogs in the yard. The criticism never stopped, no matter how hard Lutchmee tried to please her.

One evening, Lutchmee was preparing a curry in the karahi, and stepped away to get another spoon. As she returned, she saw Mamiyar take a small packet from within the folds of her sari and tip its white contents into the curry. Then, dusting her hands, she walked off quickly.

When Vikram arrived back from the fields, his mother told him how hard at work his wife had been cooking for him. But the food was much too salty. Her husband, hungry and enraged, flung his plate to the floor and shouted at Lutchmee. Miraculously, his mother produced another curry for him to eat.

Lutchmee knew that she could not tell her husband what she'd seen, as he probably wouldn't believe her; and he didn't notice that his wife went to bed hungry that night.

Mamiyar was less subtle with the lunches that Lutchmee prepared in a tiffin for Vikram. Mamiyar would stop her son before he left and replace Lutchmee's tiffin with one she had prepared. The contents of Lutchmee's tiffin would be thrown to the chickens in the yard.

After a few months with no change in her mamiyar's attitude, Lutchmee decided that she had no option but to accept her fate – but she tried to stay out of mother-in-law's way, remaining obedient and courteous while still keeping her distance. But that did not always work. 'What sort of daughter-in-law does not come and sit with her mamiyar?' the older woman would scold when she hadn't seen Lutchmee for a while. Then Lutchmee would rub her mamiyar's scalp with coconut oil and massage her calloused feet, while Vikram sat in the yard, smoking beedis by the fire.

Eight months into the marriage, Lutchmee was still bleeding every month. Mamiyar saw this as yet another sign that her new daughter-in-law was bad luck, and increased her prayers and tributes to various deities. She took Lutchmee to every sadhu in the village. They gave her potions to drink and herbs to put under her mattress, and the last Brahmin told them (in exchange for a few chickens and some rupees) that there was an evil eye over Lutchmee and that no baby would come until she had fasted by abstaining from eating meat for sixteen Tuesdays.

Her mother-in-law, inconsolable, wailed out the bad news to Vikram that evening before his wife had a chance to. He comforted his mother and impatiently urged Lutchmee to bring some sweet chai for Mamiyar, who was now so overcome with distress that she could not walk and had to have a lie-down.

Lutchmee religiously followed the Brahmin's advice, fasting and praying as ordered, but the bleeding still came exactly every twenty-eight days, while Mamiyar became increasingly venomous and Vikram took less and less notice of his wife. A baby was no longer possible anyway: he'd lost interest in her altogether.

Feeling a sense of urgency one night, Lutchmee tried to initiate intimacy with her husband. 'So you are a whore now?' was his retort as he pushed her away. She curled up on her side of the bed, crying silently.

After two years of marriage, there was no sign of a baby or any affection between husband and wife. Hardness had set into Lutchmee like an immovable boulder.

Her mother-in-law did not bother to sheath her claws in front of her son any more, instead plunging them repeatedly into her daughter-in-law's barren womb.

Lutchmee was hanging out the washing when she heard screams and shouts. Fieldworkers came running and Lutchmee stopped one of them before they got to the house. Through panted breaths he revealed that Vikram had collapsed in the field.

Lutchmee dropped the basket, gathered the skirt of her sari and ran blindly, her mind a tangle of confusion. When she reached her husband, his eyes were staring fixedly and unblinking. Lying on the dark earth, his head facing skywards, he looked like a prepubescent boy.

Lutchmee fell onto his chest in despair. He wasn't breathing. A fear gripped her, but before she had time to completely take in what was happening, she heard her mother-in-law's cries.

Mamiyar came running, her hair flying loose from its neat bun. Shoving Lutchmee aside, she snatched her son protectively towards her bosom. His head rolled against her heaving breasts. She wailed and cried into his hair, then beat on his chest, then beat her arms against her own chest. The men tried to help her to her feet but she pushed them away.

She turned to Lutchmee. 'Cursed!' she screamed, squatting in the dark earth, her eyes full of liquid fire and revulsion.

Lutchmee tried to get out of the way but was not quick enough. Mamiyar pulled her to the ground. 'It is you! You did this!' All her hatred had suddenly found a path out. Through tears and agonised shrieks, she called Lutchmee a witch and cursed her part in the marriage.

Mamiyar's spit flecked Lutchmee's tear-stained face, and the shocked young woman did not even raise her hand to wipe it off. She eventually prised herself loose from her mother-in-law's vice-like grip and stood up.

But Mamiyar was not done. 'Tomorrow you will also die! You will die on the pyre next to my son. You will burn for what you did to him! You will burn and then I won't have the burden or shame of you for a day longer!'

Lutchmee stood still, gulping for air that suddenly seemed too thick to inhale. She could not believe what she had heard. Sati had been a thing of the past, only carried out by rich families or villagers in remote areas where the British rules could not reach.

Lutchmee lay in her tiny room, waiting for first light. Musicians and mourners who had arrived the previous evening had fallen asleep on makeshift beds, some still clutching their dholaks and flutes.

Her fear was still so real that she could taste it, but she no longer felt helpless. She was not willing to die for an old lady's revenge or for a man who was too weak.

The cockerel crowed in the yard. Before long, the household would be up and getting ready. Lutchmee packed a few saris, including her bridal sari from Vikram. She also slipped the pair of gold valayals and bell-shaped jhimkis into a pouch and tied it to the inside of her underskirt. Taking the stash of money Vikram had kept beneath their bedroll and the rotis she had made the previous day, Lutchmee left what had been her marital home.

Pulling her pallu over her head to conceal more of her face, she walked down to the river. She knew it flowed all the way to Madras and the Bay of Bengal, and she'd decided she would follow its path. In Madras, she could melt away and maybe in time overcome the grief and loneliness she'd felt since she had married Vikram.

Lutchmee did not meet many people in the first few hours of walking, but as the sun rose higher, villagers came down to the river to collect water and wash their clothes. She hurried past, careful not to make eye contact; most of them ignored her.

By the evening, the rubbing of her chappals had caused her feet to blister, and she sat with her feet in a shallow pool while she ate the last of the roti and thought about where to find safety for the night. Finally, without any option, she looked for and collected a number of broken-off branches and stacked them against a tall tree, then dragged scrub over them. She crept into this makeshift lean-to, pulling more scrub after herself to conceal the opening.

The next day, after a night of broken and fearful sleep, she made her way into the next village she came across and followed the crowds to the nearest temple in the hope of getting some food. The offerings of fruit and coconuts on the steps of the temple made her stomach rumble. Waiting for a moment of quietness between groups of people, she slipped some of the fruit under her sari and made her way back to the river.

By the end of the fourth day her feet were severely blistered, with some of the little ulcers broken open and bleeding, and every step she took was painful. Early the next morning, after another anxious and disturbed night in another makeshift lean-to, Lutchmee hobbled into the nearest village, and used some of the money to buy turmeric. Back at the river's edge, she made a paste of it, and applied it to the raw wounds on her feet.

Lying on her back on the river bank, she looked up at some wispy clouds scudding across the startling blueness of the sky. Exhausted by her ordeal, hungry and in pain, fearful of the present and uncertain of the future, she fell asleep.

'Akka? Are you okay?'

The voice that woke her was young and female. Her eyes snapped open and she looked up. Two women around her own age were looking down at her, concerned. Both carried buckets – it seemed they had come down to the river to collect water and seen Lutchmee dozing there.

'Yes. I'm just tired.'

The women continued to look at her expectantly, and she saw one of them glance at her wounded feet.

'I'm looking for my husband,' Lutchmee said, pulling her feet up, out of sight, under her sari. 'He went to the market and hasn't come back yet.'

'Which market?' one of them asked.

'The one in Madras,' she replied.

The two women looked at each other, then the one who had spotted her injured feet said, 'Our neighbour is going there today. Come, we'll ask him if you can go with him. It will be quicker in his wagon.'

They reached Madras by midday, Lutchmee squeezed into a corner of the man's coconut wagon, uncomfortable but hugely relieved not to have been walking. She thanked the kindly neighbour and climbed down off the wagon, then raised a hand in farewell as she watched the big ox slowly clip-clop away into the crowds.

Despite being surrounded by throngs of people in this thriving centre, Lutchmee felt horribly alone. Before this flight down the river, she had never left her village, and the new sights and sounds threatened to overwhelm her. The roads were filthy, and beggars and wallahs flanked either side. Shops seem to have sprung up in every available area, their owners peddling an assortment of items, from scarves and saris to vegetables and coconuts. Stray animals roamed freely – cows, goats, dogs, chickens and, too often, bold rats.

For the first few nights, she rented a small, airless room in a particularly crowded and run-down part of the city. She had never lived on her own before and she enjoyed the solitude. After four nights on hard ground under a heedless sky, she slept peacefully, and only left the room to wash and get food.

She trusted no one, and when a young girl who introduced herself as Devi spoke to her in the chowk, she found that she was instantly suspicious. As busy and anonymous as the port city seemed, Madras was still not far away enough from the village, and at every turn she thought she would be found and returned to the village to face Mamiyar and certain death.

When her money began to run out and Lutchmee found herself down to a single meal a day, Devi explained that she could help. 'Madam Bandowa, she takes good care of her girls. Come, I will take you to her.'

Devi's affectionate tug on her arm and the fact that the girl seemed well cared for and in high spirits made Lutchmee feel that perhaps she had no other option. Lutchmee had heard of such women – they sometimes lived and worked in the temples. Given her situation, she found herself quickly adjusting the prejudgements she had made about them.

Madam Bandowa was a warm, motherly figure with a broad smile and hands that seemed to do most of the talking. She was stroking a rather sad-looking kitten and crooning to it gently when Lutchmee walked into the front room.

Without getting up, Madam Bandowa greeted her. 'So you are the beauty that Devi has been talking to me about,' she said, handing the kitten to Devi and gesturing to a small tray of warm rotis, potato curry and sambar. 'You want to work here? Plenty good money for a young, pretty girl like you,' she added, watching Lutchmee eat the food greedily.

'Maybe I can cook and clean?' Lutchmee suggested. 'I don't think I can see men … different men …'

'I'll tell you what we'll do … Let's see if you can do both. If you are busy with customers, the other girls will cook and clean. If you are not, then it will be you who cooks and cleans.'

Knowing that there was not going to be a better offer, Lutchmee acquiesced. Here she would have company, a bed and food, and even make a bit of money to maybe get a better job.

*

On the edge of the city, behind the lanes of the chowk, Madam Bandowa's was a well-concealed but widely known place. Poky makeshift rooms sat layered one upon another. Damp and dark, it was a pleasure palace for some, a prison for others.

Some men who visited desired beauties – younger girls – while others wanted women who were willing to do the things their wives would not. Yet others came for the two hijras with their kohl-lined eyes and their sari blouses hoiked up high to show off their trim boyish waists.

At first, the men chose her because she was attractive like a shiny coin, but for Lutchmee, every time felt like wading into icy water. She was very self-conscious and found that trying to be alluring and seductive just did not make sense, and it showed. The act itself was usually quick and hurried: they would be on top of her, fumbling like animals, writhing and bucking in a strange frenzy.

'Pretend to be interested,' Madam Bandowa's advice would echo. 'A man, even a very little man,' and here she would waggle her pinky finger, 'wants to feel that he is big and strong.' The girls would giggle.

Once the men saw that Lutchmee was cold and made little effort, she became less popular. She fell into an easy rhythm with a few regular clients, mostly teenagers. They grew accustomed to her. She knew just how to make them feel comfortable and always washed their private parts before and after.

Lutchmee had been working there for a few months when she noticed a government man wearing a khaki shirt and matching trousers lounging in a chair downstairs. She had been cooking, and came in to serve the food. The man's eyes followed her. Beads of sweat rolled down his temples and large patches of sweat stained the fabric gathered in his armpits.

'My girls are nice and clean,' said Madam Bandowa, proudly and insincerely, as the girls paraded past him and he leered at them, his mouth opened slightly like a fish. Occasionally he ran the tip of his tongue across his upper lip, pushing it against his thick moustache.

'What is your pleasure today, Anand Sir? Maybe two girls?'

To Lutchmee's horror, the man nodded at her. 'This one? What about her?'

Lutchmee looked pointedly at Madam Bandowa. 'I'm not working tonight,' she said in as neutral a tone as she could manage.

'Challo. We are always working,' the older woman said dismissively, clapping her hands. Under her breath she added to Lutchmee, 'He's a big man with money to spend,' and surreptitiously rubbed her forefinger against her thumb. Then, loudly, she said, 'Go and wash while I give this Anand Sir another drink.'

In the room, Lutchmee steadied her nerves and lit an agarbatti stick. She sat on the side of the bed and waited.

When Anand Sir arrived, he immediately removed his trousers.

'What important work do you do, mister?' Lutchmee asked, hoping that he wanted to talk. But, keeping his eyes fixed on her, he used his big body to knock her on her back onto the mattress, then he dumped his full weight on her. Wrapping a fistful of her hair in his hand, he pinned her down as he pressed his other hand firmly against her throat.

Powerless, scratching and clawing, Lutchmee fought for each breath. Her plastic bracelets jangled vigorously in protest. In the light of the moon winking in through the window, she saw Anand Sir's face, smiling, glowering, vile. Revulsion and primal fear knotted together, and with a guttural scream, she dragged her nails across his face, groping for his black, ominous eyes.

Her vision blurred, her head became heavy and she gave in to the lack of oxygen and his sheer weight. There was no final thought, only the slant of moonlight on his drenched face as he forced himself into her in one unwelcome thrust.

Lutchmee woke to soft hands caressing her, holding her up, helping her to drink. Like a multitude of deities, they swam in and out of focus. One of the hijras sat close to her and crooned softly, using a cold cloth to dab at her face and gently lifting her sari to wipe Lutchmee between her legs.

Time seemed fluid, almost feathery, as she drifted in and out of consciousness. When she was present, the throbbing pain in her groin and the rawness in her throat made themselves felt: it was difficult to swallow and her voice came out in raspy whispers.

As she spent more time conscious, she realised that her entire body hurt, it stung and seared, but the ache within her felt like she had swallowed a boulder. She tried to remember the events of that night but they were guileful and quickly darted away from her like fish in a pond.

She knew that she could not do this any more. She had come to the edge of life itself, and now that she was still alive, she could not go back. But she also accepted that she would be dead in a few weeks. With no work, there would be no food. Nonetheless, with her decision made, Lutchmee felt a sense of freedom that was both strange and unfamiliar, yet comforting.

About a week after the attack, Lutchmee waited until all she could hear in the house were snores and whispers, then she slipped out of her room. Drawing her pallu over her head, she tiptoed down the stairs without meeting anyone.

She did not want anyone to see her leave. That would be too ungrateful: their soft voices and healing hands had made the past few days bearable. She had come to care for them in a way she did not fully understand – kind hands belonging to the women and the hijras, who wore bright red lipstick and lined their eyes with kohl as soon as they woke.

In the moonlight, Lutchmee's faded purple sari appeared darker, concealing her perfectly. Apart from the occasional chinking of her bracelets, she moved silently and with ease between the sleeping forms on the side of the street and occasional rickshaw wallahs.

An unobtrusive moon looked on, shy and peeping. Peering from behind billowy clouds, it illuminated their frilly edges, creating a carefree and frivolous night. Lutchmee stared at it, wondering what it would be like to be that consistent, that certain. There was something so comforting but also so deeply tragic about it; the moon could never be or do anything else.

A wave of exhaustion and despair washed over her. Honesty about what she'd been doing, how she'd held body and soul together until just a few days ago, was not going to help. It was simple and clear. She would bury it deep within herself.

It would not be alone in its grave, she mused. Pain and humiliation had been occupants for much longer.

3
Coolie camp, Madras
May 1909

Babuji was a familiar sight in the camp. The large Indian man, with his unpolished ways and love of money, was either liked or loathed by white and brown people alike.

Leery and still hungover from the previous night's revelries at the docks, he stalked the windswept enclosure. He was on a mission, and he rubbed his head as he tried to get rid of the throbbing that the intense heat and babalaas had brought on. His skin colour was the same as most of those around him, but his eyes were red and bloodshot and his pores were still trying to get rid of the alcohol fumes.

Babuji saw himself as a leader, appointed with a true gift. So far, getting the healthy coolies to sign up and get them on the ships had proved easy and lucrative. He didn't have a desire to leave India himself, but he did have the desire and ambition to become a rich man. This made him think about his growing purse, neatly tucked into the folds of his lungi.

When he was growing up, everyone had the same. They had all lived in hovels and had just enough to feed themselves daily. Every one of his friends had run about in dirty rags and had been constantly hungry. They were clones of poverty and no one felt much different from the others – apart from Babuji. He'd been desperate to set himself apart. He already had a slight edge – his parents had a bit more than most: some chickens that laid eggs, and a friendly goat that provided milk.

By village standards, they were well-to-do, and Babuji used that to his advantage.

When he was ten years old, during monsoon season, the Palar River had been pregnant and temperamental, with muddy water that turned and swirled like a bharatanatyam dancer. For as long as he could remember, the children had been warned to stay away from the river, especially when it was in flood.

With the river thundering past, it occurred to the young Babuji that it had power, immense power, and that he could challenge it. He was no fool and he knew that he was not a strong enough swimmer, but he was bored and in need of entertainment.

'You boys, do you think …? No, never mind,' he'd said, shaking his head and looking at the ground. But out of the corners of his eyes he'd watched them carefully. Waiting.

'Tell us, Babuji, just say,' they replied, almost all at the same time.

He dragged it out a bit longer then, finally, asked, 'Which one of you could swim across the river, this bit here, where it is narrow?'

He had not needed to say any more. They were undressing and within seconds four of them had splashed into the swirling water, all thoughts and lessons about the dangers of the river forgotten. Babuji had stood on the banks watching their glossy little brown bodies battling against the current.

For a moment it had looked like they were all going to reach the other side and he'd felt a sense of accomplishment. But then, with just about fifteen yards left, they seemed to lose sight of the far bank. With arms flailing and their eyes wide with terror, they thrashed about in the cloudy water. It had all played out so fast that Babuji had not even been able to comprehend what he was seeing. In seconds, the current had wrapped its powerful arms around each tiny waist, dancing with them to some unknown song.

Babuji had done nothing. He just stood there and watched with a ghost of a smile on his face.

The four little boys had disappeared from view around a bend, and that shook him out of his trance-like state. He ran back to the village but by then it was far too late for anyone to try to swim after them.

For endless days and nights, distraught parents had combed the river banks and offered up prayers for the safe return of their precious children. In the day, with the sun blazing down on them, and at night, with the heavy moon looking on, the wailing in the village had been constant. The smell of incense and burning camphor was heavy in the air as every mother performed every puja she knew, pleading for God to spare the lives of the four little boys.

Everyone had looked to Babuji for reasons. 'I don't know why they went,' he'd said, shaking his head sorrowfully. 'I told them that the river would take them. They did not want to listen to me.' Sometimes he'd recite all he'd learnt about the dangers of the river in parrot-like fashion, showing so much regret that he actually began to believe that he was blameless. He didn't wrestle with his conscience. There simply wasn't one to wrestle with.

His mother had listened patiently from the crowd, knowing full well that he was lying. She had seen the way those boys worshipped him. They'd called for him every day and he'd barked orders at them every chance he'd got. They would even help him with his chores without his asking, carrying buckets of water from the well while his arms dangled loosely at his sides, a blade of grass stuck between his lips. She'd grown afraid of what her son was capable of.

Before he was seventeen, Babuji had left the village, putting the image of the drowning boys behind him for good. He was going to hone his craft to make himself useful and rich.

Persuasive as he could be, finding a wife for Sappani with only a day or two to go was testing even Babuji's talents. He'd asked around and spoken to a few women but his charms had let him down and they'd hurried away, their sandals clicking. By the afternoon, Babuji was thinking about how he could keep Sappani's money without giving him a new bride.

As a last resort, he decided to try the market on the outskirts of Madras.

It was not his usual hunting ground, but he was tired of the food in the coolie camp and he thought he would have an early meal there before heading back. Walking through the marketplace, he bought a mango lassi to ease his hangover nausea, then he spent some time weaving between the stalls, eating paan, taking in the gauzy fabrics and mountains of spices, and making small talk with the wallahs.

Then he saw Lutchmee. She was thin and alone, wearing a faded purple sari, and looked out of place, her eyes curious but also wary. 'Perfect,' he said to himself, rubbing his hands together.

Approaching her, he said, 'Madhiya vanakkam. Come and eat something with me. I'm Babuji.' He extended a fat arm, indicating the food on one of the stalls and gesturing for her to join him.

Lutchmee hesitated.

'What can I do to you in front of all these people?' he asked her, arms outstretched and palms up, radiating avuncular reasonableness. 'Just come and eat,' he said, smiling and pointing to the thali.

Lutchmee could smell the buttery naan and the curries garnished with fresh dhania and slivers of green chilli. She was hungry, and, as this fat man had said, there were plenty of people around – what could he do to her with all these witnesses? She sat down and took the curry and naan gratefully when Babuji passed them to her, hoping that she could eat before she had to make conversation.

'So, where are you from?' he asked.

Lutchmee did not answer as she had just ripped into the warm bread and was finding it difficult to swallow.

Babuji poured water into a tin cup for her and covertly appraised her as he watched her eat. He took in the bruises around her neck and the dark circles beneath her sad eyes that found it difficult to meet his own. Desperation hung about her like a cloudy mist. Babuji sensed it and zoned in.

When she had finished eating, she looked up at him, her sari pallu falling to her shoulders. 'Miga nandri,' she said, looking up at him, a bit more relaxed. 'You are very kind.'

He had to time this right – too quick and he would lose her – so he let his kind acts and words soften her while keeping a safe distance. He asked her questions about her village and her family. She was guarded and it was clear that she did not want him to know about her family. A runaway, maybe?

'Do you want to leave here, bahan?' he asked. 'Go somewhere nice, not have to worry about anything?' She listened in silence while he told her about what he did. 'The *Umzinto* is docked in the bay and is ready to leave any day now.'

Lutchmee had eaten every scrap of food in front of her and she knew that it was probably the last she would see for a while. 'Take me to the coolie camp, then. I want to leave this place behind,' she said tonelessly.

Babuji led Lutchmee into the camp. It was too late in the day to get any paperwork done, but he arranged with the guards that she would sleep in the quarters with the other newly arrived single women, and then be checked by the doctor first thing in the morning.

'Then you will get the paper, the proof that you can go on the ship. It is all not so hard, eh?' he said to her with a wink, then left to find Sappani.

The next morning Lutchmee joined the queue to see the doctor. He emerged from the tent mopping his face continuously with a sodden rag. His bald head was pink and blistered. 'That man has a curved spine. He's as fragile as a bird and now he wants to make the trip. I said no – he is of no use to anyone!' he said irately to an official. 'He needs to leave. Now!'

'But, doctor, the other men won't go if Gengan doesn't go. There are seven men, strong men, brothers, uncles,' the official said.

Babuji, who had found and joined Lutchmee in the queue, watched with interest. Another official joined in the discussion. They went back and forth, the doctor's annoyance clearly growing while he kept shaking his head. Finally, the doctor evidently gave in. 'Well, I've said it before and I'll say it again: once they leave here and make it to Natal, they are not our problem any more. If these fools want to make it harder for themselves, let them. Sign the papers!' Without waiting for a response, he stalked off.

When it was Lutchmee's turn to be examined, she tried to wipe her sweaty palms against her sari as she unwound it from around her waist.

'Lie on the bed,' the doctor ordered.

Looking away, Lutchmee crossed her arms to cover her breasts.

Rough fingers clad in rubber caught and held her cheeks in a vice grip, turning her head back until her eyes were inches away from the doctor's. Shoving his fat fingers into her mouth, he prised it open and pulled her lips back to check her teeth.

'Teeth seem okay,' he called out to the nurse, who was scribbling on a piece of paper.

Firmly pulling Lutchmee's arms apart, he said brusquely, 'Now is not the time to be shy,' and palpated her breasts. Lutchmee felt the sting of her tears as he pressed hard on the bruised areas on her body. 'No breaks or fractures but some bruising. No problem. It will heal.'

She felt her legs being parted roughly and bolted upright instinctively. 'I'm not finished yet,' the doctor said, mechanically, and with one flat palm pushing on her chest, he leant sideways and plunged one large gloved finger into her. Lutchmee felt a searing pain. Biting her lower lip, she lay as still as she could, tears flowing freely down her cheeks.

'This one seems in good health – no warts or sores in the genital area, but there is some bruising there too. But that will heal as well.'

The nurse, who had leant forward and poked about in Lutchmee's scalp with her pencil, added, 'No lice but she needs a wash.'

'Don't they all!' the doctor responded, laughing at his own joke. He turned away to sign the paperwork.

'Get dressed,' the nurse instructed Lutchmee, then waved her along to where she was handed a set of new clothes and a bar of soap.

Outside, Babuji was waiting for his latest recruit. Lutchmee emerged from the washing area wearing the clothes they had given her. Her hair was wet and while she looked cleaner, the shroud of helplessness still hung over her. *Chutias, the whole lot of them*, Babuji thought to himself about the medical personnel. Occasionally the way the Indians were treated bothered him, but he did not let it fester for too long. The rules – like life – weren't fair.

With time against him, he needed to act quickly. They had already begun to load the ship. 'For a single woman, this trip can be dangerous, bahan,' he told her in a low voice. 'I want to keep you safe and make sure you arrive in Natal safely, hah? See that man there? The one with the small baby? His poor wife has died.' Babuji shook his head in a show of sympathy. 'He needs a wife, and a married woman on the ship will be looked after.'

Lutchmee looked at the man Babuji had pointed out. He was not very tall and she could only see his profile. His long arms cradled a baby who had wrapped himself around his father as if he was clinging on to the edge of the world. The man was talking to his son in hushed, soothing tones, and even though she could not hear the words, she could tell that they were kind. The child's whimpering abated and she saw his grip gradually relax around his father's neck.

Babuji had walked over to the man and summoned him, and now they both turned and began to walk back towards her. The child was lying in his father's arms, close to sleep. Lutchmee noticed that he held his child carefully and protectively as he walked.

She felt nauseous with nerves. The last few weeks blurred in front of her, and as they approached, she looked surreptitiously at the man's face. He was dark-skinned, and obviously used to working outdoors. His eyes were bright, and he had a neat, trimmed moustache beneath a pronounced nose, but his cheeks were sunken and he was very thin.

Babuji made the introductions, then asked, 'You like what you see, bhai?'

Sappani looked embarrassed but gave a subtle nod. Both men then looked at Lutchmee inquiringly.

'Yes,' she said, then fell silent.

Just then the ship's horn sounded and the activity around it became a bit more frantic.

Lascars yelled at one another while men in military uniform shouted orders and swore at the tops of their voices.

'We need to rush. It looks like the ship is leaving soon,' said Babuji urgently.

Sappani and Lutchmee allowed themselves to be led to the tent of the Protector of Immigrants. Babuji prattled on, but neither of them responded. 'Leave it all to me, no need to say much,' he told them reassuringly.

'Babu, this better be important,' the Protector boomed, leaning back in his chair, which protested by creaking loudly. As he turned to face them, long scratches were visible on his face.

Lutchmee felt her breakfast rise in her throat. She took the tiniest step back and drew her pallu over more of her face until just her nose and eyes were visible, holding it in place with a trembling hand. It was Anand Sir and he loomed large, spilling out of his chair.

'Of course, Sahib, why else would I bother you when you are so busy? This man here – his wife has just joined him.'

The Protector looked at him quizzically and his thin lips twisted into a peculiar shape. He turned to Sappani. 'What's your name and number?' He reached for a book and, licking his forefinger, began turning the pages. Running a stumpy finger down a list, he tapped it when he found what he was looking for: *Sappani Mottai, number 140316, age 27.* In the line below, Neela's entry had been amended and now read, *Neela Mottai, number 140317, age 19, deceased – disease.*

'It says here that your wife died. Has she now been raised from the dead?'

Sappani choked at the mention of his wife and looked at Babuji.

Babuji answered, 'Sadly, yes, Sahib, she did die. But if this man is to work, he needs a wife to look after the boy. This lady has been checked and she is cleared to go.'

Anand Sir looked up at Lutchmee as if seeing her for the first time and casually waved his hand in the air. 'No matter to me,' he said.

'Thank you, Sahib. I know you want the ship to be filled.'

'Yes, yes, fine, but you get half for her of what you usually get.' He drew a thick, dark line through Neela's name.

Lutchmee saw Sappani's his hands tighten around his child and he bent his head. She wanted to sit down somewhere cool. She did not know if her mind was playing tricks on her but she could smell the fat man's breath on her face, his huge body pinning her down. She stepped slightly closer to Sappani so that her arm almost touched his.

They answered the remaining questions and the amendments were made by the Protector: *Lutchmee Mottai, number 140317, age 19.*

Her identity as an indentured Indian had now been logged.

'Don't forget my money, Sahib,' Babuji said, half joking. The Protector closed his book and scribbled on another piece of paper, which he handed roughly to Babuji, who said quick goodbyes and melted away, eager to get paid before the ship left.

In the bay, the *Umzinto* was a formidable hulk in the seascape. A steamship that had been modified to carry human cargo, she blew puffs of smoke from her stacks as the boiler came to life.

The lascars shouted and darted about the deck; others scurried up and down the thick ropes, double-checking knots and pulleys. Preparing for the ship to leave the dock, they pulled on sheets and blocks, their commands to each other booming over the sound of the engine. The activity accelerated and men dashed about, onto the gangway and the top deck, their shouts intensified over the rumbling from the bowels of the ship. All the supplies had been loaded, including livestock. Chickens in wire cages squawked in protest and sheep bleated balefully as they were tethered to posts – they would be the source of any fresh meat eaten on board. Barrels of fresh water, heavy sacks of flour, beans and lentils, potatoes and baskets of salted fish were stacked and stored.

For this crossing, the Protector of Immigrants on board was KB Shaw, who now stood on the deck overseeing the boarding of each Indian. A Scotsman with a ruddy face and bulbous eyes, he used a large plaid handkerchief to mop up the sweat that pooled in the folds at the base of his neck. The captain and other officials were still carrying out the checks that had already seemed to occupy much of the morning and Shaw was getting impatient.

He had completed this run many times before, and every time he did, he hoped it would be his last. 'It's a sair fecht for hauf a loaf,' he said to Captain Roberts, who watched in silence as the Indians chattered excitedly and made their way on board.

Roberts, a young, stout Englishman, found Protector Shaw to be loud and lewd, and wanted nothing more than to remove himself from the man's company. In the depot he had been insufferable, but at least there the young captain could get away from him for a while. For the next six weeks they would be crammed together on this ship, their fates like twisted vines.

The ship was divided into two sections. In the queue that led to the upper decks, 'passenger Indians' were preparing to board. A mix, mostly of higher castes, tailors, preachers, teachers, lawyers and businessmen, they had made the decision to leave India as pioneers, had paid for their passage and could return whenever they liked. They were easy to distinguish: they wore better clothes and walked meaningfully. Their possessions had already been loaded into the cargo hold, so they strolled onto the *Umzinto* unencumbered. Their laughter could be heard as they ushered young children in front of them, pausing only to wave at family who had come to see them off.

The passenger Indians' sleeping quarters were nearest to the captain's and senior officers' staterooms. Throughout the journey they would be given the best treatment, eating good food in a clean mess, and spending as much time on the decks as they wished. And at all times, of course, they would be kept away from the indentured Indians.

The boarding indentured Indians would be expected to pitch in with all chores, from preparing meals to washing the latrines, and their time on the upper deck, with its access to fresh air and sunshine, would be severely limited. The single women were put in the stern, the single men occupied the bow, and the married couples and families were accommodated in a central section.

Every indentured Indian received a jahaji bundle. For each man there were two turbans, three dhotis, a jacket and a cap, while the women were given two saris and a jacket. They also received bedding – a small pillow, a cotton bedsheet and a blanket each – eating utensils, a tin mug and plate, and a lota for holding water for drinking and washing. A wooden comb was provided for each woman and everyone received a piece of soap.

The sepoys, hired and paid for by the British colonial government, were Indian men who'd been trained as soldiers, and it was their job to ensure that there was order on the ship and to never let the indentured Indians forget who was in charge. They would stalk the decks with authority, pouncing on even the smallest of infractions. Now they ushered the indentured Indians below, sometimes roughly, snapping orders.

Forming an orderly queue, married couples and families waited to enter their sleeping areas, on the opposite side of the ship from the free Indians. Lutchmee queued quietly with Sappani, who had Seyan in his arms. She had little to carry aside from what the authorities had just given her, but others, she noted, as she looked surreptitiously around her, toted personal possessions: cooking pots, earthen lamps, herbal medicines, spices, gardening tools and even musical instruments in tattered bags and baskets.

Sappani pushed something circular wrapped in cloth towards her. Lutchmee accepted it and knelt down to place it on the deck and unwrap it. It was a shiny silver spice dhaba, and in each of the six small recesses was an essential spice: chilli powder, garam masala and turmeric, bay leaves, crushed red chillies and dhania seeds. It had been Neela's – the only item of value that she and Sappani had taken with them from their village.

Lutchmee smiled at Sappani. 'This is so nice,' she said, tracing the design of lotus flowers engraved on the lid with her fingertips. She was deeply touched by his gift, both thoughtful and sensible. Then she looked stricken. 'I have nothing for you,' she said, looking at her new husband properly for the first time. He had a generous mouth with straight white teeth like rows of corn. He walked upright, with purpose, and his white dhoti parted to show his long brown limbs. His eyes slanted downwards, and around them were dark circles that added to his sad expression. She found herself feeling reassured in his presence.

'No matter,' was his reply.

Suddenly, loud cursing broke out and could be heard above the chattering and the rumble of the engines. 'I will not live with those filthy pariahs!'

The sepoys were roughly guiding a small, angry man firmly into the family sleeping quarters. He was stocky in spite of his diminutive height, and had a dark, thick moustache that curled outwards on either side of his lips. His face was contorted with fury, and he seemed oblivious to the discomfort of his wife. Sappani recognised her as the woman who had pretended to be his wife so that he could get back into the depot the morning he'd scattered Neela's ashes.

Vottie looked around apologetically as she tried to gather together their belongings, which her husband had flung onto the deck. Lutchmee knelt down and began to help her, picking up their goods and clothes. As she handed them over, she smiled pointedly at Vottie, as one woman who understands the situation another is in.

Seeing the brief exchange between the two women, Sappani said, 'Lutchmee, this is Vottie. She has been really kind to us.'

Vottie smiled briefly at them both, then rushed off after her husband.

'He's a real maadher chod,' the woman next to Lutchmee said. 'Thinks he's better than the rest of us.'

Lutchmee watched as the frantic woman caught up to her husband, desperately trying to keep up and hold onto their belongings while he strode ahead, his arms swinging angrily at his sides. Vottie reached out for him and he flung her arm off and promptly lost his balance, falling heavily to the deck.

The sepoys laughed and one of them prodded him with a stick to get up. Lutchmee saw his wife hesitate before kneeling to help him up.

*

There was only one box left to tick for the indentured Indians before the ship could leave: each had to be checked by the doctor and declared fit to travel. It was in Dr Michael Booth's interests that all the Indians remained alive and well; if they didn't, a portion or even all of his salary would be withheld.

Appointed by the colonial government, Dr Booth took his role seriously. This was his first crossing as a ship's doctor, and he was keen that nothing went wrong. He'd set up the 'hospital' in the deckhouse and had checked that there were suitable spaces to quarantine infectious people if he needed to. He'd inspected the sleeping quarters and written up his report – not a flattering one – on the ventilation on the vessel. And, finally, he'd checked the medical supplies. He'd found that his repeated requests for more and better equipment and consumables had been ignored, and anxiety about what lay ahead, and what he may have to deal with in very much less-than-ideal circumstances, immediately set in.

By mid-afternoon, Dr Booth had personally examined each and every indentured labourer on board, and was relieved that there were no symptoms of any illnesses and all seemed healthy and well. He reported his findings to the captain, then, exhausted, went below to his stateroom, where he helped himself to a generous slug of whisky from the silver hip flask his mother had gifted him on his graduation from Oxford some years previously.

Finally, the ship was to set sail. She would leave her dock in Madras and make her way across the Bay of Bengal to the Indian Ocean, and then begin the 8-week journey to Durban – the new home for 600 indentured and 110 passenger Indians.

On the top deck, Lutchmee stood next to Sappani, both of them silent, as the vessel pulled away from the harbour and slowly made its way out into the bay. Seyan watched with mild interest, his thumb in his mouth, his arms around his father's neck.

Smoke billowed from the stacks and the sound of the sea was infused with the calls of the lascars and swirling gulls. Captain Roberts stood on the top deck, Protector Shaw next to him, as the *Umzinto* built up speed and headed out to sea, leaving a silvery trace in her wake.

From the ship Sappani could see the rising smoke of the funeral ghats. Lutchmee followed his gaze. 'I am so sorry,' she said to him.

He nodded acknowledgement and continued to stare at the receding shoreline.

PART II

CROSSING

The food, medicines and other appliances on board are of good quality, and your health, comfort and safety will be carefully attended to. The Indian Government has appointed officers who are most strict and vigilant in securing for you all these advantages.

– *Notice to coolies intending to emigrate to Natal,* 21 March 1874

4

Umzinto, northern Indian Ocean
May 1909

Soon they could not see the land any more, and the sea became more tumultuous. Lutchmee and Sappani climbed cautiously down the ladder leading into the bowels of the ship, Sappani carefully passing the boy down to Lutchmee when she'd reached the bottom.

As her eyes adjusted to the gloom, Lutchmee began to properly take in her surroundings for the first time – the place that would be her and her new family's home for the next two months. The double-tier bunkbeds were close together, with only enough room between them for a person to stand – although the ceiling, which was the floorboards of the deck above, was low enough for standing upright to be impossible for all but the shortest adults and the children.

There was a sickly smell of vomit and the air was fetid with sweat and fear. Seyan, in Lutchmee's arms, began to cry. 'Here, take him,' she said to Sappani, unable to console the child. Her inability to soothe Seyan intimidated her. She was also aware that they would all be sleeping very close to each other, and it all seemed so strange and sudden, like she was living someone else's life.

She felt nauseous and tried swallowing hard a few times before she sat down on an empty bed. She was experiencing a slow, rising sickness, from her belly upwards, which made everything spin and caused her tremble, with flushes of warmth. 'Have a drink of this,' Sappani said, offering her some water from his lota as he jostled the wailing Seyan on a hip.

As the *Umzinto* picked up speed and lurched through the waves, Lutchmee found herself next to Vottie, who was vomiting onto the wooden floor without any sign of stopping. This only intensified Lutchmee's need to vomit. Vottie's husband, Sarju, was looking on but saying nothing.

'Some fresh air will be good for us,' Lutchmee said as she helped Vottie to her feet, but they found that the gate to reach the top deck had been pulled across, locking them below.

The young Chinmah joined them, equally desperate to get above. In the early days of her pregnancy, she'd been unsure about what was happening to her body and spent much time wishing it would stop. Then, when she was first in the coolie camp, and the doctor had told her that the baby she was carrying would arrive in the next few months, she'd wished it would just go away. Now she felt it moving inside her all the time, kicking and rolling, turning and poking, and she'd become intrigued by the creature growing inside her. But she was also very tired a lot of the time, and right now she felt hot and panicky.

'Let us out, please,' Vottie begged a passing lascar who appeared on the other side of the gate. 'She is in the family way,' she added, pointing to Chinmah's belly as proof.

After hesitating, he relented. 'Just for a little while,' he said, as he let a few women up. Lutchmee grabbed Seyan quickly and took him with her.

On the top deck, it seemed that the lascars were the only ones who were not being violently sick. Most of the sepoys had never been on a ship, and they too staggered about, trying to find their sea legs.

Lutchmee gulped at the salty sea air. Seyan appeared to be calming down and taking in the view, his cries having dwindled to a sad whimper. The view was remarkable, with the ocean engulfing everything around them – imposing and beautiful at the same time.

Seyan, suddenly realising that his father was not with them, began to cry again. Trying to comfort him proved pointless. Lutchmee felt awkward around the boy and he seemed to sense this. He cried louder than ever, and she quickly hurried back down the ladder.

'Take him,' she urged her new husband, her words not coming out as gently as she would have liked.

The other women were sent back below the decks soon after. Annoyed with herself, imagining that Sappani was probably regretting his decision to take her on, Lutchmee sat down on her bed, waiting for the uneasiness she felt in her stomach and mind to pass.

Vottie and Chinmah joined her, all of them in various states of seasickness. They sat together in silence for a while, then Lutchmee raised her head and caught Vottie's eye. United in their misery, they began to laugh at themselves and each other. Their laughter caused a few others to raise their eyebrows in disapproval.

As it was getting dark outside, Sappani and a few other men were sent to carry out chores on the deck. He passed Seyan to Lutchmee, and immediately the little boy began howling like a stricken animal. 'Go, he will stop crying soon,' Lutchmee said to the boy's father with more confidence than she felt, and he left reluctantly.

Lutchmee tried in vain to pacify the child, and just when she thought she could not endure any more, Vottie said, 'Pass him here.' The teary-eyed Seyan flung himself into Vottie's familiar arms, and she cradled him gently until his cries became softer, his breathing slowed down, and he fell asleep.

Lutchmee watched with envy, her inadequacies as a new mother laid bare.

'It's going to be okay,' Vottie said. 'He just needs to get used to you.'

'I'm trying,' Lutchmee said, helplessly.

'He has lost his mother, remember,' Vottie said gently as she passed the sleeping boy back to Lutchmee.

Vottie's reassurances reminded Lutchmee of Madam Bandowa's, Devi and the hijras, and she felt a pang of sadness. She decided that Vottie, with her kind heart and willingness to help, was someone she could trust. She could not do this alone.

*

For the first two nights, the baby slept with his father. Sappani woke to tend to him when he cried, and every time he did so, Lutchmee woke as well. She needn't have bothered because the little boy would not let go of his father, no matter how much she encouraged him to.

While she did not have any love for either the child or his father yet, Lutchmee felt a deep grief for the man and the motherless baby. *I have to try*, she resolved. So, on the third night, she said to Sappani, 'Give him to me.' Seyan turned and held onto his father. Sappani gently prised the boy loose and passed him to her, then, looking stricken, walked away quickly. He too wanted her to bond with the boy, and that was why he was making himself scarce.

Seyan wailed in Lutchmee's arms for what seemed like hours but eventually, out of sheer exhaustion, he fell asleep. Exhausted herself, she gently lowered the boy onto his bunk.

The next night, as Sappani was about to settle Seyan for the night, Lutchmee said, 'Let me do it.' He agreed and this time there were not the same hard lines of concern on his face. She took the boy and quickly walked away until he could no longer see his father. She paced the length of the single women's area, carefully avoiding the bunk beds in the dark. The lanterns were still burning. Vottie watched Lutchmee but kept her distance.

It was hot and stuffy between the decks and when the sepoy on duty saw Lutchmee with the crying child, he allowed her to come up to the top deck. The night was still except for a cool breeze that fanned them; Seyan's cries began to diminish as he watched Lutchmee's face. Holding him close, she pointed at the stars and a sliver of a moon, which looked as if they had been flung carelessly by a celestial hand.

Her arms ached with his weight but she did not stop. 'Sleep, en anpe,' she crooned to him as she paced, cradling him so that he could see the stars until his eyes grew too heavy to stay open. Finally, his little head relaxed back against the crook of her arm and he fell into a restful sleep.

The wind played with a lock of his hair and he was the picture of innocence and beauty. Something stirred inside Lutchmee. She could not explain it. She brushed her lips over the top of his downy head and whispered, 'My son.'

Sappani was wide awake when she returned to lower Seyan gently into the bunk next to his father. 'Ah, good. He is sleeping,' Sappani smiled.

During the day, Lutchmee and Vottie and Chinmah had duties to perform. One of them was to clean the rice, which took hours – the women had to carefully pick out the tiny stones that were mixed in with the rice grains, one by one. They took turns to watch Seyan as he wriggled around on his belly, occasionally trying to grab fistfuls of uncooked rice. Now and then one of them would spring into action to avoid him getting hurt or stop him putting something inedible into his mouth.

Lutchmee felt a strange happiness when Seyan saw his father but still wanted to stay with her. Now that he was feeling more settled, he proved to be a happy boy, chuckling whenever they were together. He was a bit on the thin side but seemed to enjoy his food well enough. However, he would refuse to eat unless he was being carried around at the same time.

Lutchmee felt more relaxed and Sappani sensed that. When it was time for the indentured Indians to get their two hours of fresh air per day, the new little family enjoyed being on the top deck, walking around and sometimes sitting together for their meals. They looked with envy at the passenger Indians, who were kept separate, as they were allowed to walk wherever they pleased, while the indentured Indians were cordoned off in one area of the deck.

With the dawn of each day, it felt more and more as if this truly was Lutchmee's real life, not one borrowed from the ashes of a woman who had died before her time.

Suspicion hung in the air around the *Umzinto*. Caste rules had no place on the ship, but for some this could not be tolerated. Hundreds of years of routine and tradition were hard to change over the course of a few days.

'What's wrong with Sarju?' Lutchmee asked as she and Vottie found a place to sit. He'd walked stiffly away from his wife when he'd seen

Lutchmee approaching, his eyes ablaze, his face set in irritation and his moustache quivering as he clenched his jaw.

'He's seen the Brahmins that are free Indians strolling about – it's salt in his open wounds,' Vottie said. 'All his life he's never once mixed with people below his caste, so this is a struggle for him. They told him that he would be separate from the other castes on the ship, and we're all mixed in together.'

Lutchmee nodded. She'd overheard Sarju just the day before, muttering, 'These filthy men, carrying on as if we are all the same.'

From the Brahmin caste, the most respected of the classes, Vottie herself had been raised according to Vedic traditions. As the village pandit in Ponneri, her father was revered; he studied the Vedas and taught many others the Vedic scriptures. As a result of this, his only daughter had been greeted kindly wherever she went. By the age of ten she was accomplished in the art of yoga, taught to her by her mother, and in the evenings when the men were gathered, she would listen intently to her father's teachings. She was the only girl there and no one seemed to mind.

Vottie's two elder brothers were being trained to become pandits by their father, and also attended the local missionary school, where they were getting a Western education. The school encouraged children of any caste and gender to attend, but castes below Brahmin seldom did, and most Indian families sent only their sons, as daughters were needed at home to help with domestic chores.

Vottie begged her brothers to teach her the new words they were learning in English, and, an exceptionally bright child, she quickly mastered the English alphabet from the books they tossed so carelessly aside when they returned from school.

Finally, her brothers, finding the work as spiritual advisors tedious and wanting more lucrative ways to earn money, asked their father if they could drop out of school and leave the village. Although frustrated with his sons' lack of discipline, he acquiesced.

With her brothers gone, Vottie found her desire to learn growing. She was drawn to the school lessons that sometimes took place outside, when she would sit discreetly at the back and listen to the Bible stories and mimic the words she heard in a clear, crisp English accent.

Brahmin girls had never attended school in their village and had never mixed with lower castes, but Vottie was determined. She broached this with her father one evening. At first he was reluctant. 'What would people say, Vottie? It is one thing letting you sit with me in the evenings but sending my daughter to school? They will laugh at me.'

Vottie's mother argued persuasively on her daughter's behalf. She could see that Vottie was restless, and her endless questions during the day were exhausting. 'You know that Brahmins must be educated to a high level, so why not this girl too? We can then make sure she marries well,' she told her husband.

Vottie's father finally relented and enrolled Vottie in the missionary school. The child excelled, and soon could easily read texts from the Bhagavad Gita and the Bible. But what she enjoyed above all else was the time she spent with the friends she made. At the school, they played together, all castes, girls and boys.

All her life she'd lived with rituals and routines and expectations of self-control without end, and at school she found herself laughing more and enjoying the learning – not only what was being taught by her teachers but also what she was picking up from the other children. For the first time, Vottie realised that children from the lower castes were no different from her, and it seemed to her that the caste system that divided everyone served no purpose at all.

She was careful, however, not to discuss this with her father. She had often heard him talk about how 'necessary' it was for there to be order in Indian society.

At the age of sixteen, Vottie wasn't surprised when her parents arranged her marriage to a similarly young Brahmin named Sarju from the next village. It bothered her that her new husband didn't approve of the mixing of castes, and she spoke out vehemently against this. The immediate and furious slap that she received across the face from him ensured that she didn't do that again.

India was changing and Sarju did not think it was for the better. He had enjoyed the privilege that came with being from a higher caste since birth, and he was not ready to give up his entitlement. He spoke out about it as often as he could, and while those around him were adapting and adjusting, he simply could not contemplate that he was to be on the same level as everyone else.

When the arkatis had arrived to spread their message of recruitment to South Africa, they'd assured him that men of high caste like himself were given the choicest, highest-paying jobs as sirdars – overseers – on the plantations, plus the best housing, and many other perks and benefits that the lower castes were denied. So Sarju made the decision that he and Vottie would leave India; he wanted to go to a place where his breeding would be appreciated and respected. And when the arkati implied that, for the right amount of money, he could influence both the farm and the position to which Sarju would be assigned, the Brahmin was only too happy to hand over the extra cash.

But things had not been going as expected for the angry little man. It had been bad enough in the coolie camp, but at least there he could occasionally escape the stifling confines of the married quarters and get away from the vermin that surrounded him, even if it meant striding for hours alone around the inner perimeter of the camp fence. Now that they were on the ship and there was nowhere else to go, his contempt had grown.

And Sarju was very vocal about his superiority; he felt unashamed that, according to him, he was better than everyone else. Not surprisingly, as a result he'd become less than popular among the other Indians. Without any discussion, the men withdrew from him and refused to befriend him. This was unfortunate because on the ship you needed all the friends you could get.

The sea was particularly rough that evening, with the waves seeming intent on turning themselves inside out. The sky had suddenly turned an ominous slate-grey and aggressive gusts rocked the *Umzinto* as if it were made of paper. Frothy waves beat against the hull and spilt onto the deck. An angry wind swirled like a demon overhead, with dark clouds gathering quickly and thickly.

On the top deck, Captain Roberts was shouting orders at the top of his voice. While the wind and waves whipped the ship relentlessly, the lascars scurried about, shouting instructions over one another and the howling wind.

The squall had come on them so quickly that some of the Indians, sitting in the mess on the port side of the ship, eating their dinner seated at the rough wooden communal benches and tables, had not had time to get below. Sappani, Seyan and Lutchmee, and Vottie and Sarju, as well as a few other Indians, were stranded in the mess, lurching from one side to the other, holding onto one another or anything that wasn't moving. Their meals – chapati, rice, fried mutton and beans – had flown off the tables, joining others' dinners on the floor, mixing together into a spicy-smelling mush as the ship rocked and swayed.

Chinmah, who'd been sitting at a neighbouring table, stood up and was suddenly thrown off balance, her childlike eyes wide with terror. As she lurched past, Vottie reached out and grabbed her hand, while Lutchmee held onto Vottie and with her other hand grabbed a wooden beam.

The chaotic motion of the ship then upset some of the freshwater barrels, and the water cascaded onto the floors, splashing and lapping around everyone's feet. Once empty, the barrels kept rolling and smashing into everything in their path.

As terrifying as those moments were, fortunately the squall passed quite quickly and the lurching eased up. Lutchmee released her grip, and she and Vottie helped Chinmah to her feet.

Lutchmee quickly looked for Sappani and Seyan. Sappani had wedged himself into a corner bench, Seyan tightly gripped in his arms, and he now gave her a quick smile to show they were all right.

Looking around, the Indians hoped to salvage some of their meal but there was very little that was edible. Standing up and seating Seyan on the bench, Sappani was reaching for an unclaimed chapati when he found his hand being kicked suddenly. The chapati fell back onto the deck. Startled, he looked up to see Sarju.

The Brahmin was beside himself with rage. Not only were the same cooks and the same utensils used to prepare meals for everyone, there was the added indignity, in his eyes, of eating in this disgusting place with everyone else.

'Gaandu,' he hissed, looking down, glowering, as Sappani straightened up but remained sitting on his haunches. Then more words in Hindi followed as Sarju erupted into a tirade of abuse, his outrage slopping out of him without restraint. 'Bad enough that my meals are prepared by pariahs and I sleep in a room with pariahs; now I must eat food touched by this filth!'

Everyone grew silent. Vottie watched in terror for a few moments, then made a move towards her husband. Lutchmee stepped quickly to her side and held her arm tightly, sensing the danger.

Not a single person moved and even the children's excited chatter died away. Everyone watched what Sarju would do next.

Slowly, Sappani stood up to his full height, never taking his eyes off the other man. Sarju was small but his air of arrogance and the inbuilt dignity that comes with being born a Brahmin made him appear larger than he was.

Sappani, expressionless except for the tiniest crease around his eyes that showed his disdain, clapped Sarju on his back. 'No trouble, bhai,' he said. 'The food is yours.' Then he turned and walked away.

Humiliated, Sarju stood gaping. Then, seeing the looks on the faces around him, he shouted out behind Sappani: 'Now you dare to touch me! Go, you dog! Run away, you bastard!'

Sappani did not even turn around.

When Sarju realised he was not getting anywhere with the spectators, he stalked off to complain to the Protector yet again. A few of the men followed him, laughing, no doubt to see if there was anything else that would prove to be entertaining.

Lutchmee let go of Vottie's arm. As they knelt to pick up the food, Vottie said, 'That bastard man. I don't know who he thinks he is,' and she shook her head. 'He is just not a good man. He is always making trouble wherever we go.'

Will this follow us all the way to Natal? Lutchmee wondered. Today's happening served as a reminder that maybe the past and the rules of Indian society would always be there.

Later, Sappani came looking for Lutchmee, and on seeing Vottie with her, and the worried frown lines on her forehead, he reassured her, 'Don't worry. I will stay far away from Sarju.'

Lutchmee felt another flicker of warmth for him. 'Vottie, don't worry, we will move away, even below the decks, just keep a distance, you know,' she added, pressing her friend's hand encouragingly.

Vottie smiled gratefully but Lutchmee could not get rid of the foreboding feeling – this was far from over.

The next evening Seyan had a raging fever. His body was limp and only whimpers escaped his dry lips. In the medical cabin Dr Booth diagnosed the little boy with mumps. His parotid glands were swollen and he was having great difficulty in swallowing. The family had to be put in quarantine immediately in a small cabin guarded by sepoys, kept empty for this very purpose.

Sappani and Lutchmee took turns with Seyan. He cried continuously and clung to his father, refusing to be put down. They tried to keep him cool by sponging him with rags dipped in water. Lutchmee spooned a weak broth into his mouth at every opportunity, and they kept up the medicine that Dr Booth had given him to help with the pain.

Terror and dread were etched into Sappani's face – he had lost his wife to disease, and now his child was ill. Lutchmee felt helpless; she could see Sappani's fear and didn't know how to alleviate it. Seyan demanded all their attention and they took turns to sleep when they could.

On the third day, Seyan's fever broke and Dr Booth felt a bit more optimistic. Seyan's was the only case of mumps he'd diagnosed on board so far, and he hoped that the parents' quick actions in getting themselves quarantined would contain the disease.

'You must stay here with the boy for a further five days, in case one of you gets it,' he told Lutchmee and Sappani.

Making his way up through the decks towards his cabin, Dr Booth thought about what had brought him to this point. After he'd completed his education, he'd set up a small practice in London. An enquiring and adventurous soul by nature, it wasn't long before he found himself frustrated by the same complaints every day: the endless litany of hysterical symptoms among the upper-class women (most often the result of sheer boredom, he suspected), the attacks of consumption (which, despite his prescribed light diet of jelly and port, almost always ended in a protracted period of lying on a sofa, and then death), venereal diseases (passed on by their husbands, who frequented the prostitutes who worked near the ports and garrisons, and which he treated with mercury), and the bloody and often tragic horrors of childbirth.

Of course, there were also the regular outbreaks of smallpox, cholera, typhus and measles, which sometimes killed entire families, but there was nothing Dr Booth could do about these other than be as kind as possible to those suffering, and alleviate their pain with judicious applications of alcohol and opium.

For Booth, there was also the increasing pressure from his widowed mother to get married, in which he had no interest at all. He'd taken to escaping to Portsmouth over the weekends, to avoid having to sit through yet another dinner orchestrated for him to meet yet another available young lady, and it was there that he'd discovered that he liked being among the ships and other young men. He'd spent time in the docks and would often ask permission to go on board ships that were being repaired. It was in the dockyard that Booth heard about the law that stipulated that every ship carrying indentured Indians to the colonies had to have a medical doctor on board.

He signed up, sold his burgeoning London practice to a friend for a song, and within a month he was on this, his first sea voyage as a ship's doctor. It was both the adventure he'd sought and a massive eye-opener for the young Briton. Being a private man, he enjoyed the solace of being at sea, but he'd heard the stories and knew that things could go wrong very quickly.

He felt his pulse quicken. He was out of his depth here, with so many people and only him to make sure they all made it to the other side …

*

Lutchmee, Sappani and Seyan had been together for a little over two weeks now, and Seyan was almost recovered. The time together in quarantine made it seem as if they were in another world.

The sounds Seyan made in his sleep became familiar and Lutchmee found herself feeling calm and confident when the boy was in her arms. And Seyan nestling into his father's embrace was also wonderful to watch, and it made Lutchmee a witness to the love that Sappani was capable of. She felt a twinge of an emotion she hadn't experienced before. It seemed to be born out of the need to feel wanted. Gazing at the baby in his arms, she too wanted to be held and feel his strong arms envelop her.

Suddenly, she felt desperately alone as her past swam in front of her. Long gone was her sense of trust and anything that could resemble stability. The agony and rejection of her marriage, and the humiliation and pain of the two months after she ran away from her husband's mother's house were almost too much to bear, and she sensed that if she let them bubble to the surface, they could ruin any chance of a future with Sappani. She took comfort in the fact that India's shores were getting further and further away. With every inch of sea the *Umzinto* crossed, her past was being buried ever deeper. Nobody would ever need to know anything about it.

'Are you okay?' Sappani's voice interrupted her thoughts.

She smiled a yes, and indicated that he could take her place. She carefully moved into a sitting position, then slowly stood up with Seyan in her arms. As she passed the soundly sleeping child over to his father, Sappani leaned forward and lightly kissed the top of her head. Like magic, she felt her fear evaporate.

Taking her turn on the floor of the tiny cabin, she closed her eyes, laid her forehead on her bent knees, and listened to her husband's breathing slow into sleep. Some time later, his muttered cries of 'Saari, Neela, saari,' woke her, and she quickly got to her knees and shuffled over to the side of the bed. He'd turned onto his side, his little boy – whose breathing, she realised, was now slow and calm – clutched to his chest.

Gently, Lutchmee laid a hand on Sappani's back and rubbed it very lightly. His agitation eased, and he slept on. She felt the rhythm of his breathing below her fingertips and revelled in the delight of this moment. Her eyes grew heavy but she fought her tiredness, afraid that if she closed them this would vanish.

Later that night, Lutchmee woke drenched in her own sweat and both sides of her face ached. She didn't want to wake them but she felt hot and her joints ached.

Sappani stirred and she shook him awake. 'I think I'm sick too,' she croaked, her mouth dry.

He called out to the sepoy on guard, who alerted the doctor. Holding the gas lamp over her, Sappani helped her into a sitting position and began the much-rehearsed practice of trying to keep her cool, while they waited for Dr Booth.

Over the next few days Sappani took the same care of Lutchmee that he'd done with Seyan. He fed her broth that Vottie left outside for her, and swabbed her sweating forehead when her fever grew too high. Dr Booth visited often and was pleased with how quickly she recovered.

Journal of KB Shaw, Protector of Immigrants
Aboard the Umzinto, *28 May*

The northern horizon is black and the wind blaws lang and sairly – we can be sure of a squall soon. My cabin is hot and there is no breeze. I would be happier in the dreich days of Inverness than this hell.

I thought the last run would be the last. This had better be it. I've had enough of the sea and the heat. I'm pure done in with these coolies – the pay is not good enough to get them from one shore to another.

The captain, Roberts, is a nice enough lad but he's far too young.

He has let the coolies stay out on the deck longer and this can only be bad news.

They have been fighting since we left port. They fight over everything and the noise they make, all the whisky in the world cannae drown them out. Today they fought over castes and then over tobacco and blankets.

I have my work cut out for me and every day I am meting out punishments and it does not seem to be having an effect on them.

The wummin, too, fight; yesterday it was over soap. Now the lascars and sepoys have joined in and are blootered every night. I'm scunnert of the lot of them.

5

Umzinto, Indian Ocean

June 1909

The men had been drinking the kallu that had been smuggled on board. While alcohol among the Indians was forbidden, as long as there was no trouble, the sepoys turned a blind eye to it. There had been some disturbance, though: a fight had broken out and one of the Indians had injured another, breaking his jaw. The captain had contemplated chaining some of the drunk men to the top deck to set an example but decided against it. They were a few weeks into the journey and everything was going well, and he wanted to keep it that way.

It was late, and most people were settling down to sleep, but Sarju, who had spent much of the day drinking, began to get animated and loud. 'We are like pigs here; worse even,' he slurred, 'sleeping with these filthy dogs!'

In such a limited space, privacy was not possible, and Vottie knew that her husband's voice was loud enough for everyone to hear. She also knew that when he got to this stage of drunkenness, Sarju was like a performer, feeling duty bound to give the watching eyes a show. She knew only two types of drunk men: the ones who became merry, then sang sad love songs badly, then cried for someone who'd passed on – usually their mother – and finally went to bed loving everyone. Her husband was certainly not one of those; he was the type who became increasingly indignant and nasty with alcohol.

Lutchmee, Sappani and Seyan were back in the married quarters, with Lutchmee and Seyan fully recovered. Seyan had just gone to sleep in his father's arms and Lutchmee was hoping he wouldn't wake. Sappani looked over at Sarju but remained where he was, pacing quietly, rocking the baby.

'Maadher chod, every one of them! Think they are like me.' Sarju got out of bed, tottering precariously.

A sepoy came past and Sarju sat back down on his bunk, momentarily quietened.

Vottie lay pensively in her bed, waiting for the inevitable.

'Saala kutta,' Sarju said loudly, pointing in Sappani's direction. 'He thinks he is better than me. Now they are back here, bringing their diseases to us too.'

Seyan began to whimper and then to cry. This had a ripple effect, with another child starting up, then another, and the fragile pre-sleep peace was shattered.

Vottie felt uneasy as several dozen accusing, tired eyes settled on them both. 'Please, Sarju, let's just sleep now. No one wants any trouble,' she whispered to him.

'Why? Because you want to be their friend, hah?'

Vottie knew things would only get worse from here, and watched in dismay as Sarju edged closer to Sappani. Getting off her bed, Vottie hurried after him, grabbing his arm. 'Just stop, Sarju. These people are sleeping. Please.' The fear in her voice was unmistakable.

Tiny hairs on the nape of Lutchmee's neck prickled as she felt the tension. She took the swaddled Seyan from his father's arms and made for the far end of the cabin. As she passed Chinmah's bunk, she helped the pregnant young woman to her feet, then ushered her in front of her.

Sappani nodded at Lutchmee, wordlessly telling her to remain where she was with Chinmah and Seyan at the far end of the cabin.

Lamps were being quickly relit as men got out of their bunks, and a general buzz of dissatisfaction rumbled around them. Vottie stepped back as a group of them moved menacingly towards Sarju.

'Muttaa koodhi,' one of them yelled, as he shoved Sarju in the back.

'So, you are the big man, hah, the one who doesn't like us pariahs?' a second man said as he stepped in front of Sarju.

Vottie was terrified: the alcohol had loosened Sarju's lips and heightened his resentment, and being made a fool of in front of everyone wasn't going to help.

She stepped between him and the men, facing her livid husband. 'Let's just go to sleep, Sarju. These people don't want trouble.'

She tried to take his arm but he shrugged her off angrily, his nostrils flaring, his eyes ablaze. It was as if he was seeing her for the first time. For an instant, everything was silent. Then, without warning, he swung his right fist into her face. The sound of his heavy gold rings against her soft flesh was sickening.

Vottie's tiny body rocked unsteadily, and belatedly, uncertainly, she raised her hands to defend herself.

'Bitch! It's you! You like these dogs, these pigs!' he shouted, grabbing her by the shoulders, raising his right knee and landing it in her stomach.

'Aiyoo, Vottie!' Chinmah screamed.

Vottie crumpled to the floor, drawing herself inwards, wrapping her arms over her head. 'Please, Sarju,' she whimpered.

Everyone stared and a few of the men stepped back. This was not their business.

Like a predatory animal, Sarju circled her, eyes fixed and glaring, arm raised, poised to strike again.

Putting Seyan into Chinmah's arms, Lutchmee tried to push through the crowd to get to Vottie, but Sappani got there first. With ease, he caught Sarju's hand in mid-air and twisted it behind his back. Gripping Sarju's shoulder, he yanked him backwards.

Sarju kicked out towards his wife but his foot ricocheted uselessly, pushing him off balance. He fell back against Sappani, screaming, spit gathering in the corners of his mouth like sea foam. 'Behinchod! Take your filthy hands off me,' he shrieked. Straining with frustration, the veins in his neck bulging, he tried to get out of Sappani's grip.

Sappani remained unmoved. It was almost as if he couldn't hear any of the vile insults at all. His face was calm, his expression blank.

Two other men stepped forward to help Sappani restrain Sarju while Lutchmee helped Vottie to her feet. Blood gurgled from Vottie's mouth and nose as she made a feeble attempt to stand upright. She fell to the floor again and this time a few more hands helped her to get up.

Most of the lower-caste Indians on the ship had suffered at the hands of higher castes before, and, sensing the weakness of the trapped Brahmin like animals smelling blood, they began to move in on Sarju. Sappani realised the danger as the crowd closed in, but Sarju was far too drunk to be aware of his predicament.

'Let's take him to the Protector,' Sappani said, putting as much authority in his voice as he could, and quickly dragged the belligerent Indian up to the top deck.

Leaving Seyan in the care of one of the women in the married section, Lutchmee and Chinmah took the dazed Vottie to the hospital cabin.

'Her husband, he did this,' Lutchmee volunteered to Dr Booth.

The doctor nodded. Gently, he tipped a small quantity of laudanum into the corner of Vottie's mouth. The medicine took effect quickly, and Vottie flopped back onto the examining table, her eyes heavy.

The doctor looked Vottie over carefully. 'Her nose is broken,' he said. 'The cut inside her mouth will heal on its own.' He stitched the wound on her right cheek where Sarju's rings had torn into her flesh. He gently palpated her stomach and, even drugged as she was, she winced. 'I think we will have to see if she can keep any food down over the next few days. For now, just give her liquids.'

'Doctor, is she going to be okay?' Chinmah asked, worried.

'She needs rest and a bit of care,' he said.

Lutchmee thanked him, then turned to Chinmah. 'I will stay here with her. You go to bed. You need your sleep.'

Chinmah wanted to disagree, but she was also tired. 'I will come back, you can get some rest,' she said, before taking one last look at Vottie.

'You should be taking it easy yourself,' Dr Booth said, glancing quickly at Chinmah's belly.

Chinmah nodded shyly and left.

In the darkness, with the only sounds the distant churning of waves and her friend's laboured breathing, Lutchmee watched over Vottie and waited. Every time the injured woman stirred, her friend reassured her.

Meanwhile, Sappani and the other men had walked Sarju around on the top deck to try to sober him up, but he was still making a spectacle of himself. Annoyed, the sepoys had taken over. Pointing at Sappani, one of them had said, 'You come and tell the Protector what happened,' then they had half-marched, half-carried the stumbling Brahmin to the Protector's cabin, where the faint glow of a lantern was visible.

After listening with evident irritation to Sappani's account, Shaw had ordered Sarju to be put in the brig to sober up. He would be dealt with in the morning.

Sappani had placed a mug of water in the cell for Sarju before he descended to the lower deck. Seyan was sleeping deeply, as if nothing had happened. Chinmah was asleep with him, one arm protectively over the child.

In the early hours, Chinmah woke, handed the baby to his father, and returned to the hospital cabin to take over from Lutchmee.

When Vottie opened her eyes the next morning, both Chinmah and Lutchmee were sitting silently next to her bunk. Vottie stared ahead in silence for some time. Her head was heavy and her eyelids felt like lead.

Dr Booth came in to check on his patient. 'Feeling better?' he asked kindly.

Vottie stared at him. She felt herself floating away.

The doctor looked at the row of tiny, neat stitches on her cheek and peered into her mouth. 'No more bleeding,' he said. 'You can come and see me in the morning and evening here for the next few days, just to make sure there is no infection.'

Chinmah spoke, her voice louder and clearer than usual. 'Please,

Dr Booth, she can't go back to Sarju. It is not safe. Let her move to the single women's area.'

Dr Booth looked at Vottie and the various shades of bruises on her face, and nodded his agreement. 'I'll speak to the Protector,' he said.

Although Shaw was clearly unhappy about it, he gave permission for Vottie to be moved, and Lutchmee and Chinmah helped her slowly descend, step by painful step, from the hospital cabin to her new bed on the bottom cot of a bunk shared with Jyothi, a fresh-faced young girl of about sixteen. Jyothi was on the ship without family and seemed to delight in the company of the three women.

Now that the pain medication was wearing off, it hurt Vottie to even smile. She sat silently as they swabbed her cheek with the medication that Dr Booth had administered to help the wound heal.

'I'm so sorry, Vottie,' Jyothi sighed, clasping Vottie's hands in her own, her voice wavering.

Vottie nodded and tried to smile.

'Can I do anything to help you?' Jyothi asked, eager to be of use.

Lutchmee, who seemed to be taking control of everything that morning with a quiet determination, responded. 'You can help feed the big baby,' she giggled, handing Jyothi the bowl and spoon.

Jyothi began to spoon sambar into Vottie's mouth. Vottie took a few small sips then waved the food away.

'You must eat, bahan,' Jyothi said, and persuaded her to take a few more mouthfuls.

'Let's get some water and we'll wash her hair,' Chinmah said. 'I need help – this gets in the way,' she added, smiling and touching her stomach lightly. Jyothi smiled back and followed her out, finding comfort in her new-found usefulness.

When the women returned with the water, Lutchmee dipped a rag into it and carefully cleaned the blood off Vottie's face. Humming softly, Chinmah wet and lathered Vottie's hair, and Jyothi joined in. Tenderly, the women washed their friend and helped her into clean clothes. Then they shook out the linen and made up Vottie's bed, and helped her back into it.

Journal of KB Shaw, Protector of Immigrants
Aboard the Umzinto, *14 June*

The coolie Sarju is raging and being all high and mighty. The eejit had a right square go at his wifey and then wants to skelp with anybody he can. He's a roaster and the other coolie walked away cool as you like. I think Sarju will stay put in the brig and give us all some peace and quiet and give him a chance to simmer down.

His wife was braw enough before he broke her face. Now she has to be in the single wummins section so her husband cannae hurt her again. It has meant moving people around and there were complaints of course. There are complaints about everything.

I dinnae ken how I can put up with them much longer. They fight and complain and want mair all the time. Mair scran, mair water and mair time on the deck.

For the next few days, Vottie was never alone and Jyothi was constantly by her side. She combed Vottie's hair and made sure that the stitches were clean and dry, or she would just sit quietly next to her while she slept. Lutchmee maintained her daily rice-cleaning duties on the top deck, having to do a bit more without Vottie's help.

Jyothi became skilled at pilfering treats from the galley. In addition to their regular meals, she smuggled out bits of dried fish and biscuits, which needed to be mixed with water for Vottie to swallow. She had also managed to get some ganja, a common remedy in India since ancient times and one of the most beneficial drugs to heal wounds, fight malaria, cure leprosy and help mental illnesses. 'Try some,' she said. 'It will help with the pain.'

'Where did you get this from?' Lutchmee asked.

'I traded it for a few things.' She stuffed the ganja into a wooden pipe and lit it. Vottie inhaled the smoke a few times and had a coughing fit. Then she leaned back, her head feeling heavy and light at the same time. She found the women's constant chatter soothing and she allowed the cadence of their voices and their funny stories to wash over her. Flanked by her friends, she floated above her misery and physical pain. Yet she knew it was only a matter of time before she would have to face her husband again.

'It's not the first time and it won't be the last,' she said quietly to Lutchmee later that evening. 'He has done it before, many times.' Lutchmee looked at her with genuine pity as she continued. 'I lost a baby too. I was six months pregnant and he did not stop kicking me. He thought I wanted another man.'

'How did you come to be here? If he's Brahmin, surely he has land and money?' Lutchmee asked, puzzled.

'India – he did not like the way it is changing. He does not believe that we are all just the same …' Vottie sighed.

'What about your family?' Lutchmee asked.

'I left them behind. I wanted to be a good wife, and I thought maybe a new start would help. Look where that got me,' she said, sadly.

Lutchmee reached out to her, unable to find the right words to comfort her friend.

'I'm a Brahmin too, you know,' Vottie said. 'I even attended school and learnt to read and write with the missionaries.'

'I knew you were clever!' Lutchmee said, clapping her hands delightedly to soften the mood.

'Not that clever,' Vottie replied flatly, pointing to her swollen face.

Journal of KB Shaw, Protector of Immigrants
Aboard the Umzinto, *19 June*

The dunderheid captain is too young to maintain order and discipline, and Dr Booth is just a young lad too. He also complains without cease – not enough medicines, he says, and he wants us to treat the Indians like royalty. He will learn in time that it's pointless trying to do yer best. They don't appreciate it.

A wee bairn died and I had to throw its little brown body overboard. I felt like throwing it into the furnace, but you should have heard the fuss the Indians made. What a commotion! They wanted to do all their rituals and other such nonsense. The body bobbed on the surface in the ship's wake. The mother was wailing and clawing at her face and clothes. It was enough to wake the dead bairn up.

'Six lashes on the deck where everyone can see,' the Protector said to Sarju, who was standing in front of his desk, nervously playing with his fingers.

'But, sir, she is my wife. My wife,' Sarju said, fear flickering wildly in his eyes.

Ignoring his protests, Shaw waved the Indian away, and the sepoys, waiting outside the door, stepped in and took Sarju out before he had a chance to say anything more.

Order had to be restored on the ship. If the authorities heard that the Protector had not acted, then that would look bad for Shaw, like he was not taking charge. His concern was also about what would be waiting in Natal if Sarju's wife had not recovered by then. It was ultimately his responsibility to ensure that all the Indians arrived safely and in good health.

He called for Dr Booth. 'The wummin who was beaten – how bad is it? Is she going to be fit to work or is this going to have to come oota someone's pocket?'

'It was a vicious attack and really she stood no chance against her husband, I believe,' the doctor said. He could barely conceal his dislike for the dismissive Protector.

'Is the lassy going to be able to work, boy?' Shaw thundered.

Dr Booth instantly took a step back. He paused, crossing his arms. 'She's recovering, but I don't think that she should stay with—'

'That's all I needed to hear,' Shaw interrupted.

Undeterred, Dr Booth persisted. 'While I am here, sir, can we talk about the medical supplies? I'm worried that—'

'Haud yer wheesht. I have to go and make an example of that man – make sure these coolies get the message,' Shaw replied.

'If I am to make sure the Indians are well, sir—'

'Listen here, there will be no Indians to look after if they start on each other. You don't know what they're capable off,' the big Scot snapped, and he marched off.

A few people had already gathered on the deck. Word had got around quickly and many of the indentured Indians wanted to see Sarju receive his punishment. Vottie was among them, standing on unsteady feet, supported by a reluctant Lutchmee.

Sarju was led out by sepoys, who tied him to the mast. His dhoti was dirty, and his face and body unwashed.

'Let's go, Vottie. There's nothing for you to see here,' Lutchmee said to her friend.

'I'm not going anywhere. This may be my only chance to see this bastard get what he deserves. I would walk on hot coals to see this,' she shot back.

Sarju's eyes were fixed on Vottie's when the first lash struck his bare back. While he screamed and cried in agony, Vottie's face was set in stone, unmoved.

That evening, Vottie sought out the Protector. She knocked on his door and he did not hide his surprise when she stepped in. 'I am Vottie, sir. I'm Sarju's wife. I have come here to ask you to please let me go, let me be free from that man.'

Steepling his forefingers, Shaw rocked back in his chair and surveyed the damage. She certainly was not nice to look at with her bruised face and swollen nose.

'He is not a good man. Please help me,' Vottie said, quietly and pleadingly.

'Why should I interfere?' Shaw asked, his thick Scottish accent making it difficult for Vottie to make out his words. 'You are his wife and you agreed to marry him.'

'If you leave me with him, I am not going to live long,' Vottie said. 'Please, sir! I will do anything, anything you say. Just change the papers.'

'Surely yer husband has learnt his lesson now that his punishment has been executed?' Shaw said, irritably. 'Can't ye make amends?'

'I am asking you to protect me,' Vottie pressed on. 'Protect me from a man who will kill me.' When she saw by his expression that Shaw wasn't moved by her pleading, she added, in a louder voice, 'A dead woman can't work!'

Shaw felt the warm air suffocating him. Yes, he was the Protector of Indian Immigrants, hired by the British government to do exactly that. He doubted it meant that he needed to meddle in their domestic affairs, though. 'I don't have the authority to grant your request. This sort of thing is dealt with in the court,' he said. Vottie felt despair, but her heart lifted slightly when he added, reluctantly, 'But until we get to Durban, maybe it's best if you stay with the singles.'

Outside the door, Vottie hugged Lutchmee. It was a small win.

When Lutchmee and Vottie returned below decks, Chinmah was waiting for them, hot and restless, massaging the small of her back. They helped her up to the top deck for some fresh air. They found a bench near the bow and sat down.

The next moment, Sarju was striding directly towards them. Vottie froze. The women moved closer to her on either side, and Chinmah slipped her small hand into Vottie's and squeezed tightly. Lutchmee looked around quickly. Two sepoys were sitting some distance away, resting in the shade of a sail.

Sarju walked up to Vottie and stared down at her with hatred in his dark eyes. 'You bitch! You filthy bitch! Look at me. Look at what they have done to me because of you!'

The three women stared at him. 'Please, bhai, just leave us alone,' Chinmah whispered.

He ignored her, continuing to fix Vottie with his hate-filled gaze. 'So, you think you are brave, eh? You think that you can do this and I will still want you?' Without warning, he drew his head back and spat in her face.

Vottie slowly wiped the spit off her face with the back of her hand. 'You think I want you, a bastard like you, who hits a woman?' she growled.

'You are *my* wife!' Sarju shouted. 'I can keep you or throw you away like the dirt that you are!'

Vottie pursed her lips but remained silent. Lutchmee glanced past Sarju at the sepoys, whose attention had been grabbed by the shouting, but who were clearly reluctant to stir from their rest.

'This bitch,' he said, noticing Lutchmee's movement and nodding towards her, 'she's looking for her husband. Think he is going to save you? That filthy dog. I'll kill him with one hand!'

'Please, we don't want trouble,' Lutchmee said. 'Vottie is still getting better. Maybe in a few days, you can talk. You are just angry right now.'

It was not the right thing to say, and Sarju exploded. He lunged for Vottie's throat. Lutchmee yanked Vottie's arm, pulling her friend out of harm's way, while Chinmah stood up quickly and stepped away from the enraged man.

Her eyes grew wide and she gulped down her fear. 'You leave her alone,' she said emphatically. No one had heard her use that tone or speak with such a volume before.

Sarju lurched to the side, trying to grab Vottie.

'Help us, help us!' Chinmah yelled, at last stirring the sitting sepoys into action. They came running, one of them pinning Sarju's arms behind his back, and both frogmarching him off down the length of the deck. The women could hear Sarju shouting obscenities all the way.

Journal of KB Shaw, Protector of Immigrants
Aboard the Umzinto, *25 June*

It has been fair weather and the captain says that we have just passed the Reunion Islands. Supplies are low, with only dhal and some rice, which seems to be mostly stones. I don't mind the scran but I could do with a good tattie.

I've been feeling a bit hingy aw week. Sores on me tadger and I'm finding it hard to pish. I cannae go to that skinamalinky longlegs Booth – he will start up again about medical supplies. Don't want him to know my business, so will have to wait to get to the port. I should have never pumped that scabby coolie hoor!

I spend my time teaching these coolies how to be civilised. Just when I think they know how to behave, they start up again.

6
Umzinto, southern Indian Ocean
July 1909

Life on the *Umzinto* had become a succession of dawns and dusks. The weather became more temperate as the ship sailed south although during the day it was still sometimes too hot to go onto the decks; in the evenings, though, it was cool. The sea was calmer and stretched in front of them like a silky blue ribbon.

Meals had become paltry affairs. With the journey nearing its end, supplies were low and the meals, made up of mainly rice and dhal, were barely edible. The rice was broken and the stones in it made their teeth ache. The fresh animals had long since been slaughtered and eaten, and even the cured meat was finished.

The rules had become a bit more relaxed and the indentured Indians were allowed more time on deck to stretch their legs under the watchful eye of the sepoys. They would gather in small groups, play cards and sometimes even sing bhajans. With the end in sight, there was no longer a need to ration as much, so daaru and tobacco were passed generously around. In moments like these, the gloom would lift: their new lives were closer than ever.

Lutchmee, Vottie, Jyothi and Chinmah always sat together when they could. Chinmah's round face, large eyes and diminutive size made her look more like a child than an adult, but her growing bump separated her from the children. Lutchmee and Vottie were worried about their pregnant friend, as her husband, Ramsamy, did not seem to even be aware that his very young wife was due to give birth soon. He seemed to be lost in a world of his own, seldom speaking to anyone.

While the other woman prattled on about their new life on the plantation, Chinmah's fear and her unborn child were locked together, growing. At every kick she would be reminded of her condition, and she would then push the thought away. It was not that she did not love her child; she was just terrified of giving birth and did not know if she was ready to be responsible for another life.

Jyothi was alone with Chinmah, sitting on the deck. She was massaging Chinmah's back and they fell into an easy conversation. 'We are all like jahaji bhais,' Jyothi said.

Chinmah smiled. 'Are you worried at all about the husband you will find in Natal?'

'It can only be better than what I was facing in my village,' Jyothi replied quietly, and Chinmah did not push her to explain further. But Jyothi inhaled deeply and exhaled before she began. 'I fell in love with a married man. He said he would leave his wife, but when we got caught, he told everyone that it was my fault. My brothers, my father and mother, they wanted nothing more to do with me, so they all drove me out. I met an arkati and now I am here. I can never go back.'

'So maybe this is a good thing for you too – a new life,' Chinmah said.

'Talking about new life, Chinmah, is Ramsamy going to care for you?' Jyothi asked quietly, lifting her eyebrows and gesturing with her chin to Chinmah's belly.

Before Chinmah could answer, Vottie and Lutchmee arrived, and any response Chinmah may have had got drowned in the women's chatter. They found a spot to sit with a clear view of the kushti match that was about to begin.

The wrestling matches had become less brutal and more comedic due to a lack of energy in the wrestlers, although the reduced rations and awful food had not altered the appearance of the two rather large men. Their stomachs were the first to collide, their fat jangling like tambourines. Flabby arms grappled and flailed, holding on to any bit of flesh or cloth they could find. They rolled and tumbled about, looking much like elephants playing in the mud. Laughing, they began to beat on each other until one of them got the better of the other and just sat on him, his bulk spread out over the man's face.

The four women began to laugh. 'I'm going to wet myself!' Chinmah gasped, trying to cross her legs despite her big belly in the way.

There was more cheering and applause as the victor helped the loser to his feet.

Later, as the sun dipped its head below the horizon, orange and ablaze, the festive mood erupted in dancing and singing. Dholaks and tablas appeared on the deck, and a sarangi was produced by one of the women.

She began softly, her eyes closed, her bow in her right hand and three fingers of her left barely touching the strings. Everyone stopped to listen. As she lost herself to the music, the notes danced in the air around them, and the men on the tablas and dholaks joined in. A woman with a soulful voice began to sing.

A few men got up to dance, singing the words they knew and laughing as they re-enacted the love scenes. The watchers could not help but join in, and began to coax others to join in too. The younger, more limber women got up and began to dance, sometimes singing in high-pitched voices as well.

The single ladies grew bold in their numbers. They too danced with steady, practised movements, trying not to meet the gazes of the watching men. They twirled and tapped their bare feet on the wooden boards, looking like exotic butterflies. They danced kathak and bharatanatyam, their bodies like silk ribbons, losing themselves in the music and sea and space around them. Dancing gave them the freedom to be beyond earthly bounds, as close to any goddess as possible.

For each of the girls, the dancing also held a moment in their past. They recalled dancing in front of family, of fathers they would never see again; being admonished by a dance teacher, a far-reaching authority that could be heard even now.

'I used to dance in the temple as a girl,' Jyothi volunteered as she sat swaying to the music, hungrily watching the dancing women.

'Go! Go and dance, Jyothi. Enjoy it!' Chinmah nudged her.

That was all the encouragement Jyothi needed. The music and laughter floated over her and she drew herself up to her full height. She felt her apprehension lift; weeks at sea, fear, anticipation, all seemed to fade. She inhaled deeply – not the scent of the sea, but the smell of promise. A quick smile crossed her face and the evening glow highlighted her cheekbones. Gathering her sari around herself, she began to dance the odissi, the swaying of her hips and expression in her eyes paying tribute to the goddess Sarawati.

When the dancing was over, Jyothi was out of breath and her face was flushed. Her friends were delighted to see her youthfulness and exhilaration.

'You are so good! Definitely good enough to dance in the temple!' Chinmah said.

Jyothi blushed and accepted their praise. She had a spring in her step as she walked now, her face a picture of childlike innocence.

On the top deck, the solitary figure of a sepoy called Muthu had been watching Jyothi with interest. As she'd danced, lost in her own world, he'd felt his lust rising. How long had it been since he had last felt the warmth of a woman?

Much later, the Indians were finally instructed to go below to sleep. After a few protestations, they eventually made their way down to their bunks.

In the single ladies' quarters, the women were still in a state of slight euphoria, re-enacting the dancing they'd seen and giggling. They held up saris as screens as they changed out of their clothes, undoing their plaits and buns and making up their cots for the night.

Without warning, sepoy Muthu walked in. Some of the women were still undressing, and they tried to cover themselves up. Unhurriedly, he walked up and down the rows of bunkbeds, running his eyes over the women, taking his time to look closely at each face.

'Challo, challo,' he said gruffly, finally, before walking out again.

The women, unsettled by this unwelcome and unaccustomed intrusion, finished their preparations for bed quickly. As each woman got into her cot and settled down for sleep, a quiet settled over the section.

Some time later, Muthu returned, walking over to the glowing lamps that were usually left burning every night and extinguishing them.

'Bhai, we need the lamp on,' a voice said.

'Not tonight,' he replied flatly. 'We've got to save the kerosene. There's not enough left.'

Jyothi lay awake in the darkness. She did not like this dense lack of light. She listened to the whispers of the women around her, then turned on her side and curled into herself, allowing her mind to meander back to her dancing. In the darkness, she smiled as she dozed off.

Jyothi woke feeling anxious and hot. She had kicked off her blanket because the lower deck was always stuffy. She sat upright, groped for her lota, which was next to her cot. Locating it with her fingertips in the pitch dark, she gripped it and drank deeply.

She lay down again, listening to the breathing around her. She sensed rather than saw a movement in a far corner, then heard the creaking of floorboards. Somebody was moving very quietly around the sleeping quarters. Perhaps it was someone who had been to the latrines and was now trying to get back to their bed.

She was about to sit up when she felt the crush of a person on top of her. The wind was knocked out of her chest. A large clammy hand was clamped over her mouth and nose, the rough fingers pressing painfully into her face.

She bucked and writhed, trying to throw off the hot, heavy body. As she realised she was running out of air, and began clawing at the hand on her face, her attacker grabbed at her nightie, shoving it roughly up above her waist. Using his legs to prise hers apart, he fumbled with his trousers. Jyothi felt the vomit rising as her consciousness ebbed. Her heart beat wildly, as if it was trying to burst out of her chest.

His flesh against her inner thigh was sticky and foreign. The burning sensation, the unbearable thrusting, his fetid breath on her neck and sick-sounding guttural moaning into her hair, hung in a space that she could not make sense of.

He gave a final moan and slumped over her, his hand falling from her mouth. Jyothi desperately sucked in huge lungfuls of precious air. The man pushed himself off her, and she lay immobilised, listening to his retreating footsteps.

The silence rushed back into the sleeping quarters, flooding the darkness, and Jyothi once again heard the sighs and snores of those sleeping around her. It was as if no one had even been there.

Her breathing decelerated and very slowly her heart returned to its rhythmic patterns. There was stinging pain between her legs, and a disgusting wetness that she knew was part of him. She rolled sideways and retched.

He was gone but the smell of him lingered on her skin, her face, her being, as if he had swallowed her whole. His brutal attack had changed her, and she no longer felt connected to herself; his violent intrusion had unmoored something fundamental in her. She knew with a terrible and fierce certainty that she would not be able to face the procession of dawns and dusks that lay ahead of her. It felt as if she was poised over the edge of the world, without anything mooring her any longer.

Gingerly, she got out of bed and, on shaking legs and with hands outstretched to avoid bumping into the rows of bunkbeds, she walked slowly and painfully to the ladder and made her way to the upper deck.

A few sepoys were sleeping in their hammocks, being gently rocked by the sea, their legs and arms dangling like seaweed caught in nets.

It was a clear night and almost every star was visible. A cool breeze caused goosebumps to rise on her arms and she wrapped them around her torso. Her dark tresses lifted slightly in the night air.

The smell of the sea, the sound of the water lapping against the side of the ship and the gentle hum of the engines seemed to work with each other to create another existence, one far away from what had just happened to her.

Barefoot, Jyothi tiptoed to the far side of the ship, her eyes steely and moist. Calmly, as if she were in a dream, she gathered up her nightie in her one hand and stepped up onto a seat. The wind whipped her hair around her and tugged as she looked out at the black sea. Tears shone in her eyes but stayed there, and did not fall.

She peered over the edge. It was inky-dark down there, and the light bouncing off the water appeared very far below. She inhaled deeply and smiled, knowing that the feeling of being unrecognisable to herself, of being untethered from what made her her, would soon be at an end. This gave her the peace she was looking for, and she placed one bare foot then the other over the side of the *Umzinto*.

There was a splash as her body broke the surface of the black water but it was instantly swallowed up by the hum of the ship's engines.

The next morning, people emerged from below the decks, stretching and coughing, forming orderly queues, washing, praying. They performed their rituals in an automatic, perfunctory sort of way. Diyas were lit and there was chanting and the smell of incense and camphor as deities were revered and remembered.

In the galley, the women were preparing the morning meal. 'Where's Jyothi?' one of them asked. 'Go find her. Tell her we need her.'

Someone went below to the sleeping quarters, where she saw Jyothi's bed was unmade, the blanket trailing onto the floor. 'Jyothi?' she called. There was no response.

After checking in the latrines, the woman sought out Lutchmee and Vottie, with whom she knew Jyothi spent much of her time.

Lutchmee, who was busy changing Seyan, said, 'I haven't seen her this morning. The last time I saw her was last night, when we all went to bed.'

The limited confines of the ship meant that the news of the missing girl spread fast. Everyone had a theory, but it wasn't until one of the women who also slept in the single women's quarters mentioned that the sepoy Muthu had blown out all the lamps and left them in pitch darkness that Lutchmee and Vottie began fearing for their young friend. They immediately went below to have a closer look at Jyothi's bed.

Like a bad spirit being summoned, Muthu suddenly appeared behind them.

Vottie and Lutchmee turned to stare at him. 'Why did you blow out all the lamps last night? They are always left burning,' Vottie said, her voice hard.

Muthu jutted out his lower jaw. 'I don't have to answer to you,' he said, shaking his fist, and stalked off.

Some hours later, once the ship had been searched from bow to stern, with no sign of Jyothi anywhere, the bell rang for all the indentured Indians to present themselves on the top deck. Suspecting what they were there for, they all lined up quietly and without fuss. Vottie and Lutchmee wanted to retain a flicker of hope in their hearts but they both knew full well that there was only one way off a ship when it was at sea.

Shaw strode onto the deck and waited, twitching with nerves, while the sepoys counted everyone. When they reported back, the Protector's fears were realised: the girl was gone. He instructed the sepoys to question the Indians, but nobody knew anything about what had happened to Jyothi.

Groups of men and women huddled together on the deck, wondering what her fate might have been. The image of the happy young woman dancing only the evening before was still alive and fresh in their memories. Muthu, who seemed more aggressive than usual, took it upon himself to break up these gatherings, flourishing his whip to make the Indians scatter.

Vottie and Lutchmee went back below to Jyothi's bunk. They sat down next to her bedding. She had not owned much but they knew that the others would soon pick over her possessions like slum dogs over meat. Her blankets, saris and even her stash of biscuits would be argued over. The two women felt duty-bound to rescue her personal things, at least.

Folding up her bedding, Vottie's sharp eyes picked out a red streak on the blanket. Looking at it closely, she recognised it for what it was. Wordlessly, Vottie showed it to Lutchmee. The two women looked at each other at the same moment, shocked, knowing, hoping that in each other's eyes they would find a better explanation for the stain.

'We must go to the Protector,' Vottie said, her voice low and thick with rage and pain. 'He must find out who did this to her.'

'We know who it was,' Lutchmee pointed out. 'Muthu put out the lamps.'

'Then the Protector must punish him,' Vottie said.

KB Shaw was feeling exhausted. He'd already found Jyothi Ram's details in his ledger, and recorded her death by suicide, and the date. He wasn't looking forward to explaining it to his superiors when they reached Durban. He also hoped there were not going to be any more missing women.

'Come in,' he called when the women knocked at his door.

It was a sparsely furnished room, but with enough to show that he was a man with authority, with books on a shelf, and a large desk and chair that seemed out of place in the cramped space.

'We have concerns, sir,' Vottie said, ignoring Shaw's irritable expression. 'We believe that our friend Jyothi was …' She looked uncomfortable for a second, then straightened her shoulders and continued, '… assaulted by one of the sepoys.'

Shaw's expression remained almost unchanged, just his eyebrows rising a little. 'Really?' he said, his disbelief obvious. 'And I assume you have proof of this?'

Lutchmee stepped forward, her head lowered, the stained blanket in her outstretched hands. She tried to avoid this white man, and this was way too close for comfort.

Shaw recoiled slightly but Vottie persevered, pointing out the stain. 'Sepoy Muthu put out all the lamps in the ladies' quarters at sleep time. This is not normal routine,' she said. 'Why did he do that?'

His top lip curling, Shaw gingerly took the blanket from Lutchmee, holding it away from himself. Turning it this way and that, he gave a show of examining it while his mind whirred. The men were at sea for a long time, he told himself, and it got lonely for any man – Indians, sepoys and officials alike. The coolie women's paan-stained teeth and poor hygiene were enough for some men to keep their hands to themselves. But not many.

Muthu was a bully and a layabout, and he wouldn't put it past him to do something like this, but simply extinguishing some lamps didn't make him guilty.

Glancing up at Vottie, Shaw was suddenly aware of how different she was from the other coolie women – how bold and confident. Giving her a ghastly smile that revealed a set of large yellow teeth, he said insincerely, 'I will investigate. I will find out what happened to yer friend.'

Journal of KB Shaw, Protector of Immigrants
Aboard the Umzinto, *6 July*

We lost a lass last night. Killed and dumped overboard, or jumped. A few nights ago I heard some screaming coming from the lassies' lavvy but when I asked the next morning nowt could tell me a thing. The sepoys say that they saw and heard nothing and as usual the lascars say they were asleep. I find it hard to believe.

The doctor – he's a walloper. The company has to follow the rules of course and now Booth is being more of a pain in the erse. All in a flap about the railings around the bulwarks not being high enough, someone could fall over, and how he does not have the equipment he needs in the hospital cabin again. What am I supposed to do about that? We are days away from Durban – you'd think he would be relieved.

The coolie wummin from the singles quarters have the pox now. They are saying that they are getting sick from the crew messing aboot with them. Booth is aff his heid, complaining that he disnae have enough mercury to treat them all. I cannae cope with the bastards for much longer, they're doing my nut in.

*

One evening, with the ship only days away from Durban, Chinmah found herself in excruciating pain. She sought out Lutchmee, who was with Seyan on the lower deck, trying to get him sleep.

'I think it is time,' Chinmah told her.

Lutchmee sent someone to get Vottie, who was on duty in the galley. The two women were still discussing the best course of action when Chinmah's water broke, cascading down her legs and onto the floorboards. The pains came quickly after that.

Vottie ran to let the Protector and Dr Booth know that Chinmah was about to give birth, as well as to procure some basic supplies to help them deliver the baby. She returned with blankets and bowls of hot water, prepared for them by the women in the galley.

Word spread fast, and two other older women came below to help. Lutchmee sighed with relief – neither she nor Vottie had ever given birth, although both had assisted at births before; these women had children of their own. They took charge and issued orders.

Ramsamy was found on the top deck, playing cards. He was informed, but his expression remained the same and he continued playing his hand without so much as a word.

Chinmah, terrified and in agony, rode out each contraction screaming and straining. Sweat poured off her, and she hardly seemed aware of her surroundings.

The women took turns swabbing her body with cool cloths and all encouraged her, but Chinmah quickly became exhausted, crying helplessly as the hours passed and the contractions came relentlessly, one after the other.

Outside, daylight faded and the bell rang for the evening meal. A few minutes later, with a quiet patter of bare feet and without exchanging words, two women put down some food that they had smuggled out in the folds of their saris so that the makeshift midwives would have something to eat. They understood that the friends had a long, uncertain night ahead.

As the night wore on, the fear left Chinmah's eyes; they were now just two glassy, dark pools, devoid of understanding of the world of pain she was in, screaming when she could gather the strength, but otherwise weeping weak, impotent tears.

Dr Booth, who'd been happy to leave the delivery to the women, was sent for before he could go to bed. He examined Chinmah quickly while the ladies looked away. When they looked at him again his expression reflected his concern.

He tutted and stood upright. This girl still had the body of a child, and her cervix had not dilated much. He was worried about how it was all going to end. He silently began to weigh up his options and make a mental note of the medical supplies he would need. 'I'll be right back,' he said abruptly and walked out. The women stared after him.

Dr Booth was glad when he reached the fresh air. He sat down and let out a great sigh. Summoning a passing sepoy, Booth told him to inform the captain that a woman was having a baby and may not make it through the night. Then, shaking his head, Booth entered his cabin and took several hefty glugs from his silver hip flask.

Finally, he looked in his bag for his scalpels and sutures, his mind going back to when he'd practised on female cadavers almost five years before.

It was almost dawn. With the help of the doctor, the women had moved Chinmah to the hospital cabin. It was doubtful she'd even noticed. She was exhausted, fading in and out of consciousness, and her body seemed to have given up; she was no longer straining.

Lutchmee and Vottie stayed with their friend, holding her wet, limp hands. The other women sat outside the door, praying and chanting.

The young doctor looked almost as stressed as his patient. Beads of sweat were dripping down his face, which was bright red, and his throat and ears were flushed too. His blond hair stuck up like a parrot's crest. Panic was starting to set in but he tried not to show it.

'The baby is stuck,' he announced to Vottie and Lutchmee. 'The head is visible but it has not moved any further along the birth canal. Go and get the father, while I check if I have everything I need.'

Vottie found Ramsamy and shook him until he woke. 'Chinmah is having the baby and she is in trouble,' she told him.

He stared blankly at her.

'You need to come now!' Vottie said curtly, hardly able to believe how little interest he was showing.

Ramsamy followed Vottie back to the hospital cabin, then waited for some time outside before going in. He glanced at his wife, lying still and pale, while keeping his distance, which was no small feat in the cramped space. 'She is very young,' is all he said, before giving a brief bow and leaving the cabin.

Dr Booth, nonplussed, insisted that Lutchmee and Vottie stay with Chinmah. He set out all his equipment and asked Vottie to wipe it all down with an antiseptic solution. Chinmah's pulse was dropping and they needed to work quickly.

Vottie handed him the various instruments as they worked together to save the young girl's life. Lutchmee helped to raise Chinmah's legs and Dr Booth made an incision in her perineum. Lutchmee swabbed the blood so the doctor could see clearly. The baby was wedged tightly but Dr Booth was determined. He reached into Chinmah and began to tease the baby out. His coat was soaked in blood and there was a streak of blood on his forehead.

What seemed like hours later, a small, almost blue baby was pulled out of the unconscious Chinmah – an infant girl, surprisingly big, given the small parents who had created her.

Dr Booth quickly checked the baby over and stuck a finger in her mouth. She coughed and began to breathe on her own. Slowly her colour began to come in, and she let out a desperate cry. The doctor and the two women helping him let out sighs of relief, and Vottie wrapped the infant in cloths and blankets.

But Chinmah wasn't out of the woods yet. With Lutchmee's help, Dr Booth worked to stem the flow of blood and sew up the incision he'd made.

Sitting outside the hospital cabin on the floor, Ramsamy had fallen asleep. Vottie prodded him. 'It's a girl,' she said, uncovering the little one's face and leaning down to show the father. He gazed sleepily at the child for a few moments, then closed his eyes again. Vottie stared in perplexity at Ramsamy, then went back into the hospital cabin, where Booth was completing the suturing.

'The mother is going to need care. She's lost a lot of blood,' he said, addressing the women but keeping a sharp eye on his work.

'Yes, we will take care of her, doctor,' Lutchmee said.

'These stitches need to be kept clean,' Booth continued, as he tied the loose end of the surgical gut. 'She can rest here. I'll come back and check up on her soon.'

The doctor hesitantly patted Chinmah's unreceptive knee, then left the cabin.

By the next morning, the volume and quantity of the Indians' incessant chatter had reached new levels. Protector Shaw was irritated. At breakfast with the captain, they could barely hear themselves speaking. They consoled each other with the knowledge that within two days they would be docked in the harbour and rid of the coolies.

Last night the young doctor had come to see the Protector in his cabin. The woman who'd given birth was not in the clear yet, Booth had told him, and had reiterated the need for more and better medical supplies. Shaw had listened impatiently, knowing full well that nothing would change. *The doctor has much to learn*, the Protector had thought to himself as he watched the exhausted man leave. He'd seen conditions worse than this. This trip had been an improvement!

Land was in sight and a rumour was started by the lascars that they would be in Durban by the next morning. From their lofty perches, they were making crude jokes about the good time they were going to have in port. With their pockets heavy, as they were paid only when they docked at their destination, the lascars would find their solace in the brothels that lined the far side of the dock. Cheap liquor and women of all colours, shapes and sizes abounded.

In preparation for docking, the decks were scrubbed and cleared. Everyone – crew, passengers and indentured Indians alike – was responsible for ensuring that they would pass the inspections. Before a single soul disembarked, officials would come aboard the ship for a close look, and if there were any sign of illness or infection, everyone would have to be quarantined.

Despite his busy night and lack of sleep, Dr Booth wanted to see his patient. A part of him had expected Chinmah to be a corpse by the morning, so he was relieved to be greeted warmly by the women around her, their hands pressed together in gratitude and their heads bowed. Checking Chinmah's stitches, he wrestled to push the images of her battered little body out of his mind, but he knew it would stay with him forever. The cabin smelt stuffy and metallic after all that had happened in it during the night.

After the doctor had left the previous evening, Lutchmee and Vottie had stayed with Chinmah through the night, leaning over the spent young woman and stroking her forehead with cool, gentle fingers. Lutchmee had rocked the baby, which seemed unusually content and wasn't yet crying for its mother's breast – a small mercy.

In the early hours, Chinmah's eyelids had finally fluttered open as she slowly regained consciousness. When she'd taken stock of where she was, and Vottie had whispered to her all that had happened, including about the stitches she'd had to have, Lutchmee had laid the infant girl in her mother's arms. There was an instant transformation in Chinmah's eyes. They no longer reflected a child's innocence but shone with the fierce protectiveness of someone who has had to fight to stay alive. The girl was now a mother. Looking down at her sleeping baby, soon Chinmah was asleep too.

Now Dr Booth said, 'I'd like to examine the baby. Pass her here,' and as Chinmah handed over her daughter and lay back on her bed, Booth gently pulled open the swaddling, looked at the cherubic face within, and said, 'Oh, what an angel.'

The doctor examined the newborn and reassured Chinmah that, apart from some bruising, which was to be expected after all the infant had been through in order to make her way into the world, all was well.

Later, he made sure the Protector properly recorded the birth of the baby. Chinmah had named her Angel.

*

Leaving Lutchmee with Chinmah, Vottie went to find Seyan and make sure that all was also well with the little boy. Sappani was happy to hand him over for a while, and Vottie took him up to the top deck and sat in the sun with him, rocking him on her lap.

She was pensive. She'd stayed clear of Sarju for days now – her transfer to the single women's quarters had afforded her that luxury. But the end of the journey meant that she was going to have to return to his side as his wife. They'd signed on as a married couple so, of course, they would be assigned to the same plantation. Sarju was hoping to be made a sirdar, his job to oversee the work of the other Indians on the plantation. Vottie knew that her options were limited – fieldwork or perhaps work in the planter's house as a maid or servant.

She felt a deep sense of misery. With the Protector not having allowed her to officially leave Sarju, she would be forced as his wife to go wherever he went. And where would she even go if she had permission to leave him? But she did not care about that; anything would be better than staying with this man she'd grown to detest. Sarju was showing his true colours and she knew that was not going to change.

Any affection for her husband or feelings of loyalty to him had died inside her and in their place was a strong and growing desire to survive. Vottie resolved that she needed to pretend that everything was okay, to get Sarju to let his guard down, and then perhaps she would have a chance to get away from him and the torment he rained down on her.

Lutchmee appeared at the top of the stairs from below decks, moving slowly, helping Chinmah, who was clutching her baby girl – Angel – to her chest. Vottie quickly shifted Seyan onto her hip, and went across to lend a hand. The three women carrying the two infants walked slowly across the top deck, and made themselves comfortable in the sunshine.

Together, they watched the approaching land mass in the distance. Comforting and warm, the air wrapped the ship in a cloud, and for a time the three women felt safe. The sea was flat and calm.

'We made it across the Kala Pani,' Vottie said.

'I almost didn't,' Chinmah said, the dark circles beneath her eyes and her pale face a reminder of her ordeal – but then she smiled.

Vottie relieved her of little Angel, who had a shock of black curls, a pert nose and dark irises. 'Aap khubsoorat hain,' she murmured, kissing the sleeping baby on her downy head. Vottie felt the familiar yearning as she hugged the newborn to her. Her insides seemed to turn to water and a dull ache returned. But she could never allow herself to bring a child into the world, as a baby would tie her to Sarju forever.

Vottie looked sideways at both the women, briefly touching the scar on her face, then whispered fiercely, 'I am going to leave that man. I hate him.'

Chinmah looked at her, bewildered. 'But how, Vottie? He is your husband.'

'That doesn't mean I don't hate him. Chinmah, that man will kill me if I don't do something to get away.'

Chinmah looked stricken, so Vottie, changing the subject, turned to Lutchmee with a cheeky smile. 'What about you, Lutchmee?'

'Whatever lies ahead, I am ready for it,' Lutchmee said, confidently. 'It can't be as bad as everything I left behind.' Briefly, her marriage to Vikram, his dead body lying on the ground, the hatred in her mother-in-law's eyes, rising smoke from what would have been her own living sacrifice, the hunger, the humiliation and the hands tightening around her throat – these images swam through her mind.

Seyan's tiny hand slipping into hers brought her back to the present and, with a sharp intake of breath, she reminded herself that all that was over. Sappani was a good man. He loved his son, he had never been harsh to her, and he had not even tried to touch her during the journey. She felt like she could ask for nothing more.

Lutchmee and Vottie clasped each other's hands, understanding each other without a single word being exchanged. A moment passed between them, coming from what felt like the deepest connection women could feel with each other.

Angel began to whimper, and Chinmah took the baby and fumbled with the opening of her sari blouse. She pressed her nipple between her fingers and guided it into the baby's expectant little mouth. Angel latched on immediately and her sucking sounds appeared to lull her to sleep as she closed her eyes.

Chinmah winced, her pain clear as she tried to sit comfortably. There in the sun, sitting with her two friends, suckling her newborn, she heaved a great sigh, then, like a flood, released a torrent of tears that she had been holding inside her.

She cried for her lost childhood, but she also cried out of sheer exhaustion, from the weight of being a new mother and her body no longer feeling like her own. What lay ahead in Africa was unknown and scary, with the added complication of a new baby. The ship had been a haven of sorts and now it seemed as if she and her baby were about to be ejected into a place that they did not understand.

PART III

ARRIVAL

The Coolies Here

They were a queer, comical, foreign looking, very Oriental like crowd. The men with their huge muslin turbans, bare scraggy shin bones, and coloured garments, the women with their flashing eyes, long dishevelled pitchy hair, with their half covered well-formed figures, and their keen inquisitive glances, the children with their meagre, intelligent, cute and humorous countenances mounted on bodies of unconscionable fragility, were all evidently beings of a different race and kind to any we have yet seen either in Africa or England.

– *The Natal Mercury*, 22 November 1860

7
Durban
July 1909

The dock in Durban wasn't deep enough for the *Umzinto* to go all the way in, so several longboats bobbed on the surface around the ship, waiting to take passengers to the shore. In each boat sat dark-skinned African men, looking as if they were carved from the same wood as the boats themselves. The Indians gaped – they had never seen anyone darker than themselves. These men had skin like polished betelnut, with short twisted hair like the outer covering of a coconut. They had large, thick lips and flashing white teeth that caught the sunlight and sent it back across the water.

The logs and medical journals had been checked by the port officials and declared to be in order. Against his better judgement, Dr Booth had been persuaded – aggressively – by Protector Shaw not to say anything about the venereal diseases that troubled so many of the indentured women to whom he himself had given a clean bill of health at the start of the trip eight weeks before. 'Haud yer wheesht, Booth, or this will be yer last trip,' the Scotsman had told the doctor.

For Booth, it was Hobson's choice. Medical amenities on this ship had been sorely lacking, and he'd been disturbed by some of the treatment he'd seen the Indians suffer at the hands of the crew and officers. He felt strongly that he had an obligation to try to improve conditions – medically, at the very least – for future shiploads of indentured Indians, but if word got out of the pox that had swept through the single women's quarters, he would be fired – or so Protector Shaw said – and then he would be in no position to improve anything for anyone. So, reluctantly, he signed off on the medical report, stating that all five hundred and ninety-five arriving indentured Indians – six had died on the voyage; one soul had been born – were in good health.

The certificate to offload the human cargo was given, and the indentured Indians formed a slow procession on the deck of the ship. Holding onto their possessions while pointing things out to one another, they chattered amicably.

When it was their turn, Sappani helped Lutchmee into one of the small boats, then handed Seyan to her, stepping in last himself, and helping her to get seated.

'Chinmah, you come in next,' Lutchmee called, and Sappani helped her and Angel in too. Ramsamy followed, stepping in cautiously and seating himself away from the others. Vottie was also in their boat, sitting next to her two friends.

The air was fresh and warm, and although it was midwinter here, the sun beat down on them.

Relieved to be off the ship, they drank in everything around them. The land was flat and in the distance they could see the tops of tall green trees. The waves washed rhythmically up onto white sandy beaches and the port was bustling with people.

They recognised the uniforms of the British soldiers and official-looking men. Hawkers sold fruit and vegetables from stalls. 'It will be so nice to cook something fresh,' Vottie said.

The Indians' first steps on dry land were difficult; it felt like the ground was churning and trying to throw them off like wild horses.

'Get in a line!' someone behind them ordered.

They waited until they were called to the checkpoints, where their papers were inspected by the officials. Then they were moved along to the coolie camp at the far end of the port. It was a makeshift building that reeked of human waste. The indentured Indians were to remain here until the planters arrived to fetch them.

Some sirdars were already there, acting on behalf of their masters, ensuring that the newest recruits would be at work without delay. Most of the sirdars were Indian too, having worked their way up the ranks. Now they worked as supervisors over the new labourers. They wore turbans and loosely fitted khurtas.

Captain Roberts walked past with Protector Shaw, their relief evident in their huge, genuine smiles. Behind them, Dr Booth rushed to keep up. Noticing Chinmah as he passed, he stopped to speak to her and stroke Angel gently on the cheek. 'You take care now, and make sure you see a doctor soon,' he said.

Vottie and Lutchmee thanked him and blessed him by touching his feet with both hands. Chinmah tried to do the same, but he quickly caught her elbow and helped her back to a standing position.

He flushed bright red, then walked determinedly towards the office with his file tucked under his arm.

'Ramsamy and Chinmah Naik, Mount Edgecombe Sugar Estates.'

The officials had finished calling out the final destination of each indentured couple, and Chinmah could barely keep herself upright. She felt like she was going to vomit. 'I can't leave you both, I can't!' she cried, holding on to Lutchmee and Vottie's hands. 'Please, can't you change it?' she begged the official.

'It's north of Durban – not far,' he replied abruptly and moved on.

Lutchmee caught her in a tight embrace and whispered, 'You can do this. You are the same girl who just gave birth to this baby. You have to do it for her.'

Vottie's eyes brimmed with tears and she too encouraged Chinmah, who looked panicked and confused.

Quickly, Lutchmee approached an older woman who was also being sent to Mount Edgecombe Sugar Estate. 'Please, bahan, this girl, Chinmah, is very young. Please help her.'

Realising what Lutchmee was doing, Vottie also sought out other women who were destined for the same plantation, and asked them to take care of Chinmah too. 'She has just had her baby,' she added, trying to ensure maximum sympathy and support for Chinmah.

The Mount Edgecombe sirdar was eager to get going before it got much darker. Chinmah was helped into the wagon, still crying. Lutchmee and Vottie continued offering her reassurances but neither of them was sure she was listening any more.

'Apna khayal rakhna,' Vottie said to her, hugging Chinmah like a little sister one last time. The young woman now sat silent, her tears used up.

Finally, just before the oxcart lurched forward, Lutchmee pressed something into Chinmah's hand. The new mother closed her hand around it and drew it beneath her sari.

'Look – see, no callouses! I am not a common labourer.' Sarju, furious, held out his hands to the officers, urging them to inspect them. On the official paperwork, he was listed as a fieldworker bound for Stanger Tea Plantation, north of Durban. 'I even gave that bastard more money! He said it was for sure that I would be a sirdar once I got here,' Sarju whined.

'Get in,' the sirdar said, sternly, indicating the oxcart. 'You can talk to the master once you are there.'

Unwillingly, grumbling, Sarju climbed into the cart.

Vottie stood there disbelievingly. She simply could not to go with Sarju. 'I need to go and speak to the Protector,' she murmured and began to walk away.

Suddenly a sjambok snapped next to her ear and the sirdar snarled at her. 'You get in right now, too. You can sort your problems out with the master later.'

'Stanger Tea Plantation.' Lutchmee repeated it out loud, hugging her friend, so that she would remember where Vottie was.

Sappani came forward and helped Vottie up into the oxcart. 'You look after yourself, Vottie,' he said.

Sarju jerked his head back, then spat viciously at Sappani's feet.

The cart trundled off, its wheels groaning into motion and awakening the dust. Vottie craned her neck until it ached, and until Lutchmee and Sappani were tiny specks in the distance.

Vottie sat silently next to Sarju in the oxcart, her skin burning where it was touching his. She listened as he talked to the other Indians about the injustice of it all. Part of her wanted this not to be a mistake, so that Sarju could be put in his place and seen for what he really was.

'I'm a Brahmin, you know. They don't know how to treat people like me.' He went on and on, oblivious to the looks on the other Indians' faces.

There were about ten of them, men and women, who stared at Sarju, blankly, exhausted, not caring at all about who he was and what he thought he deserved. A woman was trying unsuccessfully to quieten her child who appeared to be only a few months old. She reached into her blouse and pulled out a piece of cloth that was wet with her breastmilk. She gave it to her child, who sucked on it.

As they bumped along, Vottie thought about poor Chinmah, so tiny and frail. She was certain that these bumpy roads would be causing her a lot of pain. She remembered her large, unknowing eyes, and those eyes again in Angel. She thought of Jyothi, too, and that sepoy who had not been punished. The rage within her climbed.

Lutchmee cried freely, watching her friends leave, while Sappani held on to a wriggling Seyan, one hand gently resting on her shoulder.

The sirdar for their estate, Sezela Sugar Mills, south of Durban, had not yet arrived so they had no choice but to stay overnight at the coolie camp at the edge of the dock. Food was distributed and places to sleep were assigned for the night.

Lutchmee lay awake all night. Her heart ached at the thought of her friends. Her sisterhood was now divided and strewn across this strange new land.

Sappani couldn't sleep either. He thought about the sleeping child next to him and Lutchmee. His mind flitted to the face of the angry Brahmin. 'I hope we never see that Sarju again,' he whispered to Lutchmee.

'I hope she is going to be okay,' Lutchmee whispered back. They both knew she was worrying about Vottie.

Early the next day, the immigrants bound for Sezela Sugar Estate were awakened abruptly. The sirdar had arrived on his horse and was eager to get them back. Henry Rouillard, the plantation owner, could not spare any wagons that day – it was going to be a long walk. Within half an hour about fifty Indians, men, women and children, were assembled in the dusty yard. Bleary-eyed and still disoriented, they followed the sirdar, who kept his horse at a slow trot. They walked with no idea of how far they were going. The sun was still in a state of semi-slumber as they took in the scenery.

Sappani heard it before he could see it – the whispering rustle of the sword-shaped leaves in the wind – and he felt an odd sensation, as if the sound would forever be linked to him. The land in front of them and to the sides appeared to be shifting and restless as the breeze passed on from one plant to another, the green hues changing with each movement, sometimes bright emerald, then dark khaki, then green tipped with silver. The mounds of sugar-cane plants folded and rolled out to the horizon, coming to an abrupt halt where the Indian Ocean sparkled at the very edge of it all. The sea was also shifting, but to a different rhythm.

Lutchmee looked over at Sappani, who was carrying most of their belongings. Sweat was pouring down his face. She had grown accustomed to his presence and could read his expressions: his brow was knotted in concentration, a sure sign that he was deep in thought.

She felt an odd, dizzying feeling in her stomach. He had a certain sureness of self. He didn't seem to be consumed with competition or arrogance. She felt safe around him because she knew that he was a peaceful person with simple needs. He wanted his son to be taken care of and wanted to be cared for himself. Also, she knew that he wanted to care for her too.

Sappani slowed his pace and offered to take the boy onto his back.

The sun's warming rays seemed to penetrate to the core of her heart, and Lutchmee smiled to herself. She was far away from the hurt she had once known, with a baby in her arms (even though he was getting a bit too heavy) and a good man next to her. She muttered a prayer to Lakshmi, thanking her for her protection and good fortune.

The sirdar, a serious man named Kuppen, seemed kind. He provided them with water and some food during the day, and at times allowed them to rest in the shade of the trees.

8
Sezela Sugar Estate, Natal
July 1909

Eight hours later, exhausted but still hopeful, the caravan of fifty tired, dirty Indians arrived at Sezela Sugar Estate.

Sappani stood on the stone path that led up to the barracks, indicating to Lutchmee to stand with him while letting the others go ahead. He bent down and picked up a handful of the earth. After rubbing it between his hands, he poured some into Lutchmee's hand, then into Seyan's. 'One day, in time, we will have land that's our own,' he promised, while Lutchmee, smiling, tried to stop the baby from putting the soil into his mouth.

Hill Barracks was the most recent building, ugly but more modern than the others. It sat halfway up a hill, a blot on the idyllic landscape. 'Hill Barracks houses more than 200 of the 600 workers on this farm,' Kuppen said. These 'lines', rows of buildings divided into tiny rooms, were to be their new home.

Hill Barracks had originally been one of the older coolie lines, built by the early Indians with wattle and daub, but had since been upgraded with wood and corrugated iron. The roofs, originally made of dried cane and mealie stalks, were now thatched. Each long building had ten small rooms on each side. The only ventilation was from the open doors, a small window and a narrow opening running beneath the eaves as a result of the corrugated-iron sheets not sitting flush on top of the walls. A long, narrow veranda ran the length of each building, furnished with old chairs and small benches. At the end of each line were communal toilets and washing areas, for bodies, dishes and clothes.

The road to the coolie lines was a snaking path dotted with giant aloe plants and fruit trees. The walk up the steep hill on legs that still did not feel like their own wore them out. They sat down on the grass. Seyan held on to Lutchmee's shoulders and pulled himself into a standing position. Sappani and Lutchmee drank in the view, allowing themselves to get lost in the rippling green stalks of the sugar-cane plants to the right, while over the ridge the sea came into view.

It was Sunday and the voices of Indians and the cries of children could be heard in the barracks. Older children were playing in the yard and a few Indians were bent over in the small garden. A goat, tethered by a rope and a stake in the ground, bleated, and chickens clucked to themselves and kicked up dust as they scratched in the dirt. Two shirtless boys were playing with sticks and one of them fell down and began to cry.

Kuppen left the new arrivals sitting in the shade and sped back down the hill on his horse before turning left, up the path to the main house. The sound of the horse's hooves was swallowed up by the whispers of the sugar cane and the crashing ocean.

The Indians didn't have to wait very long to meet their new master. Amid a moving cloud of dust, Henry Rouillard, the younger of the two Rouillard brothers, appeared on horseback, with Kuppen in his wake. He dismounted and handed his reins to Kuppen. The already established Indians melted back into their homes until only the new arrivals were left.

A squat Frenchman with a bushy moustache, Henry had an air of authority and self-appointed righteousness. His shirt was crisp and so white that it dazzled the eyes of those looking at him. He wore a smart, navy-coloured jacket, which must have been stifling in the heat, with gold buttons that seemed out of place. His shoes were clean and shiny, and even his hat didn't appear to have a speck of dust on it.

He cleared his throat several times, his moustache moving as he did so, then raised a hand and recited loudly, 'Poor is he who works with a negligent hand, but the hand of the diligent makes rich. Proverbs ten, verse four. Let us pray.' He bowed his head and placed the palms of his hands together. 'Our Heavenly Father, thank you for the safe arrival of these souls. Thank you for the opportunity they have here in Natal. I know that they are going to make the most of the blessing they have had the fortune of receiving. We are all your humble servants, Lord. I ask that they be obedient, just as all your servants must be, that they work hard to build your kingdom, and above all that they come to know the one true God. Amen.'

Rouillard whispered something to Kuppen, who shouted out quick instructions for the Indians to get into a line. While the master surveyed the Indians in front of him, Kuppen and other farmhands quickly and quietly brought the rations from a large shed nearby. It had two large doors that could be locked with heavy chains. The key dangled from a stout string around Kuppen's neck.

The dry goods were weighed out into smaller sacks: rice, dhal, sugar, beans and mealie rice, which the newcomers would have to work out how to cook. Added to each small pile were some candles and matches, an oil lantern, a couple of blankets and bedrolls, soap, tin plates and pots, and a few cooking utensils. In a small box, each household was provided with some ghee for cooking, some saltfish, a cabbage, a few onions and potatoes, and a fresh cauliflower. They were also given two aprons made from sacking, to wear when they worked in the fields.

Rouillard, pacing slowly down the line of Indians, made a few comments. 'You will do nicely,' he said to a young, muscular Indian man. 'A bit long in the tooth, but we will make sure you work,' he said to an older man. He seemed less concerned with the women.

Finally, apparently satisfied with his inspection, he cleared his throat again, looked up and smiled. 'Welcome to Sezela Sugar Estate. I am your master, Mr Henry Rouillard,' he said. 'My brother Phillip and I are the planters who own and run this plantation, the largest in Natal.

'You are here to work. Everyone will obey the sirdars. They work for me and they will let me know if anyone steps out of line.

'You men will be paid ten shillings each month if you work well. After each year of completed service, you get will get one shilling a month more. Women will work for the same hours for five shillings a month and will receive half the rations. You will be paid on the last Saturday of each month, no sooner.

'You can all collect your rations at the end of each month. If they run out before that, that's your problem, not mine. You get free board and medical care but that does not mean you can run to the doctor whenever you feel like it.

'Work starts at sunrise and you leave the field when the sirdar tells you to. You work six days a week. In the cane-crushing season, this may be extended. Sirdar Kuppen here will make a note of any absences, and you will not be paid for any days you don't work.

'Women with babies, you can work if your baby can stay out in the fields with you. If not, you can look after the baby at the lines but you will receive no pay, only rations.

'You will find that I am a fair master. If you work hard here, you will be taken care of, but your punishment will be most severe if you do not work well. Remember, I have paid money for you to come here, so you must make sure that I don't regret that.

'Rest today, for tomorrow your work begins.'

There was a pause and Sirdar Kuppen induced a round of applause. Rouillard then nodded at Kuppen, threw himself with ease onto his horse, and set off back down the hill, turning left where the paths forked.

Sappani stepped forward, eager to get their share of the supplies and go to their room. 'You have an important job here,' he said to Kuppen.

'I have been the master's right-hand man for some time now,' the sirdar said.

'How long have you been here, in Natal?'

'More than thirty-five years. I've worked here for Master Rouillard for ten.'

Sappani looked surreptitiously at the sirdar and tried to calculate how old the man must be. Kuppen wore a crisp white turban and a white cotton kurtha. His face was lined and wrinkled, and his eyes were milky grey.

Kuppen, quickly realising what the younger man was doing, smiled. 'I'm sixty-five this year,' he said. 'I'm a free Indian, too. My whole family is free.'

Sappani nodded as if this was information that he'd known but simply forgotten.

Kuppen called each person forward, checked their names in a ledger, and gave them their rations. 'The master wants everyone to be inside their rooms, with the doors closed, by 9 o'clock every night,' the sirdar announced. 'On some farms, the rooms are locked overnight from the outside, but the master will not do this here unless he feels he is forced to by any bad behaviour.'

Sappani, Lutchmee and Seyan had been assigned the room at the end of a line. They stepped inside. Sappani reached for their lantern and lit it, and it immediately cast strange forms onto the walls.

The room was bare and reeked of stale ghee. The walls were blackened; there were remnants of a fire in the centre of the floor. A small glass square serving as a window let in some light.

Sappani laid out their rations in a corner, and unrolled the bedrolls. 'You may want to stuff some cloth under that door to keep out the snakes and mice,' Kuppen called helpfully as he passed.

It was getting darker, and they could hear the sounds of people bustling about preparing the evening meal. The aroma of frying food reminded Sappani that they needed to eat. He set about building a fire outside, not wanting to fill their room with smoke. Lutchmee decided what vegetables she could cook quickly, and looked through the spice dhaba Sappani had given her two months previously, when they'd first boarded the boat to cross the Kala Pani.

They had a simple meal of aloo gobi and rotis around the fire. Lutchmee watched her new husband eat. 'Good, really good. Such soft roti, too,' was his verdict.

Lutchmee felt her spirits soar. It wasn't the best curry she'd ever cooked but she appreciated his response.

Once the family had eaten, Lutchmee put the dirty pot and plates in a pile, then picked it up and followed what they saw other families doing. In the washing-up area, water came from a pump, presumably supplied by a local dam or river. While Lutchmee washed their dishes, Sappani filled buckets of water and poured them into a large tin drum that stood outside their room. This water would be boiled for drinking and be used for washing themselves.

Finally, the idea of a proper wash of their bodies was very appealing. On the ship, ablutions had mostly been a case of wiping themselves down with a wet rag dipped into a small dish of water.

Sappani filled a large pot with water and stoked the fire so that it would boil quickly. Once it was heated, he carried the pot of boiling water to the washing stalls at the other end of the line, next to the latrines. Roughly rectangular, the concrete walls of each stall were hip-high, to give the bathers some privacy, while in each there was a small stool to sit on and a large galvanised dish to pour the hot water into, then the cold water could be added with water from the pump.

They decided that Seyan should be washed first, as his eyes were already starting to close. Sappani prepared the bath, feeling the water with his hands until the temperature was right. Lutchmee, who'd brought the little boy, along with a bowl, some soap and rags, removed Seyan's clothes. Under Sappani's close gaze, Lutchmee felt nervous but she'd seen this being done before: she was going to give Seyan a leg bath the way she'd seen babies in India being washed.

She hiked her sari up to her knees and sat on the small stool. She then stretched her legs out in front of her, and placed Seyan, tummy down, on her shins, in this way using her lower legs to hold him in place and freeing both her hands. She dipped the bowl into the warm water that Sappani had prepared, and poured it over the child's back. Sappani handed her the piece of soap, and she used it to wash the little boy, gently rubbing at his skin. Once his back was washed and rinsed, she turned him over and repeated the process on his front.

Not used to such a thorough bath, and also overtired from a day full of unaccustomed people and activities, Seyan began to cry, but his father reassured him and he fell quiet again. Lutchmee then washed his hair, careful to screen his face with her hands so that the soap and water didn't go into his eyes. Finally, she wiped him down, pleased with the results: his cheeky little face seemed brighter, and his damp, dark hair smelled clean.

She stood up and was ready to take him back to their room to dress him for bed, when Sappani offered to relieve her. He'd noticed that some other women had arrived at the washing stalls, some of them standing sentry while the others washed.

Lutchmee gave herself a quick but thorough top-to-toe wash, using the warm water Sappani had prepared. It felt so good to be properly clean again. Then, dressing herself, she went back to their room and let Sappani know that it was his turn.

Later, despite being very tired, many of the newcomers assembled in the yard. It was a strange new world, and some of the Indians felt curiously insecure in the absence of the many sounds of the ship, so they sought comfort from each other. A night bird called, the crickets were chirping and there were the low croaks of frogs.

Some of longer-time resident Indians gathered with musical instruments. A man with a greying beard and grey hair played a mournful tune on his harmonium. Two women began singing bhajans as their children darted around them.

The women had also gathered, good-humouredly scolding the children who were dirtying themselves after their baths. A mother pulled and tugged at her daughter's hair as she tied it into two shiny, thick plaits.

The men smoked their beedis and idly chatted. Someone produced a hookah and soon a sweet scent filled the air.

A deck of cards was shuffled and four men began a game called thunee. It turned out to be fun to watch; one of the players explained to the small audience that the card game had been created by Ramsamy Naidoo, who'd been the sirdar on the estate back in the 1870s, well before the time of the Rouillard brothers.

Lutchmee took the soundly sleeping Seyan back to their room and placed him lovingly in the bedroll. She climbed in beside him and sleep came quickly to her, despite her wanting to wait for Sappani to return. In a few minutes her and Seyan's breathing fell into the same pattern.

Sappani sat outside among those who had lived here for a while, listening, not talking, eager to get as much information as he could.

Finally, an hour or so later, each family drifted back to their separate rooms.

It was still dark when a bell rang, and the Indians were woken by the rattling sound of the sticks used by the sirdars as they walked down the lines, dragging them across the room doors.

Leaving Seyan and Sappani dozing, Lutchmee got up to carry out her puja. She hadn't prayed since she was in her village but something about the previous night had filled her with gratitude and she wanted to start the day thanking God for this new life.

Dishevelled and sleepy, in their faded saris, other women began arriving at the washing area, carrying lamps and candles. Lutchmee joined in with them in their prayers. She arranged flowers on trays with water in a lota. Then, facing east and drawing her pallu over her head, she chanted with the other women as life began to stir in the barracks.

By the time Lutchmee returned to their room, Sappani was ready to leave; they had agreed that she would look after Seyan, while Sappani went to work. She made up a tiffin for him and watched from the doorstep as he joined the other men, the bell clanging loudly to signal the start of the work day. It was 5 a.m.

When Seyan woke, he was hungry. Realising this was the first time she'd been completely alone with the baby, Lutchmee fed him then sought the company of others.

In the washing area, the women were washing clothes. Their bangles chimed in unison as they soaped the items, then whacked them against the concrete block built in for this purpose. In an array of buckets and dishes and tin drums, they rinsed their families' laundry while the conversation rose and fell – Hindi, Tamil, Telegu, they all picked up words here and phrases there, and began to weave these into a sense that they understood.

Lulled by the chatter of the women and comforting sounds of clothes-washing, Lutchmee was at ease. Even though it was early, and supposedly the cold season, the African sun was already hot. The water was cool and refreshing, and she repeatedly anointed her face and neck with it. Standing upright to relieve the mild ache in her back, she allowed it to spill out of the bucket and onto her sari and bare feet.

Seyan splashed happily in the puddles collecting around their feet, and Lutchmee felt her soul well up. It wasn't just the value of the chores she was doing, or the warm feeling of responsibility it gave her, but the knowledge that she was needed and cared for by innocence itself. She smiled at Seyan and he gurgled back at her. She was beginning to feel as if the world was welcoming her back into it again.

The women who had been there longer offered up useful advice that was greedily taken in. They spoke about the journey they had all made across the sea, where to get provisions, which sirdars to look out for, the master and his wife.

There was also something unspoken that passed between them all. As if with an invisible thread, they were bound together by their circumstances. While they were hopeful that they would be able to survive this new world, there was also fear and some regret.

But as Lutchmee hung up her family's washing on a line tied between two large mango trees, she couldn't help but feel optimistic, and she allowed the happy sensation to flit about in her mind for a while before it settled again. She desperately hoped that, not far away, Vottie and Chinmah were also feeling at ease.

That evening Sappani returned to their room after having first joined the other men who had gone to wash the day's sweat from their bodies.

Lutchmee thought he seemed distant but chose not to say anything.

She served him his plate of food and, while he ate in silence, she told him about her day. 'The women have been very kind here. They have given us spices, and look,' she held up a bunch of wild bananas, 'some of them grow their own fruit and veggies. Maybe we can—'

She was interrupted by Seyan, delighted with the colour and shape of the fruit, who was squealing and reaching up for it.

Smiling, Sappani scooped the boy up and Lutchmee handed him one of the bananas. Peeling it for his son, Sappani said, 'Maybe we can get a place to plant some food too. I will ask Kuppen.'

Later, after eating and washing, Lutchmee took Seyan and joined Sappani in the yard. The gathering point was beneath a large cycad, and Sappani shifted over a bit to create a space next to him for his wife and son. The little family soaked up the scene, not feeling a part of it yet but not feeling like strangers either.

The voices were thick and animated. Tomtoms and a dholak appeared. A few men and woman danced in a ganja-induced haze, dreamy-eyed and often losing their balance. The children became caught up in the merriment too, finding their fathers a bit softer, a bit more approachable, perhaps. They made a game of weaving between the dancing bodies and then hiding behind an adult, peeping out to see if anyone had spotted them.

A fat-faced moon was out, standing purposefully in the inky heavens. Thousands of lights flickered in the sky like fireflies. The breeze rolled and tumbled, much like the drumming and raised voices.

Sappani's arm moved lower and he placed a tentative hand in the small of Lutchmee's back. He moved her long plait aside gently but then, having felt its luxurious texture and weight, he stroked the free end, feeling the dampness in it.

Lutchmee sat still, as if frozen. Her mouth grew dry. His touch was heavenly, tender and beguiling, and it aroused feelings in her that she hadn't experienced in a long time, and some that were new and confusing.

Lutchmee and Sappani watched the others for a bit longer, then, taking the sleeping Seyan with them, they went to their room. They closed the door behind them, shutting the new world out. Gently, Lutchmee tucked Seyan into the bedroll.

For Sappani, suddenly the room felt too hot. The image of Neela's naked body had entered his mind and he remembered how he would go crazy just looking at her. She was the only woman he'd ever been with, and he was angry, angry for what he was thinking and feeling now. He told Lutchmee that he needed to get something outside.

Standing on the veranda, he found he could breathe again. He didn't hear Lutchmee come up quietly behind him. She placed her hands lightly on his back, and he turned to face her. She was wearing her long nightie; her hair, no longer in a plait, cascaded down her back like a jet-black waterfall. He knew his pain was obvious and he tried to blink back his tears.

She cupped his face in both her hands. Looking directly into his eyes, she said, 'There's no hurry.' Then she pulled herself into his broad chest, wrapped her arms around him and held herself there.

For a few moments Sappani stared up at the sky, his hands hanging at his sides. Then, slowly, he raised his right hand and stroked the silkiness of her hair with his fingertips. He felt her shiver.

He led her back inside. They climbed into their bedroll and held each other. Not a word or sound passed between them; the baby was asleep nearby, and the family next door was separated from them by just a flimsy wall.

She wanted to give in to the pleasure of it all – his smell, his sinewy legs and arms that glowed in the light of the candle – but since Madras, she could not imagine being in bed with any man without wanting to scream and run.

He was slow and gentle, but still tears sprang into her eyes and she had to fight to relax her body, which suddenly coiled up with tension like a cat ready to spring. It did not hurt physically but the mental anguish felt like a noose around her neck, tightening with each second.

Finally, his patient, tender touches began to melt away her fear and anxiety, kneading away at the hurtful memories of her past. Her pleasure came from feeling touched with respect and what now appeared to be a mutual affection.

'Is this okay?' A muffled whisper into her hair as he moved his body into hers.

He did not view her as a thing to use at his will but as a person, and that was the greatest gift he could give her. She gave in to him and felt his satisfying release at the same time as her own. They clutched each other after their pleasure had subsided, until their breathing slowed and became steady again.

Lutchmee pulled herself up on one elbow and looked down at this man, her husband. Never had she met anyone like him. There was surely no other woman in this world who was as lucky as she was. She kissed his mouth and placed her cheek against his bare chest, lulled to sleep by the thudding of his steady heartbeat.

The Rouillard brothers had owned the plantation for almost ten years. They'd bought the land from an Englishman who'd run into trouble with a native girl in Natal so had decided to return to England. The place was really Henry's alone; Phillip, who lived in Arles in the south of France, had very little interest in the sugar industry but enjoyed his share of the profits.

Becoming a sugar baron wasn't something that Henry had foreseen but the offer to planters like himself from the colonial government had made it appealing and lucrative: large grants to help with the purchase of land and the promise of a steady stream of coolies to keep labour costs low and profit margins high.

The Rouillard family's colonial-style house was set in an imposing position atop the last hill on the plantation, closest to the sea. Its white walls shone like a beacon and large bay windows both attracted the light and threw it back out. Carefully tended green lawns and giant trees fronted the house, while the Indian Ocean lay like a smooth turquoise rug at its feet. The servants' quarters were alongside the house, close to the kitchen. The slave bell at the entrance of the house compound was adorned with the family crest – two azure stars above a scarlet chevron, and two roses below on a gold background.

The barracks was to the left of the house. As far as Henry was concerned, the Indians were nothing but trouble. Granted, they were less trouble than the kaffirs, but they were trouble all the same. Depending on the wind direction, their voices would sometimes carry from the coolie lines. Their chattering and singing often annoyed him, sounding much like the troop of cheeky vervet monkeys that roamed the grounds daily. But, he conceded, sometimes it was a reassuring sound: it meant the coolies were alive and well, and that meant that the sugar cane would be crushed and milled in time.

The spacious sea-facing veranda was where Henry could be found on most days. His study opened onto this shaded space, which suited him perfectly when he wanted cool fresh air or to shelter from the fierce sun.

That morning, though, Henry stood on the veranda with no appreciation for the beauty and serenity of his surroundings. He was annoyed. The payment for the new coolies was due and he didn't have the ready cash. It used to be that planters could pay in instalments but that had changed; the colonial office wanted debts completely settled each year, and he was still paying for the coolies he'd bought back in March.

When he and Phillip had bought the plantation ten years ago, things had been different. The rates for the coolies had been cheaper, as were their daily wages, and the workforce had been more … agreeable. But there'd been fewer coolie men than women, and the men had become restless, so the British government and the planters had agreed to recruit more women.

Henry hadn't agreed with this at first, as the work on the cane fields was mostly heavy going, but once the women arrived, he found that they could work almost as well in the fields as the men, and for half the pay.

But then things had changed again, when the so-called lawyer the coolies called Gandhi-Ji had come to Natal and begun to complain about the treatment of the Indians. He'd put pressure on the Indian and British governments until they'd conceded, and a Protector of Indian Immigrants was appointed and based in Natal. To add insult to injury, the wages of the Protector had to be paid by the planters. 'Such nonsense!' Henry huffed to himself.

The Protector would carry out inspections on all the Natal farms and plantations every six months, and make decisions around any complaints and demands that the coolies had. And they had demands! First, they'd wanted a temple, and Henry had let them build one (as long as they did it on their time, not his), even providing some building materials. Now they wanted a school for their children. At the very thought of coolies who wanted an education, Henry stuck out his bottom lip and exhaled angrily, ruffling his moustache.

And now that so many Indians were free, their term of indenture having been completed, they were becoming like an infestation of rats in the colony. The plan had been that once their period of indenture was over, they would return to India, but many of them didn't want to go. He'd heard them say stupid things, like they could never return because they were now cursed: they had crossed the 'kala pani' and could never return and be accepted.

Henry was glad that he'd seen the trouble ahead of time and as a result had become more involved in the decision-making. He'd signed up as a member of the Indian Immigration Trust Board. Henry knew that in this position he could influence any further changes, in a way that protected the interests of the planters rather than those of the coolies.

Henry retreated to his study and sat down with the newspaper. He tutted in irritation – on the inside front page was yet another article about the agitator Gandhi, who was back in Durban and arranging a protest of some sort.

Henry thumped his open palm on the desk, spilling his coffee. Damn nerve! It's not like they'd been living the high life in India, had they? What had Phillip called Gandhi? 'A jumped-up coolie bastard', that was it. His brother certainly had a way with words. Henry chuckled to himself, then raised his head and roared towards the interior of house, 'Come and clean up this coffee, for God's sake!'

Within seconds a nervous African woman, head bent and eyes to the floor, came in and quickly wiped up the mess with a few sweeps of her cloth, scurrying out as soon as she was done.

Bad-temperedly throwing the newspaper onto the desk, Henry stood up and strode from his study. Today he needed to make sure that Kuppen had set the standard with the new coolies: they needed to know from day one what was expected of them.

It was early July, almost a year since the planting of this year's crop. The early plants were cuttings of mature plants that had three or four nodes, and were planted in deep furrows. While this group had been growing and tended daily, there had been no real concerns apart from an infestation of sugar-cane borer, which Kuppen had spotted early and treated mercilessly. The warm ocean current along the coast, the low risk of frost and the plentiful sunshine meant that the stout fibrous jointed stalks were now ready to be harvested.

Henry was pleased that the new coolies had arrived in time to pitch in. They had already burnt the dried leaves, making harvesting easier. The fires also served to kill the venomous snakes that lived in the fields and often bit the coolies. When this happened, not only could they not work, but they needed medical care, and that cost money.

By the time Henry got to the fields, the work was well under way. The coolies were using cane knives to cut the stalks at the base of the plant, then loading the stalks onto wagons which, once full, were taken to the mill. There, the coolies would feed the steam-powered machines with the raw stalks.

From his vantage point on horseback, he watched the oxen trundle off down the valley, dragging their loads to the mill, which belched puffs of white smoke and the aroma of sticky-sweet molasses. The colonial government had given him a grant to increase his crushing and boiling capacity at the mill, so this year was going to be a bumper one for the Rouillard brothers.

In his mind's eye, he could see the white gold filling up the silos and spilling over into the sheds and storehouses.

Once satisfied that Kuppen had everything under control, Henry rode back home, feeling happier. The new Indians were in the field and the mill was crushing the cane at twice last year's rate.

As Henry's horse trotted in through the gates of the compound, a stray breeze lifted a curl above his forehead and he patted it down with his right hand. The sound of laughter caught his attention and he turned, searching for the source. His son and daughter were running in the garden, their white clothes a stark contrast to the green lawn. Elizabeth, who was ten, was holding a toy aloft, away from her brother. William, almost four, was desperately trying to get it away from her. They were being watched by their ayah, a young Indian woman named Ellamma, although Henry had insisted that everyone call her Ella, which was just so much easier to say.

Henry watched his children for a moment. Elizabeth was too much like him, he mused. She was bold and daring and never hesitated to speak her mind. She was doing well in the all-girls school that she went to and the teachers felt she had real potential. However, the boy was a concern. He was forever at Ella's side, whingeing and crying at the drop of a hat.

Henry scowled. His son was turning out to be weak and needy. These were characteristics that he loathed above all else. To add to this, William now spoke with an Indian accent, which he'd picked up from Ella, no doubt. He said things like 'Arre ram' and it seemed that he even understood Ella when she spoke to him in whatever language it was that the coolies spoke.

He made a mental note to speak to his wife, Elise, about the boy again that evening over dinner. The child needed to spend more time away from Ella and more with his actual mother. But he knew he was going to have to tread carefully, and subtlety was never his strong point; whenever he brought up the subject it ended in an argument, and then Elise would cry, and she would sleep in the guest bedroom for a few nights. Although he was pretty certain that that was what would happen again, he felt that he had to try, because one day all this would be William's and the boy needed to be prepared for it.

*

The next morning, Henry was having his coffee on the veranda when Sirdar Kuppen arrived. 'It's the coolies, Master. There's been trouble,' the tall old Indian said, without preamble.

'Those bastards,' Henry sputtered. 'They can never just do what I ask them! What have they done now?'

'Two Indi— ... erm, coolies, Master.' Kuppen, like many other Indians, hated the term 'coolie'; thoughtlessly borrowed by the whites from the Tamil term *kuli*, it originally referred to very low wages for menial work. 'The new ones, numbers seventy-one and seventy-two,' the sirdar continued. 'We found them hanging. They did not show up for work so I went looking for them.'

'Was there trouble yesterday, Kuppen? You never said anything.'

The Indian's facial expression remained inscrutable. 'No trouble at all, Master. The new coolies did as they were told. But it is all new to them.'

A few years ago, Henry might have been disturbed by this, but now he looked up at Kuppen, who was standing quite still, his hands folded in front of him and his eyes on the horizon. 'Cut them down and bury them,' he said.

Kuppen nodded almost imperceptibly, then trudged heavily down the hill to where his horse was tethered to a tree.

Alone again, Henry shrugged to himself. The Indians struggled to settle sometimes, and during the harvest they had to work longer hours and sometimes they drank too much. Dismissing the thought from his mind, he walked into his study to look for the journal he would need for the Protector's visit. Filling his pen with ink, he turned the pages until he found indenture numbers 120671 and 120672. In neat, uniform letters he wrote the word 'deserted' next to each, then blew gently on the ink to dry it before pushing the heavy book away from himself.

*

Kuppen and two other sirdars stood next to the raised mounds in the east field. A man and a woman, both in their early twenties, were now the new occupants of this patch of earth that was far away from their home.

Acting on his master's instructions, Kuppen had had the bodies cut down, but had then allowed the Indians who'd gathered to perform some basic rituals. A small hawan and some incense were all there was time for, as the eyes of the corpses were closed forever. No one had cried when they'd loaded the limp bodies onto the wagon. A grey blanket was hurriedly placed over them, but the jolting wagon made it slip off, revealing the bare calloused feet of the man who would not draw another breath.

At the side of the freshly dug graves, Kuppen's face was firmly set as he recited the last mantra in his head. He wanted to recall the faces of the poor souls, to make some connection with them and give them the dignity they deserved by acknowledging their existence. However, try as he might, he couldn't conjure a living image of the slack, numb faces he'd covered with earth.

He'd seen this too many times. He knew that the arkatis in the Indian villages often manipulated the Indians into coming to South Africa, and told them outright lies about what life in the colony would be like, and when the immigrants arrived and were faced with the reality, the shock of it was all too much.

Sometimes they came knowingly and willingly, but weren't prepared for being so far away from home. Leaving family behind, the arduous journey across the sea, and becoming accustomed to a new way of life all took their toll, and some souls were simply unable to weather the storm. He understood why, for some, escape by death seemed a better option.

Although he knew himself to be blameless, Kuppen couldn't help but feel that there was always some blood on his hands. It wasn't that he felt any deep connection because the Indians were his countrymen and women. They were very different from him, and in his position of responsibility, he had to maintain the status quo. To keep his place on the hierarchical ladder here on the plantation, he'd had to ensure that those below him kept theirs. It was as if they were all suspended in some invisible web, inextricably linked. Rather, he felt heavy and guilty because they were people too, yet in this land, they seemed to have so little value.

Kuppen sighed. He tried to find comfort in the fact that their end had come quickly. He signalled to the others that it was time to leave.

As the sirdar, heavy-hearted, rode on to the ration house, he decided that he'd had enough, done enough, seen enough. His family responsibilities were discharged: his children had been educated, and his son now worked in a bank in Durban while his daughter was a nurse in a missionary hospital. His wife, Devi, and he lived in relative comfort on a piece of land that Rouillard had given him a few years ago, in recognition of his long service.

For a brief moment, he allowed himself to be transported back to his days out in the fields with Devi at his side, when they'd been full of dreams and fears. She had been his rock. Now her rheumatism left her in pain often. She needed him more than ever and he knew he needed her too.

He was due for retirement. It felt right, now, to be able to live out whatever remaining years he had without having to deal with any more misery and death. He was unsure of how Rouillard would respond, but Kuppen knew that enough young men were wanting to get ahead to replace him, just as he'd stepped into the shoes of the previous head sirdar a decade before.

He stopped his horse and watched the Indians making their way back from the fields after working an eleven-hour shift. Their tools were slung over their shoulders and their backs were bent.

A man and a woman with a young child caught his attention – they were some of the new arrivals, the Mottai family, he recalled. He watched them because he knew the woman wasn't working in the fields, so she and the child must have gone out to meet the father, and they were now walking close to each other. The man walked in front, turning back to speak to the woman, as they walked along the path leading to the barracks. The man placed the child on his shoulders, and Kuppen could hear the delighted shrieks as the little one's joy played out on the slight early-evening breeze. He felt a sense of warmth radiate from the little family. Or perhaps it came from his own memories of his family, when the children were still children. He couldn't say for sure.

Kuppen made a mental note to introduce them to the ayah in the barracks who would looked after small children every day for a fee. Then the woman could work as well, and bring in more money for the family.

9
Stanger Tea Plantation, Natal
July 1909

The cart pulled up to an imposing gate fronting lush gardens. The sirdar, Parma, pointed out the master's home – an elongated white house surrounded by rose bushes of various colour, with blossoming creepers on the walls. An impressive driveway wound its way to the front door.

As the oxcart rumbled around the side of the house, on the neat manicured lawn Vottie could see a table being set by domestic servants. An Indian woman polished the cutlery, while a small African boy dressed in a white shirt and trousers was trying to prevent the wind from snatching the napkins away.

'The planter, Mr Kearsney, produces most of the tea around here. It's exported all around the world,' the sirdar explained, as the worn-out faces, exhausted after the hours-long trip in the wagon, looked out on the endless acres of green shrubs around them.

'The coolie lines are over there, on the edge of the plantation. See how nice they are. Mr Kearsney just paid to do them up. They used to be made out of wattle and daub, but now they're brick.'

The oxcart jolted to a halt, and Sarju and Vottie jumped down along with their co-travellers, shaking out their stiff legs and surveying their new home. A few Indians had come out of their homes to greet the new arrivals. They spoke a mixture of languages, Hindi, Tamil and Telegu and their clothes were more colonial than Indian – some wore hats instead of turbans and some of the women were in long flowing skirts.

Sirdar Parma called each person forward and, reading from a journal, told them what their job would be. Vottie was to work in the tea factory. She waited, anxious, to hear where Sarju had been assigned, and felt an enormous flood of relief when Parma announced he would work in the fields – away from her.

But Sarju was infuriated. 'Take me to see the master now. I want to get this sorted,' he said.

'That will have to wait,' Parma replied, and, before Sarju could protest, he turned and walked away.

Their rations were assigned, and each family was shown to their quarters. Vottie went back and forth carrying everything into her and Sarju's room, while her disgruntled husband sat outside talking to the men about how poorly he was being treated. On one of the trips between the piles of rations and their room, Vottie was almost knocked off her feet when a child no older than three ran full-tilt into her. Laughing, the little girl picked herself up and ran off. Vottie thought of Angel.

In the sparse little space, she busied herself. She put all their things on the floor and made up their beds on opposite sides of the room, using the bedrolls and blankets they'd been given. Then she leaned back on her heels and looked around the room. It felt empty. She felt empty. On the ship, there had always been someone nearby and she missed that.

She'd scouted out the communal washing area and met a few of the other women, while Parma finally agreed to take Sarju to meet with the master – it was clear the sirdar realised he would have no peace until this had been accomplished.

She had just finished cooking their evening meal when Sarju returned, looking pleased with himself. 'I must start in the field,' he said. 'They will see how I work, then they will make me a sirdar.'

Vottie didn't say anything in response, quietly continuing to stir the yellow lentils in the pot.

'What? You can't speak? You were talking enough to those bitches on the ship, but you have nothing to say to your husband?'

'I'm happy for you. That will be nice for you, telling people what to do,' she said, her tone measured and even.

He glared at her but didn't take the bait. 'I am better than most of the people here and I will show you. A bitch like you is not going to stop me!' He sat down. It was a silent signal that he was ready to eat.

Vottie didn't move to dish up his food. She knew her defiance was pointless but these small acts were all she had. She watched as he realised that she wasn't going to serve him. Muttering, he dished up his own food, then left to eat out on the veranda.

That first night, Vottie tried to stay awake, waiting for Sarju, who was sitting with the men. Despite the comforting feeling of a good wash and clean clothes, all her senses were unpleasantly on edge. She dozed off but was instantly awake when she heard him cursing as he tried to strike a match to light the gas lamp. When he was finally successful, she heard him shuffle over to her, and shine the light in her face. Vottie kept her eyes closed, resisting the temptation to squeeze them even tighter. Then, thankfully, he moved away and she heard him groan as he lay down. Vottie exhaled, realising that she'd been holding her breath the entire time.

The next day was Sunday, and Sirdar Parma returned and offered to take the newcomers to Durban to pick up some essentials for a small fee. Some of the Indians had stashed away modest amounts of money, carrying them carefully across the sea, and Vottie knew that Sarju had left India with their money rolled into a small pouch that he'd tied to a string around his waist.

'We need some things, Sarju. I want to go,' Vottie told him.

'So now you can talk, when you want something? Okay, Vottie, we can go, but remember this kind thing I am doing for you,' he said.

Vottie would have much preferred to make the trip without him but there was no way she could tell him not to come without causing a fight. Instead, she simply ignored him.

The trip back into Durban was again by oxcart but this time there was a bit more room. They reached the marketplace and Parma told them what time he would meet them back at the same point. He then was lost in the crowds.

Vottie was surprised at how much was familiar, but also excited by the new. Stalls had been set up on either side of the road, out in the open. They sold vegetables and fruits, some of which she'd never seen before. She was surprised by how many people there were – Indians, whites and Africans all milling about the stalls, pressing the flesh of mangoes to test their ripeness or haggling with stall owners over prices.

Trying to ignore the bad-tempered man at her side, Vottie made her way around the market, buying fresh vegetables. At one end of the market there was a row of tiny stores, and Vottie watched as a large-bosomed Indian woman added boxes of fruit to the front of one of the shops. The signboard above the door announced 'Naidoo's General Store' in bold blue letters.

Sarju stood outside while Vottie went in. The woman, who was berating a small African boy, wore a round bottu on her forehead. Gold rings adorned her fat fingers and gold bracelets jangled on her plump wrists, while her mangulsutra, also made of bright gold, nestled neatly in her heaving cleavage.

With a smile, she took and held onto Vottie's hands as if Vottie was a long-lost friend. 'I have not seen you here before. You must have just got here, bheti. Have you found your land legs yet?' she chuckled. 'I'm Mrs Naidoo.'

Vottie nodded. 'Yes, only yesterday. I'm Vottie.'

'That trip is so quick now, with those steamships. When Uncle and I came here, it took three months on the sea! Arre, can you believe that? Three months!' As if she suddenly remembered why Vottie was there, she said, 'Come, I will show you where the freshest things are,' and led her away from the other customers, and towards some boxes at the back of the store.

As the cheerful, chatty woman accompanied Vottie from shelf to shelf, she explained how she and her husband, as free Indians, had been able to set up their own stores. 'This general store is the smaller of two, and I run this one while Uncle takes care of the other one, which is in Cato Manor,' she said. 'Now, see what you want, darling. Those mangoes are so ripe and tasty, and grown right here.'

In the Naidoos' well-stocked shop, Vottie found many of the fresh things she wanted. She bought a pumpkin, potatoes with the earth still on them, red and green mirchi, and the inviting-looking mangoes. She also bought sugar and spices for cooking.

As she handed over the money, Mrs Naidoo nodded to Sarju, now smoking a beedi outside, and asked, 'And him? What is he like?'

Vottie shook her head. They both seemed to understand exactly what that meant.

Back in their little room at Stanger Tea Plantation, Vottie reached for her spice dhaba. She splashed oil into the karahi, waited for it to heat up, then added some tiny mustard seeds. Next she added the chopped onions with the mirchi, followed by the pumpkin cut into cubes. She closed the lid and waited, wafting the little puffs of steam escaping from the sides of the pot where the lid was slightly warped and didn't sit flush.

She and Sarju ate their evening meal quickly and in silence, then Sarju joined the men in a game of cards and drinking, while Vottie sat with the women, who smilingly accepted her into their group.

She answered most of their questions about where they'd come from and what the journey had been like, but when the women ventured onto the subject of children, and why Vottie didn't have any, she wanted to scream. On leaving India, she'd hoped perhaps that this would fall away but clearly it had not.

'Don't worry. See Munichi sitting over there? She came here with no baby and now she has a second one on the way,' an old woman said to Vottie, reassuringly.

'When it is right, I'm sure God will bless us,' Vottie said quietly.

She returned to their home shortly afterwards and sat down heavily on her bedroll.

Sarju returned a few moments later, banging the door open and entering the room with bluster. 'You sleeping next to your husband tonight, Vottie?' he slurred. 'Don't think this can be the case every night,' he said, waving a hand at her separate bed. 'You are my wife!' His demeanour was calm, his voice soft and almost soothing. The sinister curl of his top lip was the only sign that he was angry.

Vottie felt a wet fear slide from her chest to her bowels. Dread coiled itself around her heart and sat blinking its cold, yellow eyes. Past experiences had taught her that Sarju wouldn't leave her alone for long. He wasn't a man to be deprived of what he saw as his right.

Facing the wall, Vottie removed her sari and put her nightshirt over her underskirt and blouse even though it was very warm and sticky inside the room. She could feel Sarju's gaze on her.

She felt her heart racing but continued to look away. 'Everyone here seems nice. There's even a lady with her son from our village. They've been here four years now.' She could hear that her voice sounded high and nervous.

'How long, Vottie? How long do you think you can keep playing these games with me, eh?' Sarju was suddenly up against her, pressing his hands into her shoulders. He swung her around to face him but she turned her head away. Grabbing her face between his thumb and fingers, he forced her to look at him. 'Look at your face. It is not even healed yet, and yet you forget that I can smash this face to pieces and no one will even know you are Vottie high-and-mighty.'

Wrenching herself from his grip, Vottie tried to make a dash for the door but he pre-empted her, catching her before she could take a single step. In one swift motion, he flung her to the floor. Her arms and legs flailed wildly. He kicked her hard, once, twice, three times, in her back.

'Please, Sarju, please don't,' she begged, curling up.

He paced back and forth in front of her, while she lay slumped and immobilised, her eyes wide and her heart racing. Then he stepped back, looking at her, surveying the result of his actions. He traced his lips with the tip of his tongue, slowly, relishing the fear brimming in her eyes. Like a cat with a mouse, he wanted to drag this out for as long as he could.

Vottie felt a warm stream of her own urine between her legs, and it quickly formed a puddle beneath her. Her bowels were turning to water too.

Sarju sniffed and pulled a disgusted face. 'Not so high and mighty now, hah?' he smirked.

Vottie began to plead again, a string of words that tumbled out of her mind rather than her mouth.

Sarju leant down and roughly grabbed her forearms. Dragging her across the floor, he flung her on his bedroll. He lowered his body onto hers, pressing his face, taut and drawn in concentration, into hers. His eyes were excited, lit up.

She shut her eyes. She had no fight left in her. As her body bucked up and down involuntarily, it was not her being assaulted on that bed, but a stranger in the gloomy, grey distance.

At last Sarju rolled off her.

Vottie couldn't stop trembling. The pain in her back was beyond agony.

She pulled herself up and leant over, then vomited on the floor. Slowly and painfully, avoiding the puddle of sick, she crawled onto her own bedroll. Lying on her back, she gulped in air and pressed her hands to her chest. Her mind was foggy. She shut her eyes tightly, willing herself to have some reaction to what had happened or to the agony that was coursing through her body, but nothing came. She turned on her side and curled up in a foetal position.

Sarju, lying with his hands behind his head, watched her coolly, without comment.

The next morning, as the first rays of light peeped through the small window of their room, Vottie tried to sit up and gasped as the pain shot through her body again.

Sarju, watching her lazily from his bedroll, pointed at the vomit on the floor. 'Clean up that mess. This place stinks.'

In the distance, they could hear the clanging of a bell, calling the labourers to work. They should have been up and ready to go. The second bell would be rung in ten minutes' time, and by then, all the workers had to be assembled in the yard for roll call.

'Get ready. We have to go. No time to eat now,' Sarju said impatiently.

Vottie desperately wanted to clean herself, to get up, to be brave, but her body wouldn't obey. She lay still, trying to quell the knife-like pains in her back.

Sarju wrapped his dhoti around his waist and left.

About half an hour later, there was a banging on the door. Vottie had just managed to sit up when Sirdar Parma walked in. Looking around, he covered his hand over his nose and mouth, suppressing the need to retch as the smell of vomit hit him. 'Your husband says that you are not sick. What is the matter with you?' he demanded, his voice muffled behind his hand.

'I can't get up,' she said.

'Get dressed. We can't keep the wagon waiting for you,' he added.

'Help me, please. I can't go on like this,' Vottie said, so softly Parma wasn't sure he'd heard her right.

Vottie tried to get to her feet again but fell to her knees instead, still clutching her ribs.

Parma looked at her, his expression softening slightly. 'No work, no pay then, but you better be ready to work tomorrow,'

'You get in the wagon', he said to Sarju.

Sarju began to say something but remained silent and left.

Taking deep breaths, Vottie got herself up onto her feet. It helped to hold her ribs and take very shallow breaths, but she was still trembling so much that she had difficulty walking. She made her way to the washing area where she struggled to fill a bowl with water.

A little girl was also collecting water, and watched her with interest. 'Amma will help you,' she said, and ran off.

Vottie sank to the ground, unable to say upright any longer.

A few moments later a woman with greying hair arrived, with the girl at her side. 'Hold on to me,' the older woman said as she helped Vottie back to her own room, which was closer to the washing area. She poured hot black tea into a tin mug and added three spoonfuls of sugar, then put it to one side to cool. The girl watched as her mother examined Vottie, tracing the bruises on her chest, then lifting her nightdress to examine her back. She frowned. 'Your ribs are broken – two, maybe three of them. Your back is hurt too but I have something that will help with the swelling and the pain.'

She handed Vottie the tea. 'Sip it,' she said, then turned her attention to the contents of a wooden box that was on the floor, selecting a range of bottles of various sizes and colours. Working quickly, she relieved Vottie of the tin cup and added a few spoonfuls of the contents of a dark brown bottle. 'Drink this for the pain,' she instructed, handing the cup back to Vottie. She then applied a strong-smelling ointment to the bruised area on Vottie's back, and finally wrapped a cloth tightly across her ribs. 'You should stay in bed until your ribs are healed,' the woman said.

Vottie nodded weakly, feeling the concoction start to do its work, numbing the pain. 'Aap-ka naam kya hai?' she asked.

'Ponny,' the woman replied.

Slowly, pausing to allow Vottie to recover her breath every now and then, Ponny and her child helped Vottie back to her room. Quietly, they cleaned up the vomit and settled Vottie in her bed.

'Dhanyavad, Ponny,' Vottie managed to say before she slipped into a blessed, pain-free sleep.

Several times during the course of the day, Ponny checked in on Vottie and brought her steaming bowls of rasso, a sour South Indian soup with ginger and garlic to aid healing. She helped Vottie sit up to eat, patiently spooning the healing broth into her mouth.

That evening, Sarju was returning from the field as Ponny and her daughter stepped out of his and Vottie's room.

'What are you doing here?' he asked.

'Making sure your wife lives,' Ponny answered, her expression grim.

Taken aback by the woman's boldness, Sarju made no further comment and let the woman and child pass.

After two days of bed rest and Ponny's nursing, Vottie was able to walk again, albeit gingerly. With her ribs firmly bandaged with strips of old saris, she was able to get out of bed and prepare meals.

Sirdar Parma wasn't pleased. He came into the yard and confronted Sarju. 'You did that to your wife. It's no matter to me, that is between a husband and wife, but she must be able to work,' Vottie heard him say.

Sarju watched Parma walk off and he spat in the dust, cursing only after the sirdar was out of earshot.

Vottie herself also knew that without work, she would get no rations, and no wages either; then she would really be at Sarju's mercy. She wouldn't give him the satisfaction.

The next day Vottie was ready when the oxcart arrived in the yard. The work in the tea factory was easy enough: they had to separate the tea leaves and then sort them into various sizes and lay them out on racks to dry. Vottie lowered herself to the ground and sat cross-legged, copying what the other women did with each batch of leaves. After a time, the pain in her back flared up again when she tried to change her position, so she ended up sitting in the same place for several hours.

By the lunchtime break, she couldn't stand up – the pain had returned with a vengeance. She coughed, and almost passed out in agony. Tasting something metallic in her mouth, she spat discreetly into her hand. There was blood.

A sirdar, walking by at that moment, caught sight of the crimson phlegm, and barked, 'You can't work here like this!' He called for the oxcart and told two women to help Vottie in.

'Take her back to the barracks,' he instructed the driver and get back quickly. In the wagon, Vottie let her tears fall freely. Every jolt shook her body, releasing new waves of torment. The ride back was endless. The fields around her and the sounds of the wagon grounded her in the present.

The driver, an African man, helped Vottie down from the wagon and allowed her to lean on him as they made their way to her door. He remained silent but there was sadness as he watched her take the last few steps to her door. Ponny's daughter saw that Vottie had returned and went to get her mother straight away.

Ponny examined Vottie. She left and came back with heated rags doused in a yellow liquid. 'This will draw out the pain but you need to see a doctor,' she said.

In her sleep Vottie's dream felt real. She was running for her life, her breath ragged, her chest heaving from exertion, her throat constricted as if being crushed under a boulder. With her hands held up in front of her face, she swiped at the plants that stood in her path, cutting deep furrows along her arms and legs. Ignoring the tide of blood, Vottie ran on, her bare feet being sliced open on the roots and debris left in the field, her bright red blood leaving a trail on the dusty earth.

She turned to glance behind her, and there he was, his face sick with sin, eyes bulging, gaze fixed and steely, threatening. Sarju was moving quickly but he didn't appear to be running; he seemed to be walking, casually strolling, even. In his right hand he clutched a long knife. It glimmered menacingly as it caught the light of the sun.

Then she was falling, tumbling to the ground with flailing arms, her foot twisting in a protruding root. His face was above hers, partly obscured by the sun. 'Thought you could get away, didn't you?' he jeered. With a single, swift motion, he grabbed the length of her hair, twisting it in his free hand, pinning her face against the ground.

Her mouth full of earth, she spluttered and gagged and tried to push herself up. It was useless. She felt the energy seep out of her body into the ground below her.

Releasing her just enough so that she could see his face again, he raised the knife above his head. This time it did not shine.

Then it began to rain. Soft tea leaves landed on her. Sarju was gone. She heard a sound. Next to her, Sarju was lying in the earth, his eyes closed. Blood was spattered across his face in neat scarlet drops, almost beautiful in their arrangement.

Vottie's eye shot open and she sat up in her bed. The room was dimly lit. Her clothes were soaked and perspiration poured down her face. As her breathing slowed, she noticed a lamp glowing in the other corner of the room.

Sarju was sitting on his bedroll, watching her.

She looked around nervously. They were alone.

He approached her slowly. 'You have been asleep for days now, Vottie.' He said it irritably, as if her unconscious state had been her choice. He inched closer and instinctively she pulled her feet towards herself, trying to find a way to place her body in a defensive position.

He placed his hand on her raised knees. His eyes were now close to hers. The smell of daaru was on his breath. 'Tomorrow you must go back to work. You have had enough rest. Maybe now you know how to be a good wife.'

'I'm hurt, Sarju.'

'The money for the doctor will come out of my wages. I'm not paying,' he said.

'Let me go, Sarju,' she whispered. 'Just let me leave. I don't want to live like this. You can get a better wife, a good one.'

Sarju laughed. 'Who is going to pay me for this wife, then, and for all the cost of bringing you here and all your fancy ideas, Vottie?' He stood up abruptly, making her flinch. 'You are my wife and you will stay my wife,' he said.

As he stood over her, she recoiled inside, unsure where the first blow would land. Instead, he went back to his bedroll and climbed in. After a few minutes, he put out the lamp.

In the darkness she could hear his breathing becoming slower and deeper and then turn to snores. She lay back, wide awake. Defeated, she was done making plans. She was just grateful that Sarju had left her alone tonight.

10
Mount Edgecombe Sugar Estate, Natal
July 1909

On their first day of work, Ramsamy slept through the bell. The estate followed a policy of no work, no pay, and the little family needed food; the rations they'd been given when they arrived two nights before weren't enough to last them for more than a few days.

Chinmah shook her husband roughly. 'Ramsamy, you must get up. They will whip you if they find you here.'

He groaned and turned over.

Chinmah shook him again, but Ramsamy grumbled, 'Leave me, I'll go later.'

With Angel in one arm and a hoe in the other, Chinmah joined the assembled Indians who were lining up for roll call. When it came to Ramsamy's name, Chinmah said, 'I am sorry. My husband is sick.'

Sirdar Kasim frowned at her. 'What is wrong with him?'

'He is …' Chinmah did not know what to say. She stared at the angry sirdar, jiggling Angel on her hip.

'Go and get him. Now.'

'He won't get up. He won't listen to me,' she said.

There was a tittering among the Indians.

'Come!' Kasim ordered, and stormed ahead of her to their room. Banging open the door, he marched to the bed. 'Moollamaari, get up!' he shouted, kicking Ramsamy's legs.

A few groans were heard from beneath the blankets.

The sirdar yanked the covers off, exposing Ramsamy's almost naked body. 'Yethava, get up or I'm going to whip you silly,' he threatened.

'Just listen to him and get up,' Chinmah pleaded with her husband, pulling on an arm. He allowed her to help him get his turban and dhoti on while Angel sat on the floor, crying.

The sirdar, making noises of disgust, marched off.

As the little party set off, walking towards the sugar-cane fields, Chinmah kept pace with her husband, whose slow steps meant he quickly fell behind the others.

Sirdar Kasim noticed this and turned back, drawing his horse alongside the couple. 'Chut marike,' he spat, flicking Ramsamy on the backside with his sjambok. 'That's your name because you are just as useless.'

Ramsamy stumbled into the dirt while Kasim looked on. Chinmah helped him up and urged him to walk quicker, before the sirdar could strike him again.

Ramsamy was instructed to weed and hoe between the rows of sugar cane but he chose to sit moodily on the ground instead. For refusing to work, he was flogged twice in one day, once in the field and then again in front of everyone next to the barracks.

The master of Mount Edgecombe Sugar Estate, Andrew Wilkington, had not been on the plantation when the twenty new indentured Indians had arrived. His wife, Maria, was in the house but she didn't get involved in the running of the plantation.

The journey in the wagons from the port had taken far longer than expected, as a wheel had come off and had had to be repaired at the roadside. It had been dark when they arrived and it was difficult to make out even the path in front of them. The Indians were made up mostly of couples, some of whom had young children, who were tired and hungry and had been crying for the last few hours of the trip.

Sirdar Kasim had quickly doled out the rations and led the group to the barracks. There had not been much land put aside for the workforce and the barracks on the sugar estate was smaller than most, with only a few coolie lines dotted about, close to the railway tracks. Kasim had pointed out the rooms for each family, and where they could wash and use the ablutions – the communal washing area and outdoor pit toilet were at the end of the row.

Chinmah and Ramsamy's room was just like the others – small and airless. It had a roughly made wooden shelf on which they found tin plates and pots that had been used by the previous occupants. There was also wood and a fire pit just outside the room.

'Can you start the fire while I feed Angel?' Chinmah had asked Ramsamy. He didn't say anything in response, so Chinmah had gone inside and breastfed Angel. Once the baby was asleep, she'd settled her in her basket. It had a thin mattress but Chinmah had covered it with blankets, hoping there weren't any lice or fleas.

Chinmah was relieved to find that Ramsamy had built a fire, and, using a thawa she found in their room on the shelf, she'd cooked a few chapatis. While she was bending over the fire, something small but heavy had fallen to the ground from her sari. Scooping it up quickly, Chinmah had turned away from Ramsamy.

It was a gold valayal, no doubt part of Lutchmee's dowry, which she'd slipped into her hand as they'd parted at the port. Chinmah had tucked it into her blouse and made a mental note to bury it in a safe place. Looking to the sky, she'd thanked Shiva for the protection that had come to her in the shape of Lutchmee.

'Enakku pasi.'

'It's ready,' Chinmah had said to Ramsamy, who'd been sitting on the veranda, staring out into the night.

Ramsamy seemed to be beset by some affliction that rendered it impossible for him to behave autonomously. Without being forced to, he found it too much to get out of bed, never mind go to work in the fields.

Every day for the first working week at Mount Edgecombe, he slept through the bell, and no matter how much Chinmah shook and shouted at him, she couldn't get him up. Royappen, a man who'd arrived at the same time as them and lived in the neighbouring lines, sometimes came to help, prodding and poking at the pile of bedclothes until the thin little man buried in them emerged and got dressed, protesting every step of the way. The Chinmah would have to urge and coax her husband all the way to the fields, walking the three or four miles with him.

One day Ramsamy did no work at all, instead hiding among the sugar cane, and the sirdar was fuming when he returned just as the sun was setting. It was at that point that Kasim decided that Ramsamy needed more than a public flogging.

The next day was a Sunday, and Kasim decided that it would not be a day of rest for Ramsamy. He caught the skinny shirker by his ear and instructed the other men to tie him to the trunk of a wattle tree that was used as one post of a washing line. Children who were at play stopped and gawked as Ramsamy's hands were tied, his face pressed against the gnarled tree trunk. As all this was being done to him, he did not resist once.

In a single motion, the sirdar ripped off Ramsamy's dhoti, leaving Ramsamy naked, without any way to cover his scrawny buttocks. Almost everyone watched, only the older indentured Indians turning away and going about their domestic chores.

Chinmah stood rooted to the spot, clutching Angel close, her hot tears falling onto the infant's head. From nowhere Royappen appeared at her side. 'Don't look,' he said and cupped his hands over her eyes. But Chinmah pushed his hands away and ran forward.

Just then, the sjambok cracked like lightning as Kasim brandished it with a flourish, and a deep pink furrow appeared as if by magic on Ramsamy's bony back. He screamed, a terrible sound from deep in his lungs. There was a pool of mud under his feet and he lost his footing, making the scene the most undignified thing Chinmah had ever seen.

More cuts burrowed into his back, some as long as an arm. Ramsamy's screams became one long wail, until he could scream no longer, and keep his footing no more, and his legs gave way, with only the ropes holding him upright.

Chinmah moved to help him, but she was held back by her neighbour's strong arms.

The sirdar stopped whipping Ramsamy, then picked up a pail next to him and emptied it over the maimed man's back. The ear-splitting scream that came out of him hung in the air and told everyone what was in the bucket: salt water.

Satisfied, Kasim looked around, then spat on the ground. 'No one feed him. I'll be back later to take him down.' As he walked back to his horse, he turned, cupped his hands around his mouth and yelled, 'Let that be a lesson to you all!'

The beating didn't change things; in fact, it made them worse. Ramsamy still refused to get out of bed, and, despite Chinmah's best attempts at cleaning his wounds and applying a turmeric paste, he wouldn't speak to her. For two days he lay in bed while she went out to the fields with Angel on her back, in a sling made of an old sari.

On the third day Kasim returned, this time with a new tactic. He issued Ramsamy with a fine – one that was so much that all the wages Chinmah had earned in the preceding eight days wouldn't be enough to cover it.

Angel wasn't even a month old yet, and still breastfeeding. This, combined with the meagre portions of food Chinmah was eating, the strain of the additional work, and the emotional stress of what she was dealing with, took a toll on her body. That afternoon she collapsed in the field, her tiny body slumped on the ground, with Angel still on her back.

The woman next to her saw her fall and untied Angel. Holding the baby, she ran to get Kasim.

When the sirdar arrived, he filled a cup of water from the communal drinking pail and threw it in Chinmah's face. When she didn't respond, he clicked his tongue impatiently. There were penalties for Indian casualties on the farms, and no one wanted a dead young mother who had not even started to repay what had been spent to get her here. 'Get her onto the wagon,' he ordered, his tone irritable.

The wagon had sugar cane on it, and the Indians moved it to one side and placed Chinmah's limp body on it. They watched as Kasim cracked his whip and urged the oxen onto the road that led out of the plantation.

Angel began to cry and the woman holding her asked around if anyone could feed her. A woman who also had a baby slung onto her back sat down and unbuttoned her blouse, easing her nipple into Angel's mouth. Angel drank without hesitating.

With Kasim gone, the Indians refreshed themselves from the nearby stream and shook their heads at the plight of the young mother who'd been carried away.

Kasim knew the master would have no problem with him taking Chinmah to the doctor: rather that than not deal with the problem and risk the Protector getting involved.

Dr James Carew, a settler from England, had made a good life for himself in his thirty-two years in South Africa. He saw his patients in rooms next to his house, just a few miles from Mount Edgecombe, which gave him the freedom to choose his work hours, and he also kept a surgery in Durban. He had a steady stream of patients from the planters as he was registered with the British colonial government as a doctor for the Indians. He'd seen most things and knew the effects of life on the plantations.

The sirdar explained that the woman had collapsed, and helped the doctor to get Chinmah into the examination room. Instructing the sirdar to wait outside, Dr Carew looked carefully at the frail form of the girl on the bed. Her hair had come loose and he raised her head carefully and tucked it back behind her head. She was stirring.

Dr Carew began his examination. He found a faint pulse in her neck first, then he loosened the young woman's blouse, noticing the stained blouse from her milk. He listened to her heart and lungs with a stethoscope. He checked her mouth and nose for any obstructions. Her skin was hot to the touch but that would be expected if she'd been out in the fields.

'Hello,' he said, shining a small torch in Chinmah's eyes.

Focusing her gaze, Chinmah moaned and a stricken look crossed her face. 'My baby,' she said.

For Dr Carew it was all making sense: this young woman had given birth fairly recently; she was undernourished and the fieldwork was too much for her, especially now, during the harvest.

He helped her to sit up and offered her a rehydrating solution. It was sweet and thick but Chinmah drank it quickly.

'You're still feeding your baby, I see, but you're too thin and weak. You shouldn't be working,' he said, kindly.

Chinmah looked at him with a blank expression. 'I have to. My husband does not want to,' she whispered.

'I think you need to rest here for a while. I'll let the sirdar know and come back to check on you.'

'No. I have to get back,' Chinmah said, her voice rising. 'Angel is alone.' She tried to get to her feet but found that she needed to quickly lean back on the bed.

'My dear, you need to rest,' the doctor said, laying a gentle hand on Chinmah's shoulder.

Outside, Carew was firm with Kasim. 'This woman should not be in the fields. I will have to let the Protector know. It's not like Master Wilkington to let this sort of thing happen.'

'Please, doctor, don't report it,' Kasim said, knowing how angry Wilkington would be if the Protector was brought into this. 'We'll take care of it, I promise. The master is away at the moment. If you tell the Protector, he'll speak to the Indians and ask them questions, and they always paint a bleak picture, as you know.'

The doctor nodded but stood his ground. 'She's still nursing, Kasim. She needs more food to eat, and she mustn't be in the fields,' he said solemnly.

'Of course, Dr Carew. You have my word,' Kasim said.

After Chinmah's collapse in the field, Ramsamy did return to work. The money he earned still had to be paid towards the fine but Sirdar

Kasim allowed him to keep just enough for the family to buy food.

After a few days of rest, and with the kindness of neighbours, Chinmah thought perhaps the worst was over. Angel was feeding well again, and Chinmah began feeling hopeful about their future. She also found that she could repay the kindness of the other women by minding their children while their mothers worked or washed or cooked.

With rest and food, Chinmah soon felt strong enough to return to the fields. During work hours, Angel would be looked after by an ayah, who also cared for other children in the barracks. When it was break time for the Indians, the ayah would bring the children to the field so that Angel could breastfeed. Things were settling into a routine.

Then, one morning, Ramsamy was slow to get ready. 'Go, go, I will bring our tiffin,' he said.

Chinmah usually prepared a tiffin for Ramsamy and herself, but she nodded and left with Angel. Tenderly kissing her baby on her head before leaving her with the ayah, she walked on to the gathering point in the yard. At roll call, Chinmah looked for her husband, but Ramsamy had not turned up. Kasim was clearly annoyed but said nothing to Chinmah about it, simply instructing her to leave with six other women to work in a specific field.

Chinmah had nothing to eat all day, and after she'd fed Angel she felt lightheaded as the sea of green blurred in and out of focus.

That evening, Chinmah picked up Angel from the ayah and made her way home. Crossing the yard with her baby in her arms, she saw Ramsamy sitting with a group of men. Chinmah wanted to go over and ask him where he'd been but thought better of it. She didn't want to humiliate him.

With Angel slung on her back, she got the fire going and then cooked a simple potato curry with turmeric and rice for their evening meal.

For the rest of that week, Ramsamy didn't go to work at all. Chinmah made sure that she prepared her own tiffin, and also that she and Angel had left the room before the sirdar came to get Ramsamy. He would be dragged from his bed or whipped to get him to work. As soon as he got to the field, though, he would slip away the first chance he got.

Every evening Chinmah saw him sitting under a tree with the other men, smoking dagga, a particularly strong strain of ganja that was easily available on the plantation. Sometimes they passed around kaffir beer, an alcoholic drink made with millet by the natives.

Sirdar Kasim finally lost all patience, as nothing seemed to spur the lazy fellow on; even fining him, and cutting his and his family's food rations, had not been enough to deter the man from shirking. When, on the Friday, the sirdar came by their room and imposed yet another fine on Ramsamy, and reduced their weekly rations even further, Chinmah felt a clammy wave of hopelessness wash over her. 'Please, Ramsamy,' she begged. 'Please do this for the child, at least?'

In his drugged state, Ramsamy was totally content, however. With half-closed eyes, he simply gave his desperate wife a sleepy smile.

By the end of their second month, the little family was worse off than when they'd arrived. The money that Chinmah earned was only enough to pay the ayah for looking after Angel every day, and to buy the tiniest scraps of food. They owed the planter more in fines than they would ever be able to pay off, and Kasim had stopped giving Ramsamy even the little bit of money he'd initially allowed to buy food. Their rations had been cut almost to nothing, and there was precious little to eat; and the neighbours' kindness could only go so far. Chinmah's milk was beginning to dry up, and Angel often cried from hunger.

Ramsamy, sitting with his new friend, Royappen – who would procure the dagga for both of them – seemed oblivious to the misery around him. And sometimes he would invite Royappen into their room, which always made Chinmah uncomfortable.

PART IV

TRIBULATION

If the Colony cannot put up with the Indians ... the only course ... is to stop future immigration to Natal, at any rate for the time being.

– *The Collected Works of Mahatma Gandhi, Vol. I*, 1958

11
Sezela Sugar Estate
September 1909

Henry Rouillard had just returned home from a meeting of the Indian Immigration Trust Board in Durban. The meeting hadn't been very interesting but at the end of it the Protector of Indian Immigrants, John Tatham, had called him aside and mentioned that there was going to be an investigation on Sezela Sugar Estate. 'You've had three times more deaths and losses than any other plantation of the same size. Why is that, Henry?' he'd enquired.

'I would think that the bottles of brandy and boxes of cigars that find their way from Sezela to your office each month would be encouragement enough for you to find a reasonable explanation for that, Inspector,' Henry had said coolly.

Tatham had fiddled with his collar and flushed pink. 'Much is out of my hands now that that blasted Indian lawyer Gandhi and his newspaper is casting a light on the whole business.'

'I heard,' Henry had said, frowning. 'He's already opposing the three-pound tax rule in the Transvaal, as if Indians could stay here for nothing after all we planters paid to get them here in the first place.'

'And the damned man has settled in Phoenix, which is only about twenty miles from Durban,' Tatham had gone on. 'He's made it his base, and he's helping Indians to become self-sufficient, and to claim the land that was promised to those who spent more than five years in indenture. He's even set up a newspaper – the *Indian View* or *Indian*

Opinion or something like that. And the Indians are reading it and getting ideas above their station.'

'I knew educating them was never a good idea. I held out on building that coolie school for as long as I could.'

'That Gandhi is a threat, Henry. Stop sending me gifts and get your house in order,' Tatham had said.

Henry had looked after him in surprise. The Protector had never spoken to him like that before …

Now, in his study, Henry took a slow sip of his brandy, relaxing as its warmth flowed down his throat, soothing and softening the lines on his face. He leaned back in his chair and reached for his cigars. He selected one and, using a strong, quick motion, cut off the end, lit it and allowed it to burn evenly. He then sucked on it deeply, his cheeks puffing out as he held in the smoke. Slowly he exhaled, watching intently as the smoky rings wafted upwards.

He decided he was mildly amused at the absurdity of it all: an Indian lawyer, fighting for the rights of the coolies. 'That's just ridiculous,' he muttered to himself, swilling his brandy around in his glass.

And, anyway, he had more serious things to think about – the matter of Kuppen, the sirdar he'd grown to trust even more than his brother, for one. Today he'd come to ask for permission to retire. True, Kuppen had been in his service for a long time – since the beginning, in fact – and he was no longer as quick or as sharp on the plantation with the coolies or the kaffirs. And he had looked tired when he'd come to see him, and had been limping heavily.

'The man must be close to seventy,' Henry mused, tipping more brandy into his glass.

The other sirdars on his estate who might have stepped into Kuppen's shoes just didn't have what it took; Rouillard always observed their reactions when the Indians were sjambokked and he could see they were all too soft. They wouldn't be able to keep the other coolies in line. Kearsney in Stanger had just had a new lot of coolies come through, and perhaps there was a man in that lot that he could buy from him — at a good rate, of course. He'd ask Kearsney at the next meeting.

Then there was the matter of Elise. Henry placed his empty glass on the dark teak desk and the cigar in an ashtray, and massaged his temples. Thinking about his wife brought on a headache. She'd been distant towards him for some time. Perhaps being away from Hertfordshire for so long had put a strain on her. He'd honestly thought that the warm climate would be good for her but since the birth of their son four years before, she'd seemed to be fading, as if the air itself was sucking the life out of her.

He couldn't understand why she wasn't happy in this paradise, this world that he'd built for them. She had the house and the servants and every imaginable convenience and extravagance, yet none of it seemed good enough any more. He felt unappreciated.

Truth be told, she wasn't doing anything that a wife or mother should do. The servants did the cooking and cleaning, and their ayah took care of William and Elizabeth. Instead, Elise slept often, and several doctors couldn't find a cause for her lethargy and melancholy. Her eyes were often red-rimmed and puffy, and some days it looked as if she hadn't bothered to even brush her hair.

Elise was a shadow of the woman he'd married some twelve years back, when she'd loved to dance, had always dressed fashionably and had taken an interest in the business. Her musical laugh, her tumble of blonde curls and her piercing blue eyes had made his knees weak every time he'd looked at her.

Now she seemed like a watercolour painting that had been left out in the rain. A gem without its sparkle. She hated going out, preferring her own company, and nothing he did would convince her even to go into town occasionally. He'd suggested that they go away, just the two of them, to Cape Town, maybe, and spend a few days in those new boarding houses that were popping up, but she refused to leave their house.

It wasn't as if he hadn't tried to reach her. Only a few nights ago, he'd tried to touch her, hold her, even. As usual, she'd just turned her back to him and frozen as if she'd turned into a marble statue. Henry couldn't recall the last time he'd lain with his wife.

Tomorrow he'd suggest that maybe a visit to her sister in England would do her and the children some good. Not having to look at her every day would also do him some good, he thought. The ships sailing to Southampton were reliable, and a first-class ticket for them would mean they would have every luxury. Perhaps he should buy the tickets and surprise her.

He peered into his empty glass dolefully, as if the wife he'd once known was at the bottom of it somewhere.

Henry Rouillard didn't set off for the mill straight away the next morning. Instead, he made his way to Durban, and at the docks he bought three tickets for his family's passage to England in two weeks' time.

In the cold light of day, the idea didn't seem as grand as it had the previous night over several glasses of fine barrel-aged French brandy, and he resented spending the money, which he didn't really have to spare, but he was a man without many options. He decided that he would rather do something than nothing at all.

When he arrived home, he held the tickets behind his back as he approached Elise, who was in bed, apparently asleep.

Henry suspected she was pretending. 'Elise, darling, I have something for you. Well, for you and the children,' he said softly.

He walked over to the window and drew back the curtains. The sun was high and he found himself wishing that she would join him at the window – it really was a spectacular view.

Behind him, he heard his wife sighing. She sat up in bed, absent-mindedly smoothing down her cotton nightie with the pink ribbons around the neck that seemed too cheerful and out of place against her pale skin.

'What is it, Henry?' she asked in a desultory tone. 'I hope it's good.'

'Here – these are for you and the children. You can book passage back here whenever you're ready, when you feel … better.'

Elise reached out and took the tickets from him. She looked at each in turn, then turned them over in her hands.

Henry found the tension unbearable. 'You are happy, then?'

A ghost of a smile crossed her face. 'Yes, yes, this may be good for us. But what about you?' she said.

Henry waved a hand and smiled. 'I've got too much to do here! Anyway, you know that I can't leave these coolies for any length of time.'

As she nodded in agreement, Henry couldn't help but think she looked … relieved?

Noticing her husband's distressed expression, Elise got up and put her arms loosely around his neck, giving him a quick, passionless hug. 'The children will get to see their cousins and I've been desperate to see Anne's new baby.'

'Yes, it would be good for you to see your sister, too,' Henry replied flatly.

'But I don't want to leave you for too long,' Elise said half-heartedly.

Henry got the impression that she was just saying this and not really meaning it. He patted her arm. 'I am going to be so busy, Elise. The time will go quickly.'

'Not too quickly, I hope,' she said, finding her gown and pulling it on. She looked more full of energy than she had in months. 'I must go and tell the children and Ella.'

'I'm sure I can find other work for Ella to do while you are gone,' Henry said.

Elise stopped before she reached the door, annoyance etched on her pale face. 'Ella comes with us, Henry. I can't look after the children on my own.'

'Are you sure it's a good idea to take Ella to England? What will she do there?'

'Help me, of course, Henry,' Elise replied. 'After all, she's almost like family.'

Henry smiled and nodded uncertainly, then followed his wife out the door, walking back down the stairs to his study.

Shortly, he heard squeals of delight and both the children came running downstairs. Elizabeth flung herself into her father's arms, her hair flying wildly. William approached his father cautiously and held out his right hand for a handshake. In a rare moment of affection, Henry pulled him close too, and realised that he was truly going to miss them. They were so innocent, and the hardness of life had yet to settle on their young, impressionable lives.

They ran off excitedly to let Ella know, and Henry prepared to ride back into town to get another ticket to England, for Ella.

Anchored in Durban harbour, the *Bodiam* looked dazzling. She was a new steamship, done up in unrivalled splendour, fully equipped with new-age technology, and visible proof of the huge success of England's industrialisation. Those gathered at the dock but not lucky enough to have a berth on the ship looked on with awe and some jealousy.

Henry felt mixed emotions. Since he'd given her the gift, Elise had seemed happier. She'd smiled a bit more and had busied herself with packing trunks and giving orders to the servants in a way that she hadn't done for some time.

The children were absolutely delighted. Elizabeth was the envy of her friends at school, and as long as Ella was going to be with William, he was happy. And, having never been on a ship before, they were excited and curious.

There was a long blast from the ship's horn and it was time to say goodbye. A quick embrace and a brush of her lips against his cheek were all Elise gave him. The children promised to be good and Ella ushered them in front of her, reminding them to walk, not run, as they descended the gangway to climb into boats that would take them out to the ship.

On the dock, the gathered crowds, dressed in their best clothes, whooped and cheered as the ship left the bay. Henry watched until it was just a speck on the horizon, and then felt a strange sense of loss. Shaking his head, he headed to the clubhouse to get a drink before setting off for home.

The Clubhouse was a favourite of all the planters and any white men with authority. It mimicked the pubs and bars they'd left behind in their home country, with heavy curtains, flowery wallpaper, carpets and rugs, ornaments, well-made furniture, paintings and plants, the whole dimly lit with oil lamps. Deals were struck here, bragging was the order of the day, and salacious gossip was shared.

As luck would have it, Henry noticed that Julian Kearsney was there, drinking with a few other men he recognised vaguely.

'Julian! Come and join me,' Henry called with forced bonhomie, signalling to the barkeep at the same time to bring a bottle of whisky. He wanted to have a word with the planter before he got too drunk. 'Good to see you. It has been a while!' Henry said, thumping Kearsney on the back as he sat down.

The bottle and two glasses arrived, and Henry made a show of pouring for both of them. Offering up his glass, he said, 'Chin-chin,' and the other man clinked glasses. 'Sorry to hear about that fire. Ever find out how it started?'

'No.' Kearsney answered shortly, clearly not pleased to have been reminded of the disaster. 'We lost everything in that storehouse – five years of hard work.'

'I'm so sorry. The tea business is a tough one. Maybe you should have gone into sugar.' Henry laughed exaggeratedly but Kearsney didn't respond.

Henry cleared his throat, then said, 'Look, maybe we can help each other. I know you got a new lot of coolies in at the same time as I did, and you must be looking to let some of them go after the fire. I need a new sirdar. Anyone in your batch who might be likely?'

Kearsney rubbed his forehead with his thumb. He'd already had a few drinks and his thoughts were a bit hazy but that hadn't stopped him immediately thinking about the new man, Sarju. Sirdar Parma didn't like him, the other coolies didn't want to work with him, and every time he saw the wretched man, he brought up the fact that he was a Brahmin and should be a sirdar. Even thinking about him now annoyed the planter.

'I may have someone,' he said. 'I'll send him your way next week. How about that? You can sort out the paperwork with the Protector on your end. I'm still paying for him and his wife,' he added.

'A wife too?' Henry laughed again. 'Keeps them closer to home, I find.'

12
Mount Edgecombe Sugar Estate
September 1909

There was one bright spot in Chinmah's life: Angel, who truly lived up to her name. The infant was an easy child, spending most of the day sleeping, and cooing when she woke. And even now, when Chinmah was struggling to make enough milk to feed her regularly, the baby didn't cry much – as impossible as it was, she seemed to understand her mother's desperate circumstances.

Ramsamy, who three months since their arrival on the sugar estate was worse than ever, put energy into only two things: his burgeoning friendship with Royappen, and his ganja-smoking. He'd now insisted that Chinmah do Royappen's washing and clean his room, and it was obvious that this arrangement ensured that Ramsamy had a steady supply of ganja from Royappen.

Often, when the two men had smoked enough to make their eyes red and their speech slow, they would arrive at the room and Ramsamy would demand that Chinmah make them both something to eat. Sometimes it was late and Chinmah, not wanting to upset Angel, would struggle to pull together a meal with the meagre provisions she had.

This was one of those evenings, and Chinmah could feel Royappen's gaze on her as she ladled the food onto tin plates; her own mouth watered, as she'd eaten hardly anything that day.

As Chinmah handed him his plate, Royappen reached out, catching her by her wrist. She turned to face him quickly, her heart racing. 'What do you want?' she hissed loudly, trying to jerk her arm free. Ramsamy sat in the corner, his eyes rolled back slightly, his jaw slack.

Royappen held on. 'How about you be my wife too, eh? Things won't be so hard for you. I can look after you and your baby nicely, no bother.'

She wasn't surprised: a few women for too many men meant that arrangements like this were made all the time. And she knew there were women who let men do whatever they wanted to with them, just to be able to feed themselves and their children – the men called these women rice-cookers. But she didn't want that to be her.

Royappen pulled her closer, so that her face was inches away from his. She heard Angel whimper in her basket in the corner and tried to wrench herself away. His plate fell to the floor with a clatter.

'Please, no, bhai. My baby needs me.'

He ignored her, grasping her more firmly. She jerked back again, but he was on his feet now and it was of no use.

She screamed.

Ramsamy opened his eyes and took a few seconds to adjust to the scene in front of him. As if in slow motion, he sat up. 'What are you doing to my wife?' he asked, his voice low and slurring.

'Nothing, bhai, nothing at all,' Royappen said, releasing Chinmah, who rushed across the room to Angel and picked up her baby, her heart thudding. 'She's pretty, eh? Just fooling around, don't worry.' With that, he withdrew a folded package from his pocket. 'Friends share, don't they, bhai? Look at this.' He opened the package, pushing the ganja under Ramsamy's nose. 'Very good. The kaffirs says it's the best stuff they are getting these days.'

'Clean this up, Chinmah,' Ramsamy mumbled, nodding slowly towards the spilt food. He then sat, mesmerised, as Royappen began to crush the ganja in the palm of his hand, tenderly picking out the tiny seeds and putting them aside.

Chinmah watched Royappen, her unease rising. Her husband was soft dough in the man's hands. She now realised how dangerous Royappen could be.

Deftly, Royappen placed the crushed ganja in a small neat row within the paper. He added the filter from a beedi, then proceeded to lick the end to seal in the contents. He rolled his creation between his thumb and forefinger, admiring it in the weak candlelight.

Ramsamy's eyes grew wide with delight, and he smiled as Royappen offered the ganja to him and held the candle up for him to light it.

Chinmah felt as if she was staring into a black hole as the pungent smell filled the room. This was her future: the man with an addiction who didn't want to work who had now become the man who would trade her off to another to meet his needs.

She needed to think.

The men were soon oblivious, and she carried Angel out onto the veranda, clutching her sleeping daughter to her chest. With her shawl over her head, she sat in the darkness. She felt indescribably heavy, as if the weight of a thousand lifetimes lay on her tiny shoulders.

It had been months since she had seen Vottie and Lutchmee. She wondered what her friends would do in a situation such as this.

When she went back into the room an hour later, the men were in a sleepy huddle, their backs against each other. She despised both of them. One was weak and spineless, the other a sickening opportunist.

She climbed into the bedroll and, curling up with Angel in her arms, tried to sleep.

Some time later, she heard her name being called. She sat up. Both men had woken and now their faces had a different look. With the effects of the dagga wearing off, they appeared to be a bit more lucid.

The men planted themselves on either side of her. Fear and dread crept up from her stomach into her heart and head. She gulped and held onto her baby, pulling her closer, wishing she could put her back inside her body to keep her safe.

The men spoke as if nothing was happening.

'The food was nice,' Royappen said, smiling.

'She's a good wife,' Ramsamy agreed, nodding vigorously.

They were quiet for a while and Chinmah made a motion to get up.

Ramsamy placed his hand on her shoulder and pushed her back down. 'Royappen wants a wife. He wants you. I said okay.'

She knew how this worked. Not only would she have to cook and clean for this man, she would even have to sleep with him. And her husband wasn't only agreeing to the arrangement, but freely offering her up. She lost all composure and began to cry and beg.

Speaking loudly to be heard above her sobs, Ramsamy said, 'He wants to have relations with you tonight. I will look after the baby.'

'No!' Chinmah cried. The sound woke Angel, who cried as Ramsamy took her from her mother's arms, then quickly left the room. She heard the key turn in the lock, and Chinmah flung herself against the door, wailing, kicking and beating it.

She could see Royappen's shadow as he moved away from the bedroll, towards her. She sensed him and turned. He watched her with intense enjoyment. Her hair had come loose and her eyes were wild with fear and anger.

'Don't be scared. I am not a bad man, see. I asked your husband nicely. I didn't just do what I wanted.'

'I'm not doing it. You can do what you want but I am not going with you.'

Something in her voice told Royappen that this may be too much for one night. He was a patient man, a man who had learnt to play the long game. A spider, he knew how to spin a web and sit patiently. He sensed that this was one of those times. 'I'm a good man. I won't force myself on you, but just know I have paid for you for tonight already.'

With that, he rapped on the door. Ramsamy came scuttling, unlocking the door and opening it a crack, and peered in cautiously.

'This one is a problem tonight,' Royappen told him. 'She won't come with me. I don't need this headache, bhai. You sort out your wife.' Pushing past Ramsamy, he walked off.

Chinmah's relief was short-lived. The door opening widened and Ramsamy came inside, striding past her and laying Angel in her basket. Then he turned and punched her straight in the stomach. 'Kena punda,' he spat as he watched her crumple to the floor.

Chinmah lay where she'd fallen, thinking that the punch was probably the most energy she'd ever seen her husband expend. She could hear him muttering and swearing. 'You want to make me like a khoodhi. You want to make a fool of me in front of my friend. I am the man in this house!'

Chinmah lay on the ground, listening to Ramsamy get into bed, waiting for him to blow out the candle, hearing his breathing, and eventually his snores. She closed her eyes and allowed herself to release a bit of the apprehension that had woven its way around her. For a moment everything was still.

Feeling her way around the edges of the room, she moved herself closer to Angel. Ignoring the pain in her stomach and the ache in her chest, she curled up and slept next to the oblivious infant.

Chinmah woke early the next morning and set off to the field well before Ramsamy had even stirred. The sirdars were still having trouble getting him to work and she didn't see him all day. But Royappen was never far away, always lurking, present at mealtimes and more often than not leering and watchful. Chinmah could sense his restlessness in his intensified gaze.

That evening, after work, she found Ramsamy alone under a tree. 'Don't do this to me,' she begged, her voice barely a whisper.

He stared at her blankly. It was a done deal; her fate was already sealed. He lowered his head as she walked away.

Wiping away her futile tears, she felt panicky. She made her way slowly back to their unit. There, on the veranda, was Royappen, sitting with her sleeping baby cradled in his arms – he must have somehow persuaded the ayah to give Angel to him.

She felt the bile rise in her throat. She swallowed hard and inched towards him. Her knees felt as if they belonged to someone else. His dangerous eyes were set on hers. 'She's a pretty one.' His voice was thick and Chinmah struggled to hear above the pounding in her ears.

'Please, please,' she whimpered as she stretched out her arms for her baby.

'You are both coming with me tonight.' Royappen's words were ice.

He stood up, holding the sleeping child, and Chinmah followed him, obediently to his room in silence. Her eyes fixed on the little brown fist that had broken free of the blankets.

Royappen's room was in the next coolie line. Holding the baby in one hand, he opened the door with the other. Chinmah thought about snatching Angel and just running, not caring where to. *But what does it matter now?* she thought, carelessly. A familiar feeling of helplessness swamped her as within her soul icy tendrils coiled and swirled.

Royappen walked in with the wriggling baby, leaving the door open. Chinmah had no choice but to step inside.

Royappen put Angel on the bedroll, then closed the door behind Chinmah, pushing the metal tongue into its groove to lock it. He pushed her heavily back onto the bedroll, next to the baby. The bedclothes smelt disgustingly of old sweat.

Chinmah tried to kick at Royappen but he grabbed her legs and roughly pushed her sari above her knees.

Angel began to cry but Royappen didn't seem to hear it. Chinmah stopped struggling and snaked her arm underneath Angel, bringing the baby closer to her. Chinmah locked eyes with her infant and waited for it to be over.

Mercifully, she didn't have to wait long before Royappen rolled off her. He smiled at her graciously, as if she'd done something they'd agreed to, as if it had been an act that was mutual and consenting.

Chinmah wondered how this could be. It wasn't that she didn't understand the needs of men, but for men to be unable to control them? He didn't seem to see the person, the girl, the young mother she was. What did he see then, to be doing what he was doing, to want her in this way, to go to such lengths?

Pulling her sari down, she picked Angel up and stood in the far corner of the room. She felt deeply ashamed and repulsed. 'Please can I go home now?' Her nerves were coiled like ropes.

Suddenly the tin door shook on its hinges, shattering the silence. It was Ramsamy, shouting and banging.

Still in no hurry, Royappen moved to the door. He slid the metal back and opened it to reveal Ramsamy, clutching the frame for support, leaning his body in as the door swung open. Chinmah had never been so happy to see her husband.

'I want my wife.' His words were slow and spoken in one breath. Rocking unsteadily on his feet, he tried to step inside.

Royappen moved his body to block his entrance.

Chinmah tried to move closer to the door, sensing a fleeting chance to get away.

'We made a deal, bhai, fair and square,' Royappen replied firmly.

Ramsamy, tears flowing down his face, 'Bhai, it's my fault, let me make it right,' he pleaded. Chinmah watched as Ramsamy held out his hand towards her.

A few lights from the neighbours came on and voices could be heard outside.

Royappen flicked his eyes at Chinmah. 'I'm done with her tonight anyway,' he said, then shoved her into Ramsamy and banged the door shut behind them.

Chinmah, seeing freedom, ran into the night like a woman possessed, her sari flapping around her ankles, her hair down. Her only comfort was the insubstantial weight of Angel in her arms. She ran until the hurt in her chest matched the hurt in her head, until she was just one big pulsating pain.

Slowing down, she heard a rumble: the train track was just beyond the grove of trees that lay ahead. It wasn't as busy at night, but that was the sound of a train not far off. Feeling suddenly unnaturally calm, she mulled over this: it felt preordained, somehow, predestined that this train should be barrelling along these tracks on this night when she was here, within easy reach of the tracks, and looking for a way to end her pain.

Then doubt set in. What if she died and Angel survived? That was too horrible to bear thinking about. She shook her head, deciding instead simply to cross the tracks before the train arrived.

As she took a step towards the grove, she heard her name faintly, carried to her on the breeze. Looking back, she saw Ramsamy, clearly illuminated in the moonlight, puffing and panting, and waving at her wildly. He was running through the undergrowth, not on the path, and as she watched, he tripped and fell.

Chinmah turned fully towards her husband. Behind her, she could feel the tracks vibrating as the train thundered past. She watched Ramsamy's mouth open and shut like a fish, whatever he was screaming swallowed up by the sound of the train.

Chinmah hesitated, then, slowly and deliberately, began walking back towards her husband.

The next morning, Chinmah left early, avoiding any conversation with Ramsamy. She left Angel with the ayah, instructing the ayah to not, under any circumstances, give the baby to anyone but herself, and especially not to Royappen, and she kept well away from Royappen during roll call.

At midday the strong spring sun was branding itself into Chinmah's curved back, her cotton sari blouse offering little protection. Sweat collected in pools under her arms and at the nape of her neck as she used all her strength to raise the hoe and dig it into the rocky earth. The job of weeding meant that every care had to be taken not to hit delicate cane seedlings while removing the unwanted growth.

Taking a sip of water, she fought the urge to pour the rest over her hair and neck. She needed it to last the day and there was still a while to go before the bell would toll to summon the workers from the fields.

Chinmah heard a faint rustle. Looking around defensively, expecting to spot a cane rat or a snake, she saw Royappen striding towards her, his gaze fixed on her.

She gripped the hoe tightly, the sturdy wooden handle offering some comfort in her sweaty hand. Her heart began to thud heavily and sour bile rose in her throat. She weighed her options. Outrunning him wasn't possible – he was bigger, stronger and faster than her, and he would easily run her down. She could scream but there was no one around and she wondered if anyone would even be able to help her. She could plead with him and throw herself on the ground at his mercy, or simply give in.

Chinmah tightened her grip on the hoe. He was only a few paces away and she knew she would have only one chance. Her hands felt like stones, yet she was able to raise the hoe above her head.

Just as she was about to swing it, she heard a cry. Angel's cry. She looked around but she couldn't see her baby. It was pitch black.

Chinmah bolted upright in bed. Her clothes stuck to her skin, and the sweat made her scalp prickle. 'Angel,' she whispered into the dark. She sensed movement on the floor next to her and groped about until her hand found Angel's tiny, warm fist. She enclosed it in her hand and moved closer until she could feel Angel's soft, sweet breath against her face. The baby wriggled, then began to cry.

Lying still, holding her baby, Chinmah felt her pounding heart begin to slow down. Her breathing came in steadier intervals. Her mind started to clear and she steadied herself.

Chinmah heard Ramsamy change his position. Since three nights ago, when Royappen had raped her, he had not touched her. He was also not smoking ganja and he seemed to be trying to keep away from Royappen.

Their money was now all gone. Chinmah's stomach rumbled to remind her that she hadn't eaten that day.

She felt her breasts. They were no longer firm under her fingertips, and they no longer throbbed at intervals with the need to feed. Without any nourishment for herself, her milk was drying up. Their slack emptiness was the cause of Angel's frustration, as she sucked hard, only to find her hunger not sated.

Leaving the weeping baby in her basket, and quickly lighting a candle, Chinmah emptied the last grains of rice into water. Stepping out of the room into the hot spring night, she quickly got the fire going, then heated up the rice and, rocking Angel to try to soothe her unhappiness, she watched it boil until it was a thick porridge. She removed the food from the heat, letting the rice mixture cool, while she paced outside, her baby becoming increasingly fractious. Finally, propping Angel up in a crook of her arm, and using her fingertips, she managed to get a small amount of the rice porridge into the baby's open mouth.

At first Angel screwed up her face and Chinmah felt her body tense as Angel moved it in her mouth, wanting to suck instead of swallow. But the little one was so hungry that, realising that it was food, she quickly swallowed it, choking a little as the thickish porridge went down.

Chinmah pressed on, knowing that it was the only nutrition that she could provide for her baby. Angel quickly seemed to adapt to what was required, sucking the rice mixture and then swallowing it, her mouth opening, like a feeble chick, wanting more.

13
Stanger Tea Plantation
September 1909

As it grew darker, Vottie waited for Sarju to go and sit with the men in the yard, then she slipped away and took the path that led to Sirdar Parma's house.

He was sitting outside, smoking a beedi, and looked surprised to see Vottie.

'Sir, I need help,' she said, unsure of how to explain her predicament.

'Don't we all,' he replied, laughing at his own cleverness.

'I need to see the Protector in Durban,' she blurted out.

He looked at her warily. 'What has that got to do with me?' he asked, squinting as the smoke went into his left eye.

Vottie sighed. Parma knew that she would need a pass, permission to leave the plantation on her own, to go to speak to the Protector. But she decided to play along. 'Sir, my husband is not a good man. You know him: Sarju.'

The sirdar nodded in a philosophical way. He'd been called to their room a few times when the neighbours had alerted him to the beatings Sarju was giving his wife. Last week he'd had to rescue this same woman who was in front of him now from almost certain death. When he'd burst into their room, he'd found Sarju with his foot on her neck, and she'd already lost consciousness. 'Most of the men here are not good men but I must admit, you are right. Sarju is worse than most.'

Sometimes the men protected each other but not in this case. None of the Indians liked Sarju, and now the men had stopped inviting him to play their card games or cricket in the clearing. The junior sirdars had no time for him either, and seemed to enjoy reporting any infractions by Sarju that they usually ignored in others.

The fool had recently even tried to speak directly to Mr Kearsney again, during one of the master's visits to the plantation, and it had not gone well. The master had given him a kick in his arse. That had been fun to watch.

'Please,' said Vottie. 'That man is going to kill me and then how much trouble will the master be in? If I can go the Protector, I can ask for permission to leave him.'

Vottie's reminder that the Protector was always ready to pounce on an unexplained death on a plantation gave the sirdar pause for thought. 'I'll see what I can do,' he said, grudgingly, then stood up and turned his back on Vottie to indicate that their conversation was over.

At every opportunity Vottie went to see Sirdar Parma with the same request: 'Please give me a pass to go and see the Protector.' His response was always the same: 'I'll see what I can do.' She beginning to realise that it was nothing more than words, that Sirdar Parma was never going to actually do anything.

One evening, Vottie was sitting outside their room, shelling peas for her and Sarju's meal as she racked her brain about how she could get a chance to present her request to the Protector. She was so deep in thought that until the bowl of peas went skidding across the ground and the little vegetables rolled out in all directions, she hadn't even realised her husband was home.

She reached out to pick up the bowl, and Sarju pressed his foot down on her hand. She looked up. The expression of hatred in his eyes had become all too familiar.

'What now?' she asked.

'Everyone is laughing behind my back because of you.'

Sensing her fear, two women sitting nearby, similarly preparing their family's supper, stopped what they were doing and edged closer.

Emboldened, Vottie said, 'I am not happy and you too are not happy. What do you even want with me? Please, let me leave.'

In one swift motion, Sarju placed a foot against her hip and pushed. She went over like a skittle, upending the second dish containing the other vegetables for their supper, the florets of cauliflower rolling into the dust. Then, leaning down, he landed two quick blows with his fist to either side of her face. She could taste blood.

The two women swarmed in on her, helping the dazed Vottie to her feet while Sarju looked on with clenched fists. They ignored Sarju and led her away.

That evening, lying on a makeshift bedroll in her neighbour's room, Vottie could only take some sips of weak dhal. It dawned on her that while her life in India had been unpleasant, there, at least, Sarju had managed to contain himself, mostly because his family was always around. In India she could busy herself and keep out of his way. Now, here, she felt like a caged animal. The more denigrated Sarju felt by his situation, the more he made her suffer. It was as if his manhood depended on what he did with his hands: if they were not put to purposes that he thought worthy of himself, she would feel that hand later as a slap or a punch.

Her face was bruised and puffy the next morning, her right eye almost swollen shut and coloured in various shades of black and blue. It was clear that she was going to need medical attention.

Dr Carew was called for and arrived on the plantation a little after midday. Examining Vottie and asking her a few pointed questions, it didn't take him long to work out what had happened. He gave her a dose of laudanum for the pain and told the sirdar that, first, Vottie was to remain where she was, in her neighbour's room, until she healed; and, second, that he wanted to see her in his surgery in town in three days' time.

Sirdar Parma was furious at the unwelcome attention Sarju's assault had drawn to the plantation. He gave the unrepentant Brahmin twelve lashes and fined him a week's wages.

*

Three days later, following Dr Carew's orders, Parma hitched up the horse to the wagon and transported Vottie to Durban. Tying the horse to a post, he left Vottie at the doctor's rooms and went down the road to an inn, to pass the time there.

Dr Carew, who was familiar with the kinds of injuries he'd seen in Vottie, and who knew all too well how difficult it was for an indentured Indian woman to escape an abusive husband, did not, in reality, have to see Vottie, but he wanted to give her an opportunity to tell him freely what the situation was. Examining her gently, he said, 'Everything is healing well, but tell me, does this happen often?'

'Yes,' she said simply. 'I am afraid that if I do not get away from him, he will kill me.'

'Have you seen the Protector?' the doctor asked, looking Vottie square in the face.

'I have tried,' Vottie replied. The doctor seemed kind but she didn't know where his loyalties lay, and she didn't want to give any man any excuse to abuse her further.

'His office is only a block away. You could go there now. If Sirdar Parma comes looking for you, I will tell him that we're still busy with you.'

Vottie looked up at him, trying to gauge whether this was a trap of some sort. The white man in front of her had no reason to offer any kindness.

'Why, doctor, would you help me?'

The doctor sighed as he sat down. He rubbed his hands over his bald head and adjusted his spectacles. 'I've seen too much of this and, like you, my dear, I am tired.'

Something in his voice reassured Vottie, and anyway, she thought to herself, what did she have to lose? It wasn't as if her circumstances could get any worse.

Overcome with gratitude, and not wanting to waste a precious second of time, Vottie left the surgery, pulling her shawl over her head. She walked briskly to the address just a street away that the doctor had given her.

It wasn't long before she was in the queue in a hot, stuffy waiting room. There were other weary Indian faces: two brothers with bandages, a family with two young children and an elderly woman who wouldn't stop crying. Vottie ignored the sounds and smells as she waited her turn.

The elderly woman, who apparently spoke only Tamil, was ushered in and out of the Protector's office within seconds: John Tatham had been unable to understand her. Vottie watched her sobbing into the corner of her sari, then approached her. With Vottie coaxing her gently in Tamil, the woman revealed that she was a free Indian. Her husband had died two weeks previously and she couldn't afford the three pounds tax to stay in South Africa.

Vottie listened as the crying woman paused to take breaths between sobs. Protector Tatham had sent her away, telling her to come back when she could explain her predicament in English.

Vottie felt her ears glow hot with anger. Ignoring the stares of the others in the waiting room, Vottie marched into the Protector's office, pulling the old lady along with her. Inside, there was already a couple with a young child. Tatham was seated at a desk laden with various papers. He was younger than Vottie had expected, in his late twenties, perhaps.

He looked annoyed at the intrusion but before he could speak, Vottie blurted out, 'Please, this woman needs help.' Turning to the Indian couple, she said, 'She has been here already and he has not helped her.'

The man opened his mouth to speak but, seeing Vottie's beaten-up face and the rage in her eyes, he decided against it and waved her forward.

Turning her attention to the Protector, Vottie said heatedly, 'Why would you not help this woman, who has suffered so much? Are you the Protector or the abuser of Indians?'

Tatham sat upright, stunned. 'You can't come in here demanding whatever you want,' he said, but his voice sounded weak and uncertain. He'd never been confronted by any Indian before, never mind a female one. He'd also noticed that she'd recently been badly injured – her eye was swollen shut and there were bruises on her cheeks.

'I'm not demanding anything for me,' Vottie said indignantly, pointing a finger at her chest. 'You saw this woman. She has nothing and no one, and cannot speak English. She will talk and I will translate for you.'

Taken aback by the sheer nerve of the person in front of him, and not wishing to go to war with a woman who'd clearly recently been badly abused, Tatham sat back in his chair and nodded. Vottie quickly explained the plight the woman was in, after which the Protector left the room and swiftly returned with some forms that he placed in the woman's hands. 'You will need to help her complete these in English,' he said to Vottie, 'then we can decide whether we will send her back to India or maybe she will get an exemption from the tax.' Looking apologetically at Vottie, he added quietly, 'But I doubt that will happen.'

Vottie, who knew that the old woman's battles were far from over, nonetheless helped her with the forms, then stood with her while she submitted them to the clerk. Finally, she wished the woman well and took up her place in the queue again.

When Vottie entered Protector Tatham's office for the second time that day, he was far from pleased. He'd had some time to process what had happened, and was resenting being bossed around by a little coolie woman. 'You again!' he said. 'What now?'

'This is a matter of great urgency, sir,' Vottie began, putting as much passion as she could into her voice. 'My life is in danger. My husband did this to me.' Although she was aware that Tatham must have noticed her black eye, she removed her shawl completely so that he could see the rest of her face. 'If no one helps me, he is going to kill me.'

'Does your master know that you are here? Let me see your pass,' Tatham said, holding out a hand.

'I do not have a pass,' Vottie admitted, trying to still the tremble in her voice. 'The sirdar did not want to grant me one. I asked him many times.'

'So you don't have permission to be here, and yet you have not only come to complain but you have also meddled in the affairs of others.' Tatham looked pleased with himself, as if he'd come to a startling and revolutionary conclusion.

'Please, I'm begging you, sir, what you see here is nothing,' Vottie said, indicating her battered face. 'He has done this to me so many times that I don't even remember them all any more. If you don't give me permission to leave him, I will die at his hands.'

'I could fine you for coming here without a pass, and I could report you to your master, and you would be in serious trouble,' the Protector said, ignoring Vottie's desperate pleas. 'It's been a long day and I have seen too much of you already. Indians cannot just do whatever they like here.' With that, he took up a pen and wrote something on a piece of paper in front of him, while waving his other hand in dismissal of Vottie.

Vottie felt her opportunity slipping away. 'Dr Carew said I should come here.'

Tatham stopped writing and looked at her. 'That old fool should know better,' he growled. 'Close the door behind you when you leave.'

Out in the waiting room, Vottie needed to sit down before her knees gave way beneath her. Once she'd recovered sufficiently to stand, somehow she found her way back to the wagon and climbed in to wait for Sirdar Parma. Confused and lost, she didn't know where to seek help next. Her body ached and her gut felt like it had turned to water.

The sirdar, in a jolly mood with a bellyful of cane spirits, returned to the wagon, and they made their way back to the plantation.

Sarju was silent when she entered the room. In her experience, this was more dangerous than when he swore and threw things.

'I've got to get the meal ready,' Vottie said, grabbing a few ingredients and putting them into a tin plate, then pushing past him to the outside before he had time to cross over and shut the door.

14
Sezela Sugar Estate
October 1909

Lutchmee was preparing their evening meal. She snipped the tender spinach leaves for the saag bhaji while Sappani rocked Seyan to sleep. Although she had bought the vegetables for this meal, she hoped that she would shortly be able to harvest food from their own little patch. Kuppen had allotted them a space behind the coolie lines, and, working with borrowed tools, she and Sappani had prepared the soil, then planted seeds and tubers donated by kindly neighbours. Even after a long and gruelling day in the sun in the sugar-cane fields, they always set aside time to tend their patch, bringing water from the pump, removing weeds, pruning and staking. Everyone with a veggie patch traded seeds with each other, which meant that theirs was soon going to be full of food that they could cook and swap too: garlic and onions, green beans, spinach, tomatoes, potatoes, pumpkins and squashes.

Sizzling in the pan, the browning onion slices began to shrink in the ghee. For an instant, the aroma took her back to her village, Thiruvallur, and once again she was a young girl cooking, squatting at the fire, listening to the chattering of the women and feeling the heat that nestled her in the bosom of Mother India.

She would have loved to add a few gnarled black cardamom pods, a sundried bay leaf, a splatter of jeera seeds and a pinch of turmeric – it would really help the flavour. But she had none of these ingredients, so instead she tipped in some red curry powder with garam masala.

She moved the karahi deftly off the fire and adjusted the coals. It was too hot and the spices would burn, making the curry inedible. 'Curry leaves,' she muttered, adding them to her mental shopping list and hoping that should could find them somewhere in this new land.

Slicing the green chillies from top to bottom and exposing the tiny uniform seeds, Lutchmee tossed them in, followed by a pinch of salt. Diced into cubes, the potatoes tumbled in with a hiss – they took the longest to cook.

She replaced the karahi on the fire and the little family sat in companionable silence for a while, listening to the food in the pot gather energy and come to a simmer. She lifted the lid of the karahi and gave the contents a stir before adding some peas and cauliflower florets. A bit more water from the lota, and she put the lid on and let it all simmer. Steam escaped in puffs from crevices where the lid and karahi edge didn't meet.

Twenty minutes later, Lutchmee removed the karahi from the fire, then tasted the curry by dabbing the end of the spoon into her open palm and licking it. It was ready.

The two adults sat and ate by the fire, occasionally glancing affectionately at Seyan, who was asleep. It was Lutchmee's favourite time of the day – just the three of them. She intently watched her husband's face, highlighted by the rise and fall of the flames. He sat on his haunches close to the fire, his plate in both hands, occasionally using one hand to deftly place curry on a chapati and carry it to his mouth. Within minutes his plate was as clean as if it had never held food.

Lutchmee was stacking their used dishes together, ready to wash them, when Kuppen arrived. 'This is for you. It came this morning,' he said holding out a letter.

Taking it, Sappani glanced at Lutchmee in some surprise – who would write them a letter? – but said, 'Nandri, Sirdar Kuppen. I am most grateful.'

'Nalladhu. No trouble,' he replied.

Sappani tore it open. 'It's from Chinmah, with an address to write back to her.'

'I didn't know she could write English – and so young!' Lutchmee said.

'She didn't write it. Her neighbour did. She says Chinmah and Angel are in danger. She is writing to us at Chinmah's request, to tell us where she is and that she needs help.' Sappani glanced up at his wife. 'We are not going to sleep now, are we? You want me to write back to her straight away, yes?'

Lutchmee nodded and pulled her husband closer to her. 'I am so worried about them,' she said, and Sappani held her in a tight embrace, wishing he could do something to ease his wife's anxiety.

The next day, when Sappani and Lutchmee arrived for roll call, there seemed to be some sort of commotion.

'If the master hears about this, there will be trouble,' Kuppen was saying to three men lined up in front of him, their heads down, their expressions dull. 'You need to get to work.'

The harvest was finally almost at an end, and even though it was Sunday, everyone had been instructed to pitch in. The wagons had to be loaded and sent to the mill as soon as possible. It was also the time to dig the troughs for the seed cane in the fallow fields, and every pair of hands was needed.

'We were told that we would have the day off. So far we have not had one day off. We are tired,' said one of the men, crossly kicking his bare feet in the sand.

Kuppen tried to reason with the men but they were adamant that they were not going to work. Eager to avoid a situation in which more Indians would refuse to work – these protests seem to spread like wildfire through the lines – he called out instructions for all the others, including Sappani and Lutchmee, to head out to the fields, and sent the millworkers on their way. He instructed the striking men to stay where they were, and rode up to the big house on his horse to tell the master about the problem.

Henry Rouillard was setting off to church wearing a suit and a smart top hat, and was anxious to deal with the matter quickly. Scowling, he rode back down to the yard with Kuppen's horse on his heels. Bringing his horse to a halt in a cloud of dust that kicked grit into the eyes of the three men squatting there, he shouted, 'What the hell's the matter now?'

'Please, Master, we are tired. We work every day. Can't we at least rest for one day?' one man, evidently the spokesman of the group, said, raising his voice but keeping his eyes lowered.

'You can rest when you are dead,' was Henry's reply. Shouting back over his shoulder to Kuppen, he instructed, 'Whip the lot of them till they know who is in charge here,' then, wheeling his horse in another cloud of dust and grit, he galloped off down the road towards the plantation gate.

Realising what was about to happen, the three Indians tried to run, but Kuppen's helpers rounded them up quickly, corralling them as if they were sheep. The first man screamed for the whipping to stop after two lashes, and, weeping, began to stumble towards the fields. The other two quickly gave in, following their sobbing friend with heavy footfalls and slumped shoulders.

After the church service was over, Henry galloped back along the country lanes to his farm, his red face set in an ugly scowl, his temper rising with each mile the horse covered. He was so sick and tired of the bloody coolies. Nothing was ever good enough for them.

Urging his horse in through the plantation gates, he galloped towards the field. He was going to make his presence seen, heard and felt. These coolies must know who the boss was around here.

Lutchmee heard the sound of the approaching hoofbeats at the same time as the master's instruction: 'Get up! Am I paying you to sit around?'

She had been separated from Sappani and had been cutting cane. It was the last of the fields and this cane needed to be cut into smaller pieces. It had to be done accurately, as each piece needed to have new shoots that would give rise to the cane plants that would produce the next harvest. Till now she had been weeding and stacking the cut cane into the wagon, so she had never held a cane knife before, and after only a few hours, her hands were raw and bleeding. She'd just sat down, and, tearing a strip of cloth from her underskirt, had begun to wrap it around the wounds, when Henry had appeared out of nowhere on his horse.

He cracked his sjambok close to her head and she dived to the ground to avoid its cruel bite. Her makeshift bandages lying in the dirt, she scrambled to her feet. 'Sorry, sorry, Master,' she said, holding her bleeding hands outwards in front of her face, anticipating another sjambok attack. But Henry just stared at her with cold, furious eyes, his lips a thin, tight line.

Lutchmee picked up the cane knife, wincing as her unprotected hands made contact with the wooden handle. Biting hard on her lower lip, she turned and continued to hack at the cane, knowing that her performance would determine what happened next.

Henry watched her for a few moments, then called out to Kuppen, who had approached to see what was happening, 'No wages for this one today.'

Lutchmee kept her head bent low and focused on the burning pain in her hands as the master rode away. Lutchmee listened, continuing to cut, until she could no longer hear the sound of his horse's hooves. Still terrified to stop, she kept on, looking through her tears at the blood running over the handle of the cane knife and dripping into the earth.

That evening at the barracks, Sappani took a closer look at Lutchmee's hands. 'You sit here. I will try to clean them or else they will get worse,' he said.

'What about Seyan? You need to get him from the ayah.'

'I will, I just don't want him to see his mother crying like a big baby,' Sappani said with a gentle smile, and kissed the top of Lutchmee's head. Yet more tears welled up in her eyes and, despite the agony in her hands, she felt her heart lift.

'His mother?' she asked.

'Yes, his mother,' Sappani said.

He made a fire and heated water, then poured it into a small dish. He then removed his turban and cut strips of it with his cane knife. He used one of the strips to clean Lutchmee's wounds, dipping it into the warm water and wiping gently. He then made a paste of turmeric and water, and applied it to her injuries. Finally, using the rest of the strips, he bandaged her hands. 'Too tight?' he asked once he was done.

'Just right,' she replied, already feeling the healing sting of the turmeric paste.

Sappani brought both Lutchmee's bandaged hands to his chapped lips and kissed them gently. Then he cupped her face in his hands and kissed her softly in the centre of her forehead.

Lutchmee blushed and her ears grew warm and a sweet contentment settled in the pit of her stomach.

Sappani raised her face to meet his. 'It's going to be okay,' he said. He nuzzled her face, kissing her forehead again. Then he stood up and went to collect Seyan.

Lutchmee watched him as he walked away. She noticed the muscles in his back, shiny with sweat, the hair on his neck damp. He turned to her and smiled. She smiled back.

But then, quickly, her feeling of bliss was displaced by one of fear: she was afraid that all this would end. Sappani didn't know who she really was or what she'd done in her past. He'd never asked her and she'd never volunteered the information. As long as this was the case, she knew she would always doubt his feelings for her.

She decided that she would tell him about her past. Maybe not tonight but soon. After that she would know how he really felt.

Sarju stepped down from the front seat of the wagon and surveyed the fields around him, taking special note of the big house on the hill that looked out to sea.

The news that he and Vottie would be leaving Stanger Tea Plantation and moving here to Sezela Sugar Estate had been sudden, but welcome: finally, someone had evidently recognised his worth, his value. Here, he was to be a sirdar. 'Sirdar Sarju,' he repeated to himself. Things could not have worked out better – a gift from the universe, no doubt. He'd been doing his prayers diligently and there were days that he felt closer to God than the people around him.

Even his wife seemed pleased, although that was maybe because she would be closer to her 'friend', the wife of that useless pariah whose name he would not befoul his tongue by saying. Maybe now Vottie would stop her nonsense and settle down and be a good wife.

Kuppen was there to greet them, and introduced himself to the couple as the sirdar.

'The old sirdar, you mean,' Sarju corrected him.

Kuppen ignored him and turned his attention to Vottie, who was lifting their possessions out of the back of the wagon. 'You can leave your belongings there. They will drop them off in your room in the lines.'

'No, take them, we will carry them. We don't want the bastards stealing our things,' Sarju said.

Kuppen stared at him quizzically, then nodded. 'As you like.' He helped them to offload their belongings and sent the driver off on his next errand. They watched the cart rumble away, kicking up dust.

'The master wants to see you. It's not often we take anyone from another plantation this late,' Kuppen said. 'I will leave someone here to watch over your possessions.' The old Indian gave a few words of instruction to one of his helpers, then, indicating that Sarju and Vottie should follow him, began walking towards the imposing white house on the hill. 'It will take a few days to learn the job, as growing cane is different from tea planting,' he continued, as they walked. 'I hope you are not trouble.' Kuppen had heard about this man on the estates grapevine, and didn't want him to do anything to make the master regret letting him retire.

'No, not at all. My wife and I are very peaceful,' Sarju replied unctuously, belatedly realising that he should probably keep the old sirdar on his side, at least until he'd completely taken over control of the role.

Up close, the house was lovelier than any Vottie had seen before: with its white walls and shiny windows, it seemed to sparkle. She was mesmerised and stopped to watch and hear the song of tiny sunbirds, some with scarlet breasts and others iridescent green, as they flitted between the fuchsia trees and bottlebrushes. *What would it be like to live here?* she wondered. She gazed out at the undulating hills that swept all the way to the shoreline, and inhaled deeply.

'Vottie!' Sarju called bad-temperedly, breaking into her reverie.

Gathering up her long skirt, she caught up with him and Kuppen. Sarju smiled joylessly at her but she did not return it. While her old bruises and scars may have healed somewhat, her heart had not. It contained only hatred for her husband.

In his study, with the three Indians standing in front of his desk, Henry Rouillard tried to get a measure of the new sirdar. He sat in his large chair, his fingers steepled, and watched them. Vottie stood as still as a statue while Sarju, attempting to impress, vacillating between staring straight into the master's eyes and lowering his lids as if he were about to fall asleep on his feet. Kuppen's expression was inscrutable, as always.

'You understand that this means that your term of indenture starts from today? Five years from today?' Henry said.

'Yes, Master,' said Sarju. 'We are grateful to be working for such a good man and on such a nice big plantation.'

Henry pushed a piece of paper across the desk towards Sarju. 'You can read?'

'Yes, I can read. I'm no regular coolie, Master,' Sarju said. Vottie stepped forward as well, but Sarju gave her a quick warning look and she stepped back. He scanned the document alone. The paper stated the terms and conditions of their new indenture to their new master, and that it had to be registered with the Indian Immigration Trust Board.

Sarju signed it for himself and Vottie, and pushed it back across the desk.

'What happened to her?' Henry asked, nodding towards Vottie. Her head shawl had fallen to one side, displaying the fading bruises on her face and the scar on her cheek.

'A horse, Master. I got too close to the wrong end,' she said quietly, drawing her shawl over her head again.

'Silly woman. Not much good sense,' Sarju added, tapping his own head for emphasis.

Henry adjusted his position in his seat and interest flickered in his eyes. Never before had he heard an Indian woman speak such good English. He smiled at her. 'What's your name again?'

'Vottie. I am Vottie, Master,' she replied softly.

'And what work do you do?'

Sarju glared at her. Kuppen looked out of the window, his expression the one that people wear when they find themselves in a place they do not want to be.

'I was working in the tea factory on the Stanger plantation but I can work in the house too. Your house is beautiful, the nicest I have ever seen,' she said, aware of his unexpected interest in her but not yet sure what it meant.

'That's good to hear. Kuppen, maybe we can use Vottie in the house? There seems to be dust everywhere.'

Now Sarju smiled and pressed his palms together and bowed to Rouillard. 'We are glad to be of any assistance, Master,' he said. 'I will keep your field in order, and my wife, she will keep your house in order.'

'That's settled, then. Vottie, you will start in the house tomorrow. Sarju, you start with Kuppen in the fields, learning how we do things around here.'

Standing up and making his way around the desk towards them, the master walked over to Kuppen and addressed Sarju. 'Maybe you can be as good as my man Kuppen, here,' he said, slapping the tall old Indian on his back. 'It may not have started well, but you were a quick learner, weren't you, Kuppen?'

Kuppen laughed along but, recalling his first morning as a sirdar with the master, found no humour in it. Back then, breakfast was given to all the workers, and they ate together in the yard, so they had the energy to do the day's work. That morning, Kuppen's first on the job, the Indians had been given porridge that they did not want to eat. It was plain cooked mealiemeal without sugar or milk.

'You would have to be starving to put even a spoonful of this to your lips,' one of the men had said, and a few others sitting near him nodded in agreement.

Kuppen had walked over to them to try to get them to settle down. It was his first day and he didn't want their complaints to reach the master's ears but it was too late. Henry Rouillard was dismounting his horse, and Kuppen could still remember the sickening feeling in his stomach when he saw the tight, ugly expression on the master's face.

Henry reached the seated Indians, 'What's the problem here?' he'd asked, his irritation umistakable.

'We cannot eat this, Master,' said the man who had already complained to Kuppen. 'We need some sugar, at least. Isn't this a sugar plantation?' A few men stifled their laughs.

With a sardonic smile, the master had unbuttoned his pants and taken out his penis, then proceeded to urinate directly into the Indians' bowls, walking casually around, ensuring that at least a few drops of that steady stream of warm, yellow urine landed in each bowl.

Someone retched.

Tucking himself back into his trousers, Henry had said to Kuppen, 'Where are the kaffirs with the sjamboks? Bring them.'

The Indian men had stared, confusion and fear playing on their faces, while the Africans, each holding a sjambok, arrived. The master had ordered them into a line behind the seated Indians. 'Whip them until those bowls are licked clean,' he shouted.

No one moved.

Everyone, Indian and African alike, had stared at Henry as if unable to comprehend what he'd just said.

Then one of the Indians had tried to get up, and the movement seemed to break the spell.

The African behind him was on him at once, his sjambok flailing, not caring where it landed.

Kuppen had watched in revulsion as the Africans had whipped the Indians. The sounds of the individual men's screams quickly merged into a single cacophony of pain, assaulting his ears.

Then the master had reached for his own sjambok, and started in on the Indian men too, whipping indiscriminately, and stopping only when the men had been reduced to nothing but a crying, writhing mass on the ground, their dhotis a mixture of human excrement, blood and dirt.

'Stop!' Henry had screamed, and the lightning sound of leather snapping in the air, and the repeated, sickening noise of flesh being flayed, stuttered to a halt. In the ensuing silence, the Indian men's crying had been louder – raw and childlike.

Sweaty and red-faced, the master had then signalled for Kuppen to come and stand in front of him. The sirdar had not known what to expect but the first lash, which had caught him across his arm, was not it. The next whipped across his chest.

Then they just kept coming, all over his body. It felt as if the beating went on for hours, although afterwards Kuppen realised it was probably minutes. The depth and volume of his screaming had more than matched those of the stricken Indians.

Henry himself had said not a word during the punishment, the only sounds he emitted being grunts of exertion.

When it was over, he'd wound up his sjambok and pushed it into one of his saddlebags 'Now you will remember, you need to keep them in line. That's your job,' he'd said. Then he'd remounted his horse, kicking his heels into its haunches, and galloped off.

Kuppen had got up. He'd called for others to help, and the beaten Indians had been assisted back to the lines, where they were cleaned up. Then Kuppen had summoned them, made them line up, and walked the broken, snivelling men in single file into the field to begin the day's work.

*

From his study, Henry Rouillard watched the three Indians leave. It was barely midday but he felt thirsty. Pouring himself a brandy, he raised the crystal glass to eye level, swirling the amber liquid pensively.

Over the past ten years, many Indian women had come to the plantation. They came from all over India: Mumbai, Jaipur, Andhra Pradesh and Bangalore, and other places he didn't know or couldn't recall. In them he saw nothing but hands to cut the cane and weed the fields, and occasionally hands that gave him pleasure. He'd certainly never looked at their faces, never mind remembered any of them. They were inconsequential.

Yet here he was, thinking about the woman who'd just been standing in his office. Her smooth skin, like a polished walnut; her eyes, almond-shaped, with their long elegant lashes; the arch of her eyebrows that suggested a deeper, more knowing side to her; her full lips, dipped in the middle, revealing a hint of perfect, pearly-white teeth; her lustrous black hair flowing down around her shoulders. Despite the bruises on her face and the scar on her cheek, she was quite beautiful. His mind's eye lingered on the memory of her hips, small and sensuous, hinted at through her pink sari.

Henry stepped out onto the veranda, where he hoped the sound of the Indian Ocean and the sway of the umdoni trees would soothe his mind as usual. But not today. He couldn't recall when last he'd felt captivated by a woman in this way. Something drew her to him in a way he couldn't understand. She was bold, no doubt: poised.

Henry quickly drank down the brandy, then went back into his study and refilled the glass from the decanter. More, this time. It sloshed over onto his hand. An image of the Indian woman splayed on her back stood on the edge of his mind, dancing about provocatively, teasing to be allowed in or be rejected. He found himself feeling constricted in his trousers.

He drained the glass, wondering how he could relieve himself of his erection …

*

It was the afternoon and Lutchmee was washing their clothes when she heard a scream – not of fear or pain but of elation. She turned, drying her hands on her sari, and in a flurry of black hair and pink skirts, she was enveloped in a soft, warm, tight embrace.

Other women in the washing area stopped what they were doing and stared. Vottie and Lutchmee hugged each other and cried into each other's necks. Talking over each other and laughing, they touched each other's hair and face, to make sure it was real. Lutchmee stepped back and held Vottie by her shoulders to take a better look at her. She saw the bruises on her face but didn't say anything.

Seyan toddled over to see what all the fuss was about. Vottie scooped him up and smothered him with kisses. Caught unawares, he reached out to Lutchmee and called out, 'Amma!'

Vottie laughed happily to see how far Lutchmee had come since she'd first tried to be a mother to Seyan.

The two women walked back to the barracks, arm in arm, chattering to each other without stopping. Seyan, on Lutchmee's hip, decided he was pleased with the attention from the new arrival, and giggled with delight when Vottie tickled him under his chin.

'I'm going to live here now,' Vottie said. 'Sarju got a job here as a sirdar, and we are living over in the sirdars' quarters.' The sirdars were often allowed to build their own houses, and the one allotted to her and Sarju had been well constructed by a previous occupant. It had one room to sleep in and another, smaller room next to it for cooking, with a small indoor fireplace and a chimney that led up and out of the galvanised roof. The nearby communal washing area was small but served only the head sirdar and his family, and some of his helpers and theirs.

Lutchmee felt joyful, then apprehensive, then guilty. It was so good to have her friend here, but it also meant that the man she despised was now closer to her and her husband. Sappani and she had been doing well, working hard in their garden and trying to get settled here. In the evenings, Sappani was even helping on the school that the master had given permission for the Indians to build – it would be for all the Indians. He had even mentioned Seyan and his brothers and sisters being educated there.

Their lives were mostly peaceful. It wasn't much but they were starting to feel like they were a part of something.

Sarju's arrival could mean trouble.

Shaking her head as if to get rid of the nasty thoughts, she smiled and hugged Vottie again, wrapping her arms tightly around her. 'I will do all I can to help you settle in,' she said.

In Lutchmee and Sappani's tiny room, the women chattered on, catching up. 'Any news from Chinmah?' Vottie asked.

'Yes, she sent us her address and said that she was in trouble. There is nothing we can do,' Lutchmee said sadly, 'but I made Sappani write back to her that very day. Now that you are here, you can do the writing.'

'Okay,' Vottie said. 'I will write tomorrow, and see if there is a way we can get to see her. Maybe she can meet us in Durban? They say that Diwali there will be almost like it is back home.'

Kuppen didn't expect to be heading back to see the master again so soon, and especially not this late. Instead of taking the horse, he decided to walk. The memory of his first day as sirdar was still on his mind and he hoped that the walk would prepare him for what he had to tell Rouillard.

Four men hadn't returned from the field at the end of the working day, and had been absent from evening roll call. Kuppen had gone to look for them, and had found all of them hanging from the trees, like guards of honour in some sort of hell. In his mind's eye he could still see their slack bodies and the dense clouds of flies that rose when he began to cut them down. He also saw the fresh welts from the sjambok on their backs and legs.

He knocked on the front door and a servant let him in, going ahead of him to warn the master that the sirdar had arrived.

When the servant ushered Kuppen into the study, the sirdar found Henry seated at his large desk, eating his supper with a napkin around his neck. Wiping his mouth, Henry demanded, 'What is it, Kuppen?'

Kuppen could see no way other than to wade right in. 'Four of the coolies have hanged themselves in the far field,' he said.

Henry picked up his fork and knife and sawed through a thick piece of meat. 'You know what needs to be done, Kuppen. Why are you even here?' He forked the food into his mouth and stared at Kuppen, chewing with his mouth slightly open.

'They are the four men who were beaten on Sunday morning,' Kuppen said.

Henry's jaws stopped moving and he stared at the sirdar, and despite his resolve, Kuppen felt a shiver of fear run down his spine. He had known this was information that his master wouldn't want to hear, and that he, Kuppen, would also be expected to keep it from the Protector, but he felt now that he was soon to retire that he had little to lose – and even Rouillard, whose cruelty had become almost legendary, would surely not whip an old man like himself? But Kuppen suddenly wondered if he'd overestimated his master's ability to see the Indians – any of the Indians, including him – as actual people, deserving of mercy.

'I don't like where this is going,' Henry said. 'If they were beaten, it was for good reason. They took their own lives, and that is no one's fault. The Protector doesn't have to know – it will just cause problems nobody wants. Say they died fighting each, or for a woman or food or a drink or something.'

Kuppen listened silently.

Henry shrugged and began chewing again, speaking around the food in his mouth. 'Let the coolies do their prayers and bury the bastards in the north field. It will be fallow for a few more years.' Then he looked up at the sirdar and said, 'Do you understand what you have to say to the Protector, Kuppen? He will come here once we report their deaths.'

'Yes, sir,' Kuppen replied, his head bowed. He couldn't look at the master directly. He feared that doing so would unleash the rage that had been building up inside him since the morning.

Watching him closely, Henry said, 'I would hate for there to be another coolie buried in that field.' The threat hung in the air for a bit, then the master nodded to the door, indicating it was time for Kuppen to leave.

15
Durban, Port of Natal
October 1909

Arriving at Durban station, the little party of celebrants left the train, and Lutchmee and Vottie squealed with delight to see Chinmah waiting there for them, with Angel in her arms. Ramsamy was standing awkwardly at her side.

Vottie threw her arms around Chinmah. She felt her young friend's body tighten momentarily, but then they held each other, Angel wedged tightly between them. Lutchmee joined the group hug, and the three women stood for some time, touching each other, revelling in the warmth and solidity of each other's bodies.

Finally, the three friends broke apart. Vottie eased Angel into her own arms, immediately concerned at how light the baby was, barely a scrap of humanity with almost no weight to her at all, and how limp she felt.

Lutchmee held Chinmah by the shoulders so that she could take a good look at her. 'Chinmah, you are just skin and bone. What has happened?'

Chinmah was definitely even smaller and thinner than before. Her sari hung loosely on her hips and her cheeks were hollow.

'We need to get you some food!' Vottie said, only half joking.

Ramsamy greeted Sappani with a curt nod and ignored the women. 'I will meet you back here at seven,' he said to Chinmah and walked off.

Chinmah stared after him, and the look she gave him wasn't lost on Vottie and Lutchmee.

*

The preparations for this special day had begun at sunrise that morning. Lutchmee was in high spirits – it was her first Diwali in Natal and as part of a new family. For many of the immigrants, Diwali was the observance that was most closely tied to family and a sense of home.

She'd awoken at sunrise. Seyan was still asleep, one arm thrown casually behind his head, and Sappani was also fast asleep, on his stomach. Giving them a last, loving glance, she'd gently pulled the door closed and stood outside in the yard. The roaming chickens ruffled their feathers, and pecked and scratched in the dust. A goat, tethered to a wooden post in the ground and destined for the pot, looked at her disinterestedly with its odd horizontal pupils. Dogs stretched and hauled themselves onto all fours as they began to follow the humans in the hope of food.

The other women had also woken early and begun to prepare, following the naimittika rituals, important for any auspicious occasion. Lutchmee had joined in as they washed in the communal bathing area, chatting about what they were going to cook and sharing recipes.

Returning to the room, Lutchmee had offered up bananas, pawpaw and coconut, placing the fruit on a tray in the corner of the room. She'd knelt and lit the camphor that she'd bought for this prayer, releasing its familiar heady scent into the room. With her head covered and bowed, she'd softly chanted the mantra of Lakshmi, her namesake goddess. 'Om shreem maha Lakshmiyei namaha!'

With the morning light coming in faster now, she'd carefully prepared the oil and wicks in the diyas. How thrilled Seyan would be to see them after dark, symbolising the path that the exiled Rama and his faithful wife Sita had taken out of the forest, teaching all Hindus that whatever the challenges faced, good would always overcome evil.

For the preceding week Lutchmee had been mixing colours and using natural dyes to tint the sand and stones for her rangoli design. The last one she'd made had been for her own wedding. Now, using a stick, she'd traced the outline on the ground, then begun from the centre with a warm golden lotus flower, its petals open invitingly. Her idea to add dimension had worked, as she'd gently placed the smooth pebbles she'd died with turmeric overlapping each other. She'd then arranged the blue and green crushed stones in the shape of three peacocks – two adults and a baby – whirling outward from the lotus flower.

Standing up, she'd stretched her spine and stepped back, admiring her handiwork.

'Mika alakana, Lutchmee.'

She'd turned to see Sappani standing at the door, his hair still tousled from sleep.

'You like it?' she'd asked, her eyes smiling with his compliment.

'It is the best I have ever seen. Seyan is going to love the peacocks,' Sappani had replied.

'Don't wake him yet. I still have so much to do.'

While Lutchmee continued with her rangoli artwork, Sappani had lit the cooking fire. Outside the front doors of the barracks, many women had been hard at work preparing the best midday meal they could, hunched over their fires, poking at the wood and coals, and fanning the flames to accelerate the bubbling in the pots. The air was redolent with the smell of spicy curries, frying samosas, puris, hot rotis and chapatis.

When Lutchmee had stepped up onto the veranda to begin cooking, the woman next to her had smiled her welcome. 'Sukra hai, the master said we could celebrate. This is nice, yaar?'

Another woman had added, 'I heard that the Muslims' Muharram was a huge celebration but instead of praying, they had street fights and the Indians didn't show up for work the next day. I thought they were going to give us nothing, but they let us have Diwali – more peaceful, and less trouble for them too.'

It was to be the first officially recognised Diwali for the indentured population of Natal. Although successive waves of Hindu Indians had petitioned the authorities to allow them to celebrate this special holiday, the colonial government had thought yet another 'coolie Christmas' – the dismissive name they gave Muharram – was unnecessary. But Swami Shankeranand, an important Hindu missionary who'd visited from India, wouldn't give up, and finally, earlier this year, he'd organised a massive

Ram Navami spring festival celebrating the birthday of Shree Rama, an avatar of the god Vishnu. Joyful Hindus had met at the Umgeni Road temple, and after the speeches, a crowd of thousands had marched cheerfully through the streets of Durban, before returning to the temple for a feast and entertainment. The authorities had been impressed with both the organisation and the orderliness of the celebrations, and the powers that be had finally agreed to grant employees a day off to celebrate Diwali. It didn't take long for the planters to follow suit – they knew when they were beaten.

'Are you going in to Durban for the big festival?' Lutchmee had asked the other women.

'Yes,' one of the women had said. 'They're going to have stalls and all sorts of nice things to buy and eat.'

'Food is always tastier when you don't have to cook it yourself,' Lutchmee had added.

Another woman had told them, 'Natal Government Railways has put on extra trains for us to travel there and back.'

Lutchmee had fussed over her little family as they'd sat down to eat the lunch she'd prepared. It was simple vegetarian fare. Seyan was delighted when she placed a roti in his hands, the melted butter running all along his arm as he tried to cram it into his mouth and totter about at the same time.

They'd cleared up together after the meal and Lutchmee had taken the dishes to the washing area. She'd returned with them, cleaned and dried, when Sappani had said, 'We have something for you.' Seyan had appeared carrying a square box and handed it over excitedly.

Opening it carefully, Lutchmee had seen a purple-and-silver silk sari. She'd wiped her hands on the old sari she was wearing, then gently lifted the new one out of the box. It had felt luxurious to the touch, and she'd let it glide over her hands as she'd examined the simple silver beadwork on the pallu.

She'd looked at the Sappani, unable to express the rush of emotion she felt.

'It's the colour of the sari you were wearing the day we met.'

Lutchmee had blinked back tears.

'You don't like it?' he'd asked, nervously.

'Help me to try it on. I am going to wear it when we go in to town.'

Lutchmee had quickly slipped into a clean underskirt and Sappani had helped her to gather the pleats of the beautiful new sari and pin them at the waist. The blouse was a perfect fit and the silver beadwork highlighted her long, slim arms. Sappani and Seyan had watched her as she'd tried different styles with her hair, then settled on a loose bun at the nape of her neck.

Her eyes had shone with happiness. It wasn't about the sari. It was about feeling loved. 'I feel like a maharani,' she'd said, adjusting the pleats yet again.

'You look like one too,' Sappani had said and he kissed her tenderly on her forehead.

The excitement had been growing in the barracks. Children were scrubbed clean, fires were doused, and dogs and chickens were locked away. The Indians put on their best clothes, ready to catch the 3 p.m. train to Durban. On this day, the passenger train stopped at certain points near the plantations so the Indians could climb aboard.

'I thought Vottie would be here, ready to leave by now,' Lutchmee had said impatiently. 'She knows we can't be late. Chinmah is meeting us there. Vottie wrote to her neighbour, and it's all arranged.' She'd thought for a few moments, then said, 'I'll go over there with these mithai and see what is taking her so long.'

'Be careful,' Sappani had cautioned. They had managed to keep a safe distance from Sarju and he wanted it to stay that way.

When Lutchmee arrived at Vottie's door in the sirdars' quarters, there was no sign that she and Sarju were celebrating Diwali: no rangoli patterns, no lamps along the steps.

As Lutchmee raised a hand to knock, Vottie had opened the door, stepped out of the house, and quickly closed the door behind her. Her eyes were red and swollen. 'Oh, thank you, that looks so good,' she'd said in a strangled voice, reaching out for the plate.

They had both heard shuffling from behind the closed door, and glanced at it. It was suddenly flung open, and Sarju's furious face appeared. 'What? Now the pariah bitch is at my door!'

'Just go, Lutchmee,' Vottie had said. 'I can deal with him.' She'd pushed the plate back into Lutchmee's hands and ushered Sarju back into the room, shutting the door behind her.

It was then that Lutchmee had noticed that outside Vottie's door were ladoos, burfi and poli, covered in dust and flies. Lutchmee picked up the jharu that was leaning against the wall and swept up the food.

When she got back to Sappani, he'd looked at the plate of food untouched in her hands. 'Did he cause trouble?' he asked. 'Is Vottie okay?'

'I don't know. She told me to go. I am worried about her. That man is just not right.'

But there was no more time to act on any concerns if they were to make the train, and Seyan was squealing to be carried by her, so she'd picked him up and slung him onto her hip. Even though Lutchmee was involved in conversations as they walked with other Indian families to the train stop, she'd kept looking back, thinking about Vottie.

When they reached the stop, Lutchmee looked around once more for Vottie, in vain. 'There's still time,' she'd said to Sappani. I can just go—'

'No, Lutchmee, there is no telling what that man will do,' her husband had replied in a tone that indicated the discussion was over.

Just as the train was pulling in, drawing slowly and noisily to a halt, Lutchmee had seen Vottie weaving her way towards her. Lutchmee waved at her friend, and Seyan copied her.

'Are you okay? I was worried about you,' Lutchmee had said, pulling her friend into her arms.

Vottie didn't looked dressed for the occasion. She was wearing a faded blue sari and had draped her hair over her shoulders and front to hide a rather tattered blouse.

'Everything is all right,' Vottie had replied, then gently pushed Lutchmee away and held her at arm's length. 'Look at you!' she'd said, admiringly.

Lutchmee did a little twirl. 'Sappani got it for me. Isn't it beautiful?'

Then she'd looked seriously at Vottie. 'Where is Sarju?' she'd asked in a low voice.

'The haraami is at home and he doesn't know where I am. He thinks I am working in the big house. I could not miss being with you all and Chinmah too!' Vottie had said.

'What if he finds out, Vottie?' Lutchmee had asked, worriedly.

'What else can he do to me that he does not do already?' she'd replied flatly. 'Let's forget about him today, please.'

Finally in Durban together, the excited group of four adults and two children made their way out of the station, walking and talking over each other, towards Victoria Street, where the crowd was also heading. There, they wandered between stalls selling imitation jewellery, shawls and saris in colours that would make a rainbow envious. They ran their hands over the brocade and embroidery work of the fabric, a sensual journey for each one of them, these familiar things that had made their way here and rooted in this foreign place.

The air held the smells that everyone missed, with street vendors selling delicate Indian sweetmeats, large pots of oil bubbling as stall owners deep-fried samosas and bhajias, selling lassis of all flavours and cups of milky, sweet chai, with mounds of boondi, sticky jalebis and coconut burfi on offer.

Chinmah pulled Lutchmee to the side and pushed her mouth closed to her friend's ear. 'Angel needs milk. I have nothing left, nothing for her to drink,' she whispered, holding her hands over her breasts. 'Do you think we can buy her some milk here?'

'I'll send Sappani to go and buy some, don't you worry. When Angel wakes up, we will make sure she gets her feed,' Lutchmee said reassuringly.

Angel, strapped securely across her mother's body, seemed to be fast and peacefully asleep, and because Lutchmee hadn't held the child in her arms herself and felt how tenuously she was clinging to life, she had no idea of how serious the situation was. And Vottie, whose fears for Angel were profound, hadn't yet had a quiet moment to share her concerns with Lutchmee.

Lutchmee handed money over to a vendor and bought gulab jamuns for them all to try. Sappani watched as she gently broke off pieces and fed them to Seyan. 'Look how he likes it!' Lutchmee said as Seyan's arms shot out as an indication that she should feed him quicker.

Sappani nodded and smiled but for an instant he was taken back to the image of the fallen gulab jamuns in the dirt, on that day so many months ago in the coolie camp, when his beloved Neela had died.

They stopped at a stall that sold aromatic vegetarian biryani and bought enough for everyone, then found a shady spot to sit down to eat. They all noticed how greedily Chinmah gobbled up the food, scooping handfuls into her mouth as quickly as she could. But their relief that she was getting some nourishment quickly turned to alarm as Chinmah, her starved body rejecting the rich food eaten so fast, promptly leaned over and vomited it all up onto the grass.

'Chinmah, what is happening? Why are you so thin? Is Ramsamy not giving you money for food?'

'I will get her some nimbu pani to settle her stomach,' Sappani said.

'You have to tell us, Chinmah, what is happening?' Vottie pleaded.

'It is so bad, I don't know how to start,' Chinmah said, and burst into tears. 'We have no money. Ramsamy refuses to work, he just smokes ganja every day and I just can't …' Her tiny shoulders began to shudder and Lutchmee pulled her closer while Vottie paced with Angel in her arms.

'That maadher chod! Wait till he comes back!' Vottie threatened.

'I can't feed Angel,' Chinmah sobbed, her words muffled by Lutchmee's embrace. 'She needs milk and I have nothing,' she said, clutching at her breasts.

'The valayal I gave you – didn't you manage to sell it?' Lutchmee asked.

'I couldn't get away from the estate until today,' Chinmah said. 'And I had to make a deal with the devil to get money for the train. I kept the valayal buried, and I dug it up last night, after Ramsamy went to sleep.' Chinmah reached into her blouse and brought out the piece of jewellery, which she handed to Lutchmee.

'You don't need to worry. Vottie and I are going to help you,' Lutchmee said, brushing away Chinmah's tears.

Sappani returned with the nimbu pani, and Vottie and Lutchmee left Chinmah on the grass to sip it while they conferred in low voices. 'This is where being a Brahmin is going to be useful in this country. Here,' Lutchmee said, passing the valayal to Vottie, 'you go and get the best price for this. I'll stay here with Chinmah and Angel. Take Sappani with you.'

Vottie nodded in agreement, and she and Sappani immediately set off towards the rows of jewellery shops displaying a glittering array of Indian jewellery, the valayal safely hidden in the folds of Vottie's sari.

The pair entered the first shop they came across. 'This is some of the finest twenty-four-carat gold you will ever see,' Vottie told the shop owner confidently, as she put the bracelet down on the counter. 'The workmanship is unmatched anywhere in this country.'

The owner inspected the piece closely, running his fingers over the filigreed work, trying to hide his enthusiasm. Although Vottie had made up her sales patter, she was actually very close to being completely correct.

The jeweller named a price, and Vottie stared at him with open contempt. 'Leave it then,' she said. 'I am not parting with it for such an insulting sum. Come,' she said to Sappani who, worried that they had just turned down what seemed to be a very good deal, stood uncertainly.

'Wait!' the jeweller said, and named a figure almost double the first one.

'That's better,' Vottie said, haughtily, and handed over the valayal.

Sappani stared at her in open admiration.

In triumph, Sappani and Vottie returned to the group on the grass, where Chinmah had recovered a little, and even managed to eat and keep down a bit of biryani.

Vottie then led them all to the Naidoos' general store, where Mrs Naidoo appeared from behind the counter to speak to the women as soon as they walked in. Her ample bosom appeared to be bursting out of her pale-blue sari blouse, the hooks and eyes straining at the back and the sleeves tightly hugging her arms. Her belly hung over the top of the folds of sari at her waist and jiggled rhythmically as she walked.

'These are my friends. We met on the *Umzinto*,' Vottie explained.

'Ah, come in, come in,' Mrs Naidoo said, breathlessly. She offered the little group some figs, then pointed to some upturned boxes and invited them to sit down.

Vottie took Mrs Naidoo aside and explained the situation with Angel, and the plump shop owner bustled off immediately, returning about ten minutes later with a bottle containing warm milk. Sitting down next to Chinmah, she took the young mother's face in her hands, looking closely at her with soft eyes. 'How old are you, chellam?' she asked, and when Chinmah told her, Mrs Naidoo's eyes misted up. 'I have a daughter the same age,' she said. 'She's at school in Durban, and has plans to be a lawyer some day.'

The indentured women looked at each other, understanding the vast chasm that lay between their situation and that of Mrs Naidoo's ambitious free-Indian daughter.

Mrs Naidoo watched with motherly concern as Chinmah gently released her still, pale baby from her swaddling, and held the bottle teat against her lips, rubbing it backward and forward to release a few drops of milk, which trickled into Angel's mouth. Unresponsive at first, the baby seemed to realise that food was on offer, and finally she began weakly but determinedly sucking on the teat.

A customer rapped on the counter, and Mrs Naidoo hurried off to serve him. Lutchmee caught her on her way back to them. 'Do you have anything to bring her milk back?' she asked the plump store owner, darting her eyes at Chinmah, whose relief that her baby was finally getting some nourishment was plain for all to see.

'Yes, yes, of course,' the kindly Mrs Naidoo said. 'Methi seeds mixed into a cup of milk will be good. Let me make some for her now.'

Mrs Naidoo bustled away again, and returned in a little while, offering the restorative drink to Chinmah and also handing out biscuits and cups of sweet milky chai for the others.

Mrs Naidoo's incessant chatter made them feel welcome, and watching her serve customers, haggling with them and sometimes swearing under her breath when they annoyed her, made them laugh.

Leaving the little ones with Sappani and Mrs Naidoo, Lutchmee, Vottie and Chinmah then did some grocery shopping, selecting vegetables, fruits, grains, nuts and spices from the abundant choice in the shop. When Mrs Naidoo totted up their purchases, she gave them a big discount, and Vottie used some of the money she had got for the valayal to pay.

Finally, 'We need to get Chinmah to the station,' Sappani reminded them.

'You look after yourself and that beautiful baby,' Mrs Naidoo called after Chinmah, who now had a faint but genuine smile on her face. 'If you need anything, you just get a message to me,' she added, as they all waved to her. 'We sisters have to help each other.' She waved back from the front door of her shop.

At the station, it was almost time for the northbound train to leave and Ramsamy hadn't reappeared. The friends knew they couldn't leave Chinmah to get back to her plantation on her own, as she wouldn't be able to carry the baby as well as the food they'd bought. Instead of staying to watch more of the festivities, Lutchmee and Vottie decided that they would take the train with Chinmah and then return to Durban and take the southbound train to their home.

Sappani was not entirely pleased with this idea but when he looked at the frail figure of Chinmah, he knew she would need help. He agreed to meet his wife back at their barracks and, taking the overly tired Seyan with him, set off for Sezela Sugar Estate.

The train was almost empty, as the most of the Indians were still in town and would only be returning later. The three women found seats together, and Chinmah, with Angel nestled on her lap, felt a familiar warm feeling.

They all agreed that Mrs Naidoo was their new hero – the way she handled the customers, how firmly planted she appeared to be, each one wishing that they too could catch some of that certainty and determination, just by being near her for that small amount of time.

'But none of it happened overnight,' Vottie reminded them, sensibly. 'She also began as a coolie. She and her husband had to build up towards what they've got today.'

The women fell quiet for a while, all of them lost in their thoughts of their present and future. Then Chinmah, as if suddenly realising something profound, looked at the two of them. 'Who will look after Angel if I die?' she asked.

Vottie and Lutchmee stared at her. 'Why are you talking about such things, Chinmah?' Lutchmee asked.

'I need to know ... I need to know that she will be safe,' Chinmah stuttered, unsure why this sudden feeling of terror had gripped her when she was safely sitting with her two dearest friends.

'We both will,' Lutchmee said to her, taking her hand.

Vottie nodded agreement, then said, 'Pagal,' and playfully tapped her head. 'Nothing is going to happen to you.'

When they arrived at Chinmah's stop, Vottie and Lutchmee got off the train with her. 'Are you going to be okay?' Vottie asked.

'See those people?' Chinmah said, indicating a group of Indians standing nearby. With parcels at their feet and tired children in their arms, it was clear they had also been in Durban and were about to walk back to the estate. 'They live right near me. You two need to get back to your own homes. I will ask them to help me.'

'We will come to see you soon, Chinmah,' Vottie said, handing the sleeping Angel, the skin over her full tummy now drum-tight, and her breathing deep and content, to her mother.

While Vottie and Lutchmee were speaking to the small group of Indians, introducing themselves to the women and explaining how Chinmah needed help carrying all her purchases and her child back to the estate, the southbound train arrived. With some last hugs and encouraging words to Chinmah, Lutchmee and Vottie boarded.

'Send a message to us,' Lutchmee called out the window. As the train chugged slowly up the track, she watched the slight figure of Chinmah being swallowed up in the dark.

'She will be okay,' Vottie said.

Lutchmee frowned, unconvinced. Then she looked at her friend and said, 'And you? Will you be okay?'

16
Mount Edgecombe Sugar Estate
November 1909

Seeing Vottie and Lutchmee had buoyed Chinmah's spirits. And now there was food and she was able to pay off her debt to the ayah for looking after Angel. And she still had some money to spare, hidden away from Ramsamy.

It was the end of the week, and Chinmah was heading home from the fields, eager to see Angel. A man she didn't know was scurrying out her front door. He was carrying a bag of flour and a few tins.

'Bhai, where did you get that from?' she called out.

He glanced in her direction but didn't answer, instead quickening his pace and disappearing around a corner.

Ramsamy was standing in front of their room and, on seeing her, he hurriedly shoved something into the folds of his dhoti and slunk off.

Chinmah began running. She threw open the door of their room and looked around, willing her eyes to adjust more quickly to the dim light. When they did, she could hardly believe what she saw.

There was nothing left: not a scrap of the food they'd bought with the money from the valayal remained. Ramsamy had sold it all.

Eating properly had meant that Chinmah's milk had returned, and she was feeling stronger than she had for some time. But now it was all gone.

Spinning on her heels, she ran out, her eyes darting this way and that. Ramsamy was sitting in the yard, crushing ganja between his right thumb and the centre of his left palm.

Chinmah rushed into him, knocking him over into the sand. He scrabbled around on the ground, trying to grab at the flecks of ganja that were now mixed into the sand.

Chinmah's fists rained down on his head and back as she wept with fury. 'How could you do this to your own wife and child?' she shouted.

The neighbours had begun coming out of their rooms to watch. Then a baby starting crying, breaking into Chinmah's fury. It wasn't Angel but it reminded her to go to her child.

Leaving her useless husband lying in the dirt, Chinmah ran to the ayah's room. The old woman was standing at her door with Angel in her arms, her face grim. 'She has been like this all day,' she said, as she passed the limp baby to her mother. 'Something is wrong.'

Chinmah scooped up Angel and took her home. In the room, Chinmah stripped off the baby's clothes. Her body was hot, her little eyes closed, her tiny chest rising and falling as her breath come in little gasps.

'Angel, look at me!' Chinmah begged. 'Angel, open your eyes! Please, open your eyes!'

With rising panic, she dipped her fingers into the water in the lota and tried to drip some into her baby's mouth, but there was no response. Continuing to speak to Angel, cooing and coaxing her to open her eyes, Chinmah pulled her blouse aside and held the baby to a breast. She tried to open Angel's slack jaws so that she could latch on but the little girl was unresponsive.

Chinmah massaged her breast until drops of milk appeared and, to her enormous relief, Angel closed her mouth and began to suck weakly. She drank slowly and without her usual greediness but at least she was sucking. The feed didn't last long, though, and within just a few minutes, Angel's head fell away from Chinmah's breast and the baby went back to sleep.

Chinmah felt a ghastly chill. If she didn't do something, her baby would die, she was sure of it. A life without her baby was not worth living. She needed help.

Gathering up the infant in her arms, she ran back to the ayah's room.

'Please keep her,' she pleaded, pushing Angel into the woman's arms. 'I need to get her help.'

Without waiting for a response, Chinmah ran to Royappen's door and hammered her fists on it.

He opened it, a plate of food in his hands. 'I knew you would come back,' he said with a leery smile.

'My baby …' Chinmah gasped. 'Please, you need to help me. Something is wrong.'

Royappen, sensing victory, was enjoying the moment. 'Come inside and eat something,' he beckoned.

'Angel is sick,' Chinmah said, stepping into the room. 'Please, I need to get her to the doctor.'

'I can help,' Royappen said, lazily, putting down the plate of food, 'but, Chinmah, you must be my rice-cooker, eh?' He stared straight at her and she couldn't help but think how much like a frog he looked, with the folds of fat around his neck and his bulging, watery eyes.

Chinmah allowed herself to be led to his bedroll. In no particular hurry, Royappen unwound the dhoti from around his waist and folded it neatly, putting it to one side. Then he lay back on the bedroll and indicated that Chinmah should climb on top of him.

Chinmah stifled a wave of nausea. This frog-man was now her saviour. She moved towards him and lifted her sari above her waist, then sat over his body, her gaze fixed in front of her.

Royappen leant back onto his elbows as she lowered herself onto him. He moaned and adjusted his position, grabbing her hips to keep her in place.

He was still thrusting inside Chinmah, his eyes rolling back in his head, when a deafening sound interrupted his movements. The door to the room came off its hinges, exploding inwards and crashing to the floor.

Chinmah turned and saw Ramsamy. He was holding a hoe above his head. Screaming, she tried to get off Royappen, but he was trying to stand up at the same time, with her still on top of him. She fell to the floor, her legs splayed wide.

Ramsamy stepped over her, his eyes fixed.

She pulled her legs towards herself and cowered on the floor.

In seconds, it began to rain blood. Royappen had the chance to scream just once.

Chinmah had never seen Ramsamy look so intent on doing anything. He usually looked weary and empty-eyed. The man in front of her was staring fixedly at the soggy mess he was creating. Like a butcher, he kept bring the hoe down on Royappen. He was almost methodical and each blow was well timed, with a sense of purpose that she'd never before seen in him. Bits of flesh, fragments of bone and sprays of blood flew in all directions.

Chinmah buried her face in her hands and wept in horror.

Then, finally, he stopped. Wrenching the square blade of the hoe out of Royappen's chest, Ramsamy turned slowly, staring down at his wife cowering on the floor. His eyes radiated hatred.

The bodies of Royappen and Chinmah were found less than an hour later, the bloodied hoe that had been used to kill them discarded on the floor beside the mutilated corpses. The ayah had become concerned at the lateness of the hour, and, with the sick baby in her arms, had gone looking for the mother.

She, like many of the other Indians, knew that Royappen had been after Chinmah for some time, so when she couldn't find the young woman in her own room, she'd made her way to Royappen's. When she saw the caved-in door, she'd walked straight in. In disbelief at the slaughter before her, she'd let out a blood-curdling scream and the neighbours had come running.

Word of the gruesome double murder spread rapidly across the barracks, just as the Indians were settling in for the night. Sirdar Kasim was sent for, and in the short space of time it took him to reach Royappen's room, a few of his neighbours had already sneaked in and helped themselves to the dead man's rations and belongings.

When Ramsamy couldn't be found, Kasim realised that there was very likely a murderer still on the loose, and he sent a helper up to the main house to call the master.

When Mr Wilkington arrived, his necktie loose and his boots untied, he took in the shocking scene. 'What the bloody hell is going on here now? Are these husband and wife?' he asked, turning his pale face to Kasim.

'No, Master. The man is a bachelor. Her husband is missing.'

'Jesus,' the master said, rubbing a hand over the stubble on his chin. 'Okay, put these bodies in sacks. We can bury them tomorrow. And we'll look for the husband tomorrow, too.' Turning to the Indians gathered at the door, he raised his voice. 'You've had your fun tonight. Get back to your rooms. Now.'

As Wilkington turned to leave, wondering how he was going to explain this latest mess to the Protector, an old Indian woman stepped in front of him, a baby in her arms. 'This is her child, Master. I think she is ill,' she said as she offered the baby up to him.

'This nightmare is never-ending,' Wilkington said. 'What must I do with a coolie child? Can't you keep her?'

'I am just her ayah, Master. I don't have enough to feed my own children, and she is sick,' the woman said, pushing the baby at him again.

'Any family? Relatives?' Wilkington looked around, annoyed, at the gathered Indians who had not obeyed his command to return to their rooms. 'Anyone here able to keep this child?' he said more loudly.

This time, the Indians, who'd been reluctant to go to their rooms in case they missed out on any further drama, suddenly melted into the dark; another mouth to feed wasn't something any of them wanted, and especially not when it was a child whose mother had just died in this terrible way.

Wilkington sighed. 'Okay, give her to me,' he said, taking the bundle awkwardly. It was lighter than he'd expected but then he didn't know what to expect; he'd never held a child this young before.

'Her name is Angel,' the ayah offered, clearly relieved to have been unburdened. 'She is usually a happy baby.'

Wilkington glanced at the infant. Swaddled in a dirty blanket, her brown face was only partially exposed. Her skin was waxy and her eyes sunken in. Her mouth was open slightly, and he could hear her faltering breath.

He would take her back to the house. Maria, who'd once worked as a nurse, would know what to do.

That night, a wind howled through the plantation. It caused the precarious roofs to rattle and the wattle-and-daub houses to sway. Trees were torn out by their roots and flung to the ground.

In the barracks, the occupants viewed this as a sign. They stayed up later than usual, chanting and praying for their own safety. The souls of the dead were restless.

When Andrew had arrived home with the near-dead baby, Maria thought her husband had lost his mind. There'd been no time to argue, though. The baby's heartbeat was barely audible and her breathing was erratic. Maria's instincts as a nurse told her that the mite wouldn't make it through the night if she didn't get some nourishment into her tiny body.

Andrew himself seemed to be in shock. She knew her husband wasn't cut out for this cruel existence, no matter how hard he tried. It was just not in his nature.

Maria poured him a brandy and sent him to bed. Without protest, he climbed the stairs, barely able to put one foot in front of the other. Then, pulling a shawl over her shoulders, Maria went to find Leleti, their African servant, who had retired to her quarters some hours earlier.

Seeing the tiny, still child in her madam's arms, and the concern in her eyes, the young servant quickly put on her shoes and a doek to cover her hair, which had sprung up like a black halo. 'Where is the mother for this child?' she asked, as the two women walked back to the house together.

'Dead.'

In the kitchen, Leleti peeped at the baby. 'Is she going to live, Medem?'

'I don't know,' Maria said, as they both peered down at her wan little face. 'We can give her something to rehydrate her, a bit of salt and a little bit of sugar mixed in boiled water. You hold her while I make it,' she said, handing Angel over.

Maria quickly prepared the solution and found a small medicine dropper in the medicine chest. She showed Leleti how to dribble the solution into the side of the baby's mouth, with her head slightly raised to avoid choking her. Then, leaving Leleti with the baby in a chair in the kitchen, she went upstairs to her own bedroom. Too worried to lie down to sleep, she dozed off in an armchair.

About an hour later, she was awoken by a timid knock on her bedroom door. 'Medem!' Leleti called, softly.

Maria jumped to her feet. 'What's happened?' she asked.

'It is okay. The baby is alive,' Leleti said, gently moving aside the swaddling so Maria could see a tiny fist. She heard a mewling sound and realised that the little girl's eyes were open.

'And I have an idea, Medem,' Leleti continued. 'My cousin, Nomazizi, the one who does the washing – she had a baby, he is about six months now, and she still has lots of milk. She can feed this one too.'

'Good!' Maria said, taking Angel from the servant's arms. 'Hurry, go and get her.'

Leleti returned with another woman who had clearly been hustled out of bed and was trying to keep up with Leleti's quick pace. She had a sleeping baby tied snugly to her back.

On seeing the coolie baby in the white woman's arms, Nomazizi grasped the problem. She sat in the chair offered to her by the madam and gestured for Angel to be put into her arms. Exposing an engorged breast, she rubbed the swollen nipple against Angel's lips. Liquid spurted from the nipple, most of it running down the baby's chin.

Angel paid no attention to the food, but fixed a stare on Nomazizi.

'I think she knows this is not her mother,' Leleti said.

Nomazizi persisted and finally Angel's eyelids flickered and she moved her tongue. She seemed a bit more interested and her hands rolled into little fists. She turned her head on her own, towards Nomazizi's bare breast, and rooted around, making tiny snuffling sounds, searching for the source of the milk.

*

By noon the next day, the master had had a visit from Sirdar Kasim.

'We found the husband, sir. It was Ramsamy, the coolie who never wanted to work.'

'Did he admit to killing them?' Wilkington asked.

Kasim shook his head. 'The men found him hanging from a tree at the edge of the plantation. When I saw the body, it was covered in blood. A lot of blood. And it wasn't his – he had no injuries except a few cuts on his hands. I think we can safely assume that the blood belonged to the two dead coolies, and that he killed them.'

PART V

HOME

To take from this country helpless men and women to a distant land, to assign them there to employers ... and to make them work there under a law which they do not understand and which treats their simplest and most natural attempts to escape ill-treatment as criminal offences – such a system, by whatever name it may be called, must really border on the servile. I strongly hold therefore that the system should be done away with altogether.

– *Proceedings of the Imperial Legislative Council, India*, March 1912

17
Sezela Sugar Estate
November 1909

In the house on the hill, the African servant had shown Vottie where things were kept and what needed to be done. There was the dusting and polishing of the heavy furniture, ensuring that the linen was always clean and fresh, sweeping and washing the floors, and making sure that the windows in every room were always shiny and clear.

On her first day at work, the master had been away and Vottie was alone, able to examine everything at her leisure and take in the luxury of each room. She'd marvelled at the rosewood clock that stood guard in the entrance hall. It no longer worked but it was tall and sturdy and made the entrance seem formal and imposing. Vottie ran her cloth over the glass and admired the clock's face. The circular silver inlay was exquisite, with the numbers etched in black, and filigreed gold in each of the four corners of the square face. Maybe it had been damaged on the ship being carried here from England, she'd thought; it had seemed a shame that it hadn't been restored.

Vottie looked at her reflection in the glass. Sadness seemed to be a part of her face as much as her eyes and nose were. When had this happened? She couldn't recall. She looked older than her twenty years and felt an unwelcome stiffness in her shoulders and neck.

She moved on to dust the furniture in the study. The room, dominated by the teak desk, was tidy and smelled of leather, tobacco and brandy. She liberally spread wax over the desk, then buffed it to a gleam.

Opening the doors to the veranda and inhaling deeply, she drank in the view: the tumble of hills moved with the rippling of sugar-cane plants that stood like flimsy sentries. The ocean below stretched out like an infinite turquoise ribbon, the sky the palest blue dotted with white seabirds. After a time, she turned back into the room, leaving the doors ajar and humming while she wiped the pewter ornaments above the fireplace and plumped up the brocaded cushions on the sofa. With the sound of the crashing waves, she began to hum softly to herself.

She heard a cough behind her and froze.

'Vottie,' said a male voice. The master had returned home.

Vottie turned, feeling her cheeks and ears heat up with unease and embarrassment. It wasn't that she'd been doing anything wrong, but she'd allowed herself to slip into a place where her guard was down. Surrounded by these beautiful things and with the view still lingering in her mind, she'd been peaceful and relishing the moment.

'Excuse me, Master,' she said, bowing her head and attempting to slip out of the room through the space on his right. But he moved quickly, stepping in front of her before she could leave.

Vottie looked up at him, slightly panicked. He must have seen this, as he put both of his hands up in a gesture of surrender and smiled. 'Are you liking it here?'

The question was odd. Vottie didn't know how to respond. Her mind wouldn't throw up an answer so she didn't trust herself to speak. Eventually, she nodded.

Stepping lazily aside and allowing her to leave the room, Rouillard called out behind her, 'Bring me something to eat. I'm starving.'

Making himself comfortable in his leather-covered chair at the big teak desk, Henry poured himself a generous glass of brandy and, sipping it, removed his boots with his free hand and threw them into the far corner, where they landed with a thud. He thought back to his meeting in Durban. Things hadn't gone as well as he'd wished.

The meeting had been between the planters and the Indian Immigration Trust Board, and it seemed that the planters were losing the fight.

They wanted the earth, those damn coolies: better living quarters, education, more wages. Who was going to pay for that? There'd already been some strikes, and now there was talk of stopping indenture altogether. The planters had pointed out that if the empire wanted more sugar, labour was needed to plant, grow, harvest and process it, and the only way forward was to carry on with the indentured coolies.

Making things worse was that that agitator, Gandhi, was gaining a growing following, and his *Indian Opinion* newspaper was even making its way to London, where the politicians were getting nervous.

There was also the vexing issue of the number of deaths on the farms. The coolie Protector, that bloody Tatham, wanted to carry out more frequent inspections of the plantations, as if two visits a year weren't enough.

Shaking these unpleasant thoughts from his head, Henry turned his mind's eye instead to the little beauty, Vottie. Moments earlier, when he'd caught her unawares in his study and had stood in silence, watching her, he'd wondered anew at the strange stirrings she provoked in him.

Her back had been towards him as she'd drawn back the curtains, humming softly, and opened the large doors to the veranda. As his eyes had hungrily followed the outline of her body, he'd wondered, not for the first time, if sending his wife away had been a good idea.

The thought of the last few nights in the town danced in his mind. He remembered the dark room, the smell of cheap perfume and the way that woman's hips had felt beneath his hands as he'd clutched her. How she'd moved – my god, how she'd moved. Money well spent, he mused, trying half-heartedly to recall the woman's face, without success.

Vottie's return interrupted these thoughts. She was carrying a large silver tray set with an elegant tea service, and a platter of sandwiches and a jug of freshly made lemonade that the cook had prepared as soon as she'd heard the master's horse canter up to the house – she was familiar with his appetites. Vottie placed the tray on the far side of the desk.

The master was standing at the open veranda doors, exactly where she'd been standing when he'd arrived back, lost in thought.

'Anything else, Master?'

'That will be all,' he said, and then added, as if it was an afterthought, 'Ah, but I think that you may have to come up to sleep there.' He nodded towards the servants' quarters, which adjoined the house and were accessed through a door at the far end of the scullery.

Vottie bit the inside of her mouth and looked at him enquiringly.

'That native woman is useless. She can't even get up the stairs to wake me in the mornings.'

Although Vottie would have loved nothing more than to escape Sarju, she felt certain he wouldn't agree to her sleeping up here. 'My husband, Master, I must look after him,' she said, looking at her feet.

'Don't be daft,' he retorted. 'He's a grown man. He can look after himself.' He turned away, signalling that the conversation was over.

Vottie found his comment odd – wasn't that exactly what she was going to do for the master: look after him?'

Vottie had never thought that she would be afraid of leaving Sarju, but there was something about the way Master Rouillard looked at her that made her uneasy.

As the days went by, Vottie tried to stay as far away from the master's study as possible. But when he rang the bell, he expected her to respond to it, and she had no choice but to do so.

Today he wanted a towel, as he was going swimming in the sea. Vottie fetched it from the large airing cupboard in the scullery, and when she returned to the study, Rouillard was no longer there.

'Out here!' he called. On the veranda, he was holding a glass of brandy, as usual, and seemed relaxed as he looked out over the magnificent view. The sun was setting and the sky was a dusky pink.

His face was a bit more flushed than usual, Vottie noted, as she quietly placed the folded towel on a chair, and quickly turned to go.

He was quicker.

She felt his hand close firmly around her wrist and he pulled her towards him. Vottie squirmed silently but furiously in his grip. Then, suddenly, he let her go. She staggered backwards, staring at him, wild-eyed.

'Master?'

'That will be all,' he said hoarsely and turned his back on her.

Vottie left immediately on fast feet, her heart and mind racing. She'd seen that look in men's eyes before but never in a white man's. It scared her.

From the safety of the upstairs bedroom, she watched the master make his way down the path that led to the beach. There was no telling what he was capable of, but if experience had taught her anything, it was that any man is capable of anything. She felt her mouth go dry.

She felt unnerved and scared – with Sarju, at least she knew what to expect.

That evening, Vottie went to see Lutchmee. Lutchmee was massaging Seyan, part of his pre-bedtime ritual. Vottie sat on a stool across from her and watched as she dipped her hand into a bowl of coconut oil and greased both her hands, rubbing them until they heated up. She then began rubbing the little boy's back and he stretched out, enjoying her touch. She massaged his legs, kneading in small circles.

'Now that he is walking, he wants to just run everywhere,' she said to Vottie, smiling, never taking her eyes off the child. She moved on to his arms and he lay still as the women chattered, his eyes growing heavy.

By the time Lutchmee was gently rubbing the oil into his scalp, he was sound asleep. She covered him and ushered Vottie outside onto the veranda that ran alongside the front of the barracks, where they both sat.

It was a warm evening and the light drew insects to it. They swatted them away.

'He called me Ma today,' Lutchmee reported, her voice light with happiness.

Vottie squeezed her hand. 'He could not have a better Amma.'

Lutchmee returned the affectionate squeeze, then said, 'Now, tell me, what is bothering you? You did not come here to see me rubbing Seyan, did you?'

Vottie took a deep breath, not knowing how her friend was going to take what she wanted to discuss with her. 'The master, Mr Rouillard ...' She looked uneasily at Lutchmee.

Lutchmee now took both her friend's hands in hers and said, 'Vottie, there is nothing you can tell me that will make me love you any less. My own life has been far from blameless. I will not judge, I promise.'

'Working in the big house means I barely have to put up with Sarju these days, but I am worried I have left one hell to jump into another,' Vottie said, the words tumbling out in a rush. 'Mr Rouillard has been … paying attention to me. He is the master and I can't refuse, and I've been scared. But I was thinking about it today, and I've got an idea … a plan.'

Vottie didn't look up as she spoke – she didn't want to see any expression on her friend's face that would stop her talking. 'I need to … win the master over and get him to see that Sarju is trouble, then I can be rid of that bastard once and for all.'

Hearing Vottie talk about 'winning over' a man, and realising what it would probably mean, reminded Lutchmee of her own past, and her heart went out to her friend. She felt so grateful, once again, that Sappani was not like Sarju.

'I understand, Vottie, I really do,' she said, earnestly. 'Look at me.'

Vottie turned her worried eyes to her friend's.

'I understand,' Lutchmee said again, and nodded. 'I'm just worried that winning over the master will mean that you will, indeed, exchange one bad set of circumstances for another.'

Vottie nodded. 'I've got a plan for that, too,' she said.

On Saturdays, after completing her chores in the master's house, Vottie returned to her own home in the sirdars' quarters. Sarju was always very curious about what went on in the big house and but she didn't want to answer his endless questions about the master and how he lived.

'Be grateful, Vottie, that you were not out in the sun today,' Sarju told her. 'A baby was born, right in the fields. It died right there too.' Vottie was horrified by how matter-of-factly her husband reported this tragedy, but she did, in fact, feel grateful and she was glad that she didn't have to witness such harshness. Those in the fields also had to contend with the terrible heat, and the whips, while she was in the cool house, surrounded by lovely things. For once, maybe Sarju was right.

'Once his wife gets back, are you coming back here?' he asked. 'I need my wife here.'

Vottie shrugged. 'You ask him, see what he says.'

'I will ask him tomorrow,' Sarju said, irritably, knowing that if the master chose to keep Vottie in his house, there was nothing he could do about it. And he comforted himself with the thought that Vottie working in the big house could only enhance his position on the estate.

When he'd finished eating, Sarju went to sit outside the unit while his Vottie tidied their dinner dishes away.

She was still inside when she heard Sarju's voice. 'Where do you think you two are going?' she heard him growl loudly.

Sappani kept his voice low. 'We need to see Vottie.'

Surprised, Vottie went to the door and was concerned that Lutchmee was also there. They'd agreed that it was best for the both of them to keep away from Sarju.

'Get back to your room,' Sarju said. 'You have no right to be here in the sirdars' quarters.'

'I need to show something to Vottie, please,' Lutchmee said, desperately.

'It's okay, Sarju, I'm just here,' Vottie said, placatingly, as she moved towards Sappani and Lutchmee.

Wordlessly, Lutchmee handed her a letter in a pink envelope, and they watched her as she extracted the single sheet and held it under the lantern.

Lutchmee
I am Maria Wilkington, wife of Master Andrew Wilkington of Mount Edgeombe Sugar Estate. I found your address among the belongings of Chinmah Naik.
Chinmah and her husband Ramsamy are both deceased. Their baby daughter, Angel, has survived and is getting stronger every day.

Do you perhaps have any contact details for family? It is a matter of some urgency, as we need to secure the future of the infant.
I look forward to your prompt reply.
Maria Wilkington

Vottie looked up at Lutchmee, her eyes wide in disbelief, her grief immediate and crushing. 'I cannot believe this, Lutchmee,' she said, her voice breaking. 'What has happened?'

'I don't know but Angel cannot be alone in this world now.'

'What is happening, Vottie?' demanded Sarju, who'd been standing nearby, glowering.

'It's Chinmah, the young girl with the baby. She is dead, Sarju,' Vottie said flatly, knowing he would not care.

Sarju stared at her. 'And this is your business?' he asked, his voice like flint.

'Sarju, the baby is still alive. We need to speak to the master about going to fetch her,' Vottie said, sorrow and desperation putting a pleading note into her voice that made her husband smile coldly.

'Why would the master care about the news of filthy pariah?' he sneered. 'Anyway, I am the sirdar here, and I am saying that no one is going anywhere.'

Vottie's tears suddenly stopped and her face changed – the other three could almost see her back straighten in determination. Waving the letter at Sarju, she said, 'I am going back up to the master's house. If you stop me, I will have to tell him, and he will not like that. He is your master too.'

Sarju glared at his wife, his loathing plain, but he knew he was defeated so he turned his attention to the other two. 'You pariahs,' he snapped at Lutchmee and Sappani. 'All you can make is trouble. Get back to your rooms before I go and find my sjambok.'

Up at the house, Vottie, breathless from running all the way, went directly around to the door that led to the master's study. He was sitting outside, smoking his pipe.

Stepping out of the shadows and into the light of the oil lamp, she allowed her skirt to rustle loudly.

'Vottie,' Rouillard said. Several emotions ran across his face in succession: puzzlement, delight, concern. 'What are you doing here? I did not call for anything.'

'I am sorry to bother you, Master, but there is a letter,' Vottie said, between pants for breath, pushing the pink sheet towards Rouillard. 'It was sent to my friend, Lutchmee, who lives in the lines.'

Reaching for his spectacles, Henry read the letter, his expression giving nothing away. Once he'd absorbed its contents, he looked up, studying Vottie, taking in the scoop of her blouse revealing the caramel mounds of her breasts. Her hair was loose, not plaited as she wore it during the day.

Vottie shifted uneasily, still trying to slow down her breathing from her mad dash up the hill.

'Come,' the master said, going into his study and seating himself at the big desk. He opened a drawer and took out a sheet of paper, then wrote across it quickly while Vottie looked on. He folded the paper, placed it in an envelope, and put the envelope in Vottie's hands, along with the original pink letter. 'Permission for you to go in the morning to fetch the child,' he said.

'Thank you, Master,' Vottie said, gratitude and relief bringing tears to her eyes. She clutched the documents to her chest with both hands and looked towards the veranda door, but Rouillard got up and moved closer to her. His gaze felt like a hot iron on her skin.

'Thank you, Master,' she said, again, smiling the most genuine smile she could muster, then turned to leave.

He let her get as far as the door before she felt his weight directly behind her. Pushing her into the wall, he forced her head to the side and pushed his face into hers. His breath reeked of brandy.

When he realised that she wasn't struggling, he turned her gently towards himself. He was smiling. 'There is always a price to pay, you know. Always,' he said.

Vottie pushed her shoulders forward and brushed his hands away from her. She sighed. 'Of course there is. I am not a fool. What is it, your price?'

Her eyes were suddenly glittering with both fear and rage, and Henry was taken aback by her expression and her reaction. He hadn't expected anything like this, and he was dumbstruck, feeling more like a boy than a man.

Seeing his unease and realising that for a precious moment she had the upper hand, Vottie put a hand flat on Rouillard's wide chest and gently pushed him out of her way. Then she walked over to the brandy decanter, poured a small measure of the amber liquid into a glass, and walked back towards Henry, her head held high. She took a sip, then handed it to him, allowing her hand to linger on his for a moment.

He accepted the glass, his curious eyes not leaving her face.

Giving him a last smile, she turned and walked out.

Henry stood where he was, the glass gripped in his hand, struggling to comprehend what had just happened.

Outside, Vottie vomited into the flower bed.

18
Mount Edgecombe Sugar Estate
November 1909

In Nomazizi's room, the African servant was ready to feed, her body now producing milk for two babies. Maria watched her, mesmerised. Nomazizi seemed perfectly comfortable to feed a child who wasn't her own.

Standing in the corner, Maria felt like an intruder but she couldn't stop watching. Angel was drinking steadily now, in big gulps, so much so that she began to choke.

Maria stepped forward but quickly saw that her help wasn't needed: Nomazizi lifted the baby and patted her back gently. Angel burped and began to cry, a sound that filled both women with relief. Nomazizi settled the infant back onto her breast and Angel began suckling again.

Watching Angel, Maria felt overcome with sadness and loss. She thought back to a few nights ago, when she'd sent Leleti to find out exactly what had happened to the baby's parents, and also if anyone knew of any family.

Leleti had reported back within a few hours: 'Both the mother and father are dead, Medem, just like the master said. They say the husband went mad.'

'Did you find out if there are any relatives?'

'No, but I went to their room and there was nothing left there except for these things,' Leleti said, placing a small bundle in Maria's hands. There were a few of Angel's clothes, the parents' indenture certificates, and two letters addressed to Chinmah Naik, care of the estate.

Maria opened the first envelope, which had the return address 'Lutchmee Mottai, c/o Sezela Sugar Estate', and took out the single sheet.

Our dear Chinmah
We were glad to hear from you but we are concerned about your health and Angel's. What is happening there? Is Ramsamy looking after you both? We will try to get permission to leave our plantation and come to visit. Please look after yourself and give Angel a kiss from us until we can see you.
Lutchmee and Sappani

The second letter, with a return address of Vottie Singh at the same farm, was dated only a month ago, in early October.

Dearest Chinmah
I hope this letter finds you and baby Angel in good health. I am now with Lutchmee in Sezela and we want to see you. We are taking the 3 p.m. train into Durban for Diwali. Meet us there if you can.
Vottie

Back in her own house, Maria looked down at the mewling baby. 'You poor thing,' she crooned. If only this baby had been born a different colour, she pondered sadly. But then, as she soothed the baby, walking to and fro in her bedroom, taking in her lush eyelashes, her perfect skin as soft as a kitten's fur, her darling rosebud mouth, a gaping hole in Maria's soul began to close.

Perhaps it would be possible for her to raise this baby as her own, she thought. The little thing was already so at home here, in Maria's bedroom. Leleti had helped her get the cot out of the store shed alongside the house, where Andrew had dumped it after her last miscarriage. Together, the two women had heaved it out into the sunshine. It was dusty but intact.

Maria had then gone through the wooden boxes, searching for the layette she'd collected during her pregnancies. She'd never disposed of it, remaining hopeful that perhaps it would still be used one day for a baby of her own.

She decided that she would talk to Andrew that evening.

Waiting for the right time, Maria pushed her food around on her plate without bringing it to her mouth. Andrew, sitting across from her, had been quiet all evening and she wondered if this evening was the right time to discuss this after all.

'The Protector came today. There's going to be an investigation,' Andrew suddenly said. She looked up, noticing how old and tired he seemed. 'Kasim says that he spoke to the Indians and told them what to say … well, God knows what story he concocted, but I can't see how we can come through this. Two murders and a suicide, and now an orphaned baby. Perhaps it would have been better for the baby to have—'

Maria gasped and put her knife and fork down with a clatter. 'Don't even say such things, Andrew! She's a completely innocent soul.'

Andrew looked stricken – he often forgot what a tragedy his wife had had to go through recently, losing their own baby so late in the pregnancy. Quickly getting up from his chair, he walked around the table and knelt next to her seat, clasping her hands in his. 'I wasn't thinking. Forgive me,' he said.

Maria stroked his head and said, 'I've been thinking … Maybe the baby can be ours …?'

Abruptly, her husband stood up, went back to his place and refilled his wine glass. Not meeting his wife's eyes, he said, 'The harvest has been good but it is still not enough.'

'What does that have to do with us keeping Angel?'

'I'm all out of options, Maria. I can't get any more loans and there's a real possibility that I'm going to have to sell the plantation.'

Maria's eyes widened. 'I didn't realise things were so bad,' she said. 'But the baby, we could—'

Andrew raised his hand and shook his head, stopping her before she could go any further. 'I'm sorry, darling,' he said, as gently as he could.

'We've used our life savings on this venture and now it's time to cut our losses. We can't return to England with another mouth to feed, and a coolie baby at that. She would not belong.'

Later, in her bedroom, Maria sat at her writing desk for a long time, thinking. She thought about the baby that could so easily have been hers. She could already feel the seeds of affection taking root in her heart.

Angel, blissfully unaware of how close she'd come to perishing, and of the dire circumstances she was now in, was fast asleep, her tiny fists raised on either side of her head.

Finally, sighing, Maria took some of her pale-pink stationery out of the desk drawer. Dipping her pen in the ink, she began to write.

Maria was looking at the baby's clothes that Leleti had neatly arranged. Angel was gurgling in the cot and blowing spit bubbles, her little hands grabbing at something only she could see. The light was streaming in the window and her brown eyes were bright and curious.

The doctor had been to examine the baby, and declared her small for her age – which Andrew had finally been able to establish by contacting the Protector and asking him to look at the *Umzinto*'s records. They revealed that the birth of Angel Naik had been difficult. But the doctor now declared the child relatively healthy, given all she'd been through.

Now, Maria looked up as there was a tap at her bedroom door.

'A woman is here,' Leleti announced, knowing that this was going to be hard for the madam.

'Tell her to wait in the kitchen. I'll be down shortly,' Maria said, her voice breaking and betraying her at the end of the sentence.

When Leleti left, Maria stood above the cot and sighed. She'd played out every possible scenario and there wasn't a single one in which Angel could stay with her, and she could raise this bonny little infant as her own.

She lifted Angel onto her right shoulder and let the happy baby grab her blonde hair. She inhaled the scent of her and touched her silky head. 'I'll miss you, little one,' she said, as she buried her face in Angel's hair and wept softly.

When Maria walked into the kitchen with Angel ten minutes later, there was no sign that she'd been crying.

She examined the Indian woman in front of her. Leleti had clearly offered her water and the woman was now seated in a chair, sipping slowly from a tin cup.

'Angel!' the woman cried, jumping up and reaching out to take the baby.

Maria stepped back, clutching Angel closer to herself. 'You're Lutchmee?' she asked.

'No, I'm Vottie. I am also a friend.'

'Yes. I found your letter,' Maria replied. She felt hot and flustered. *I should have asked Andrew to be here*, she berated herself.

'Is Angel better? What happened to her?' Vottie asked, the concern clear in her big brown eyes.

'She's recovering well and she's such a good girl,' Maria said, and Vottie could hear the genuine warmth in the white woman's voice.

'Chinmah was our friend on the ship,' Vottie told Maria. 'We were even there when Angel was born. She is like our own. We will take care of her.'

Leleti had crossed over to the madam and now she slowly eased the baby out of her arms. Maria was silent. She swallowed hard as Leleti placed Angel in Vottie's arms.

'She looks just like her mother,' Vottie said, looking down at the infant and brushing away tears with her free hand. 'Please, if you don't mind, could I see where Chinmah is buried?'

'Of course,' Maria replied. 'Leleti, take Vottie. I'll keep Angel and give her her bottle.'

'It is very sad. Everyone is still talking about it,' Leleti said as they walked down the path that led to Chinmah's grave. Without prompting, Leleti explained the circumstances surrounding Chinmah's death.

Vottie listened, trying to make sense of it as she wiped away her dusty tears. Silently, sorrowfully, fervently, she wished that she and Lutchmee had not let Chinmah return to Ramsamy that day after their Diwali trip to Durban – but at the same time, she knew that, in reality, there had been nothing the two women could have done. If Chinmah hadn't returned, there would simply have been trouble all round, and then probably a fine, at least, and cut rations, and maybe even whippings. Vottie cried even more tears at the powerlessness of herself and her fellow immigrants – they were utterly at the mercy of others in this foreign land so far from home.

Leleti stopped at an empty field that looked like any other, with clumps of weeds and wildflowers in places, and neat mounds in untidy rows. She pointed to three mounds of earth, darker than the soil around them.

By Hindu rites they should have been cremated, but Vottie had come to accept that rituals weren't practical on the plantations. She stood in silence, staring at the mounds – there wasn't even a name or number to denote which was which, so she didn't know which grave contained her friend, which the husband who had abused her, and which her rapist. She herself wasn't going to end up like that, she decided; she wasn't going to be beaten to death by any man, and her remains weren't going to be shovelled over in a weedy field in a strange land.

Vottie recalled the last time she'd seen Chinmah, her painfully thin body, and the fears she'd had about Angel. 'We will take care of your baby,' she whispered into the sky.

The two women walked back to the house in silence.

Maria was standing on the veranda, holding Angel against her chest, waiting for them. Her eyes were red and her face puffy but set in a serious expression.

'She's just been fed. That should hold her until you get back to your plantation. I've packed some things for her,' she said, looking down at the bag at her feet, in which she'd put all the clothes and bedding that had once been intended for her and Andrew's own little babies. In the bag she'd also put the small bundle that Leleti had found in Chinmah's room.

She kissed Angel lightly on her forehead, before putting her gently into Vottie's arms and walking stiffly into the house. She didn't look back.

19
Sezela Sugar Estate
December 1909

'We can start again. A new place, a new beginning.' Sarju's eyes searched hers for a response. 'This baby could be ours, you know, then maybe our own will follow.'

Vottie looked coldly at the man in front of her and attempted to veil her utter resentment. He saw it and bristled under her gaze.

'I'm not ready to be a mother,' Vottie said quietly. She thought about the many times she had paid for the foul-tasting extract made with ground black cohosh mixed with dried and powdered acacia seeds. It brought on her bleeding so that she could be certain that Sarju's seed wouldn't grow inside her.

But this felt different. Angel was in her arms, already flesh, already loved.

More than anything, she wanted to put the hurt behind her. Hatred and sadness were weighing her down, and she felt as if she could hardly keep her head up some days. With Angel in her arms she felt hopeful. The child was like a soothing balm, and while she'd remained asleep for most of the journey, her eyes were wide open now and innocent.

Sarju watched her coolly. 'I am saying that we can keep that baby and it will be ours, Vottie. You and me, its mother and father.'

The sun was setting and Vottie knew that she needed to get back to the master. She also knew that she couldn't bring Angel into the hell she endured with Sarju.

'Chinmah wanted Lutchmee and Sappani to raise her; she told us that herself.' Before Sarju could say anything else, she picked up Angel's things and left the room.

Lutchmee and Sappani were sitting outside their room, waiting, a lantern at their feet.

'Is she okay?' Lutchmee asked, as both women peered at Angel.

'She is perfect,' Vottie said, smiling and putting down the large bag containing all the baby would need for the next few months. 'Mrs Wilkington looked after her well.'

Taking the baby from Vottie's arms, Lutchmee held out Angel for Seyan's inspection. 'This is your new sister,' she said. Looking unimpressed, he nevertheless put his face closer to inspect the tiny arms and face.

Watching the happy little family scene as Sappani and Lutchmee fussed over Angel in the dim light seemed to gnaw at Vottie. This was a picture of everything she did not have …

'Here,' Vottie said, pushing some money into Lutchmee's hand. 'Buy the children what they need for Christmas.'

'Where is this coming from?' Lutchmee asked.

'I don't have to give Sarju any money and the master is generous.'

'Thank you, Vottie,' Lutchmee said, then, lowering her voice, added, 'What happens when his wife comes back?'

'I won't be here then,' Vottie said and turned away, making it clear that the subject was closed.

Seyan yawned – he'd quickly lost interest in the new arrival – and was soon asleep.

Angel sucked on her hands while Sappani heated up the milk to prepare her bottle. Then, cradling her in her arms, Lutchmee fed Angel who stared at her with wide eyes.

'She's a hungry girl,' Sappani said warmly.

Once the child had drunk her fill, Lutchmee changed her and then rocked the baby until her eyes closed.

With both children now asleep, the parents sat out on the veranda, having brewed a pot of tea. This had become their ritual and it was a time they both looked forward to every evening. To have this sort of magic every night was irresistible to them both. When it was that late and quiet, it seemed as if they were the only people in the world. Sitting next to each other in silence was blissful.

Sappani stroked Lutchmee's hair; still slightly damp from her bath earlier, it fell over her shoulders like a heavy black cloth. He caught the scent of coconut and inhaled deeply.

'Are we going to be able to look after Angel, another mouth to feed, Sappani?'

'She is ours now, part of our family,' he said, reaching for her hands and enclosing them in his own.

She nestled her head against him. 'You have given me everything I could have hoped for,' she said softly.

She knew instinctively that now was the time for her to speak out, to tell her truth. Looking straight ahead and pausing only for breath or to hold back her sobs, she told him about her past – her marriage to Vikram, her mother-in-law, the sati she'd escaped.

Sappani listened without interruption

She took a deep breath and told him about her time in Madras and how she had come to the coolie camp. She didn't say it with any shame; it simply rolled out, as if it had been another life or was someone else's story rather than her own.

When she was finished, she sat in silence, her cheeks wet with tears.

Sappani sat absolutely still, staring into the darkness.

Certain that she'd pushed him away forever, Lutchmee made to stand, but Sappani gently pulled her towards him. He buried his face in her hair. She held him and closed her eyes. She'd never felt so connected to anyone in her life, as if they inhaled and exhaled the exact same breath.

When he pulled away, he left her hair wet with his tears. 'We never need to speak of this again,' he said.

Standing, he held out a hand and helped her up, and together they walked inside. There, he kissed her in the centre of her forehead and then inside each of both her open palms.

Sarju had on new trousers that he'd bought with his first sirdar's wages – so much more than the lowly workers got. 'Better for the work of a big man,' he said to Vottie when he showed them off to her.

It had been three weeks since he'd started as sirdar on this estate, and he felt like he was finally coming into his own. Secretly, he'd hoped that he would be an overseer in charge of the line gang that Sappani was in. He wanted to rub his success in that man's face. But he was prepared to be patient.

'Kuppen came to the fields today to tell me that I am overworking the Indians. I had to tell him, it's not your job!'

Vottie listened, sitting on her haunches next to the fire, hoping to get his supper ready quickly so that she could return to the master's house.

'I told him to go back to building that school that he and that pariah care about so much, to leave the real work to me.'

'They are trying to do good, something for the children,' Vottie said, without taking her eyes off the pot.

'Never a good word to stay about your own husband, but every other man is very good,' he spat, then stepped over to where Vottie was crouching and, using his heel, pushed her forward.

She reached out to break her fall and the palm of her right hand pressed into the bright orange embers of the fire. She screamed.

The pain was unbelievable, as if a thousand chillies had been rubbed into the raw flesh of her palm. Scrambling to her feet, cradling her hand, she fled, up the path to the master's house, not bothering to look behind to see if Sarju was chasing her.

In the kitchen of the big house, she felt safe – Sarju would never dare to follow her into the master's house. She slammed the door behind her, letting her tears come freely. She reached for a bowl but her uninjured hand was trembling so badly that the bowl clattered to the floor.

'Vottie, what's going on?' Rouillard, disturbed by first the slamming of the door and then the sound of the breaking bowl, appeared in the kitchen doorway.

Vottie, intent on filling another bowl with cold water in which she could dunk her burning hand, said nothing.

'Vottie!' Henry said, grabbing her by the hand – her burnt hand.

Vottie pulled away.

Seeing the shocked expression on her master's face, she turned her palm towards him. 'He did this to me,' she choked. 'He pushed me into the fire.'

'Who? Who did this?' Henry said, taking in the burnt flesh that was now forming a large blister.

'Sarju. It is always Sarju.'

Rouillard rummaged about in the cupboards, directed by Vottie, until he found a length of bandage, which he used to wrap her injured hand. There had been several complaints from the Indians about the new sirdar, Sarju Singh. This wasn't unusual when there was a change at the top of the ladder, and Rouillard had thought things would settle down once Sarju understood how the plantation was run.

Yesterday, the Indians had approached him while he was in the fields and complained about their wages being docked, and had also shown him fresh sjambok wounds on their legs and backs.

Usually, Rouillard had no issue admonishing a sirdar but this was Vottie's husband, and a small part of him wondered if the overseer was aware of the advances he'd made towards his wife. He pushed that thought aside. 'You are not to go back there, Vottie, not even to cook for him,' he instructed. He led Vottie back to his study and poured them both a brandy. 'This will help with the pain,' he said, as he passed the drink to Vottie.

She swallowed it in one gulp.

'Come and sit here, next to me,' he said, and patted the plush sofa.

Half an hour later, Henry was watching Vottie sleep. She'd had two neat brandies, which had lulled her into drowsiness.

Brushing her hair away from her face, Henry felt a now-familiar tingle of confusion and elation down his spine. This feeling had sprung on him repeatedly since he'd met her. She was getting under his skin in a way that he'd never felt before. It was beyond being attracted to her. She was different.

When she walked into the room to dust or bring his meal, he found himself sitting up straighter, a flush of colour rising to his cheeks and his ears glowing red hot. She didn't even need to say a word.

Yesterday, he'd gone to his bedroom and found her staring out the window, lost in thought. She'd been mesmerised by the ocean, sparkling at the bottom of the cliffs on either side of the house. He loved that view, and had drunk in the sight of her appreciating it as well.

'Like what you see?' he'd asked, his voice soft and soothing.

Vottie had nodded. 'It is beautiful. I love the sea.'

Henry had then joined her at the window, and they'd stood watching the ocean for a while. He'd pointed out to her where his land ended. He'd also pointed out the path that led to the tidal pool that was visible from their elevated view. Some evenings, when he was restless, he would take a servant and wander down to the tidal pool, along the makeshift path weaving through the undergrowth and across the railway line, created by his and his children's tracks. A little stream trickled under a small bridge, and just as you turned the corner, a slice of paradise would be revealed, dotted with boulders, mangroves and umdoni trees. 'You must come down there with me,' he said.

Vottie had turned to face him, her eyes revealing her interest in his invitation – and in the man himself.

'Soon,' she'd said, smiling, confident.

He'd taken both her hands in his, the contrast in their skin colour accentuated by the light streaming in through the windows. His touch had been gentle and Vottie had not seemed afraid.

Now, with her blissfully asleep beside him, he wanted to savour every moment – but then reality intruded, and, with a last glance at the sleeping beauty, he got up and walked over to his desk.

He wrote to his wife, urging her to stay on in England a bit longer. There was much illness on the plantation, he wrote, and he didn't want the children to be at risk. He added that he was travelling a lot, so was not going to be home much over the next few weeks. He hesitated slightly, then signed the letter, 'Your faithful husband, Henry.'

The next morning, when Henry returned from the post office in Durban, where he'd personally seen the letter on its way to his wife, he went to find Sarju. The new sirdar was leaning back on his elbows in the shade of a tree, meditatively chewing on a blade of grass. When the master's horse pulled up in front of him, he scrambled to his feet.

Henry tugged on the reins, pulling the horse to a halt.

'What's the meaning of this, Sarju? I don't pay you to sit around.'

'The coolies are all at work, Master. See for yourself. All is in order. They know who the boss is around here.'

Something about the man rubbed Henry up the wrong way, and he didn't think it was only the feelings he had for his wife. 'There have been complaints,' Henry told the sirdar, relishing the look of irritation that crossed his face.

'Tell me the bastards' names, Master, and I will fix them.'

'No. The Protector is coming to inspect us soon and we must not give him any reason to fine us, you understand? No more beatings, no more punishments, you hear?'

Sarju stared up at the master, mumbling irritably to himself.

Henry grew impatient and flicked his riding crop at Sarju. 'You are not the master here, I am, and you need to learn that. No more punishments, and if I hear one more complaint, you are gone.'

As Henry pulled at the reins, instructing his horse to turn, Sarju stepped forward and gave him a strange look. 'Master, there is also the matter of my wife,' he said.

'What matter is there? She will be busy in my house till Madam returns. I'm not risking her not being able to do her work because of another burn or some other injury you inflict on her, you understand?'

Sarju looked at the ground, furious in defeat. 'Yes, Master,' he mumbled.

'Speak up, coolie bastard.'

'Yes, Master,' Sarju said, a little louder, but still refusing to meet his boss's eyes.

It was fiercely hot and humid that evening. Henry felt stifled in his study, even with the doors open to the veranda. Restlessly, he paced to and fro, occasionally looking at the sofa on which Vottie had slept the previous night. He had dozed in his big chair behind his desk, happy to simply be in the same space as her.

Finally, unable to bear it any more, he summoned her, using the little brass bell on his desk. 'Bring my dinner to the tidal pool,' he ordered her, trying to ignore the strange feeling of bubbles popping in his stomach. 'Something cold. Chicken sandwiches maybe.'

The sun was dipping low on the horizon as he made his way down the hill. He stripped off and sat in the water, which retained some of the relentless heat of the day. It was delicious.

Thinking about his feelings for Vottie, he decided not to fight them any more. Instead, he was just going to wallow in them. He was drawn to her, and for whatever reason – it mattered not – she also seemed drawn to him.

His back was to the clearing, so he heard her approaching before he saw her, and was able to turn and drink her in. The wind teased her hair and her faded cotton dress pressed against her lithe body. She seemed more like a being who'd stepped out of the sea than a creature of the land.

Vottie didn't see him straight away; she was taking in this paradise in front of her. The waves were gently lapping at the shoreline and occasionally larger ones crashed against the red boulders and patches of sandy beach.

Henry called out to her and she walked slowly towards him, placing the wicker basket on the ground. He waded out of the pool to meet her and together, in silence, they stared at the ocean for a few moments. Then he moved towards her slowly, reaching for her hands and pulling her towards him.

Vottie didn't struggle as he slipped off her cotton dress. Henry was gentle with her and she found herself enjoying the look of want on his face. The experience was certainly not like what she was used to with Sarju: although it wasn't pleasurable, it wasn't painful either.

Afterwards, she slipped back into her dress and they sat still together on the sand, watching the stars as they began blinking above the ocean.

Later, once they'd shared the sandwiches and wine Vottie had carried down, Henry carried the empty basket back up to the house, Vottie at his side. Leaving the basket on the desk in his study, he took Vottie's hand and led her upstairs, towards the master bedroom.

Vottie paused on the landing, her hand still in his. 'I can't go into the madam's bedroom, sleep on her bed.' Suddenly the moments they'd shared on the beach seemed far away. This was now more real and illicit. 'I'm married,' she added, in a small voice. 'He is my husband, no matter how much I hate him.'

Henry said, 'You won't have to worry about Sarju. Once that blasted Protector has done his sniffing around and things have died down a bit, he will be gone.'

Vottie looked at Rouillard enquiringly as he interlaced his fingers into hers, unable to let go. He brought her hands to his lips and kissed the back of them.

'What about your wife? She will come home soon. What then?'

'Another worry you do not need to have,' Henry said as he led her across the bedroom threshold.

After Henry was spent for a second time that evening and began to snore, Vottie wriggled out of his arms and stood at the window, watching the moonlight glimmer over the black sea. She thought about his reassurances about her not having to worry about Sarju, or his wife's return, and pondered on how empty they seemed. As captivated as this white man may seem with her right now, she had to wonder how long it would last – how long it would take the master to relegate her once again to being just another coolie, a number, and eventually an unmarked grave whose existence meant nothing to him.

She thought about Chinmah, her girlish giggling on the ship, her adoration of her baby; then her mind went to the anonymous mounds of earth that had been her fate. She thought too about the dancing Jyothi, now no doubt in her own watery grave.

The next evening Henry told her that he would not be back for his dinner, as he was visiting a nearby planter, and Vottie took her chance to see Lutchmee.

It was late, and both the children were asleep while the women sat on the veranda smoking a hookah pipe. They watched the smoke swirl around as the crickets chirped in the nearby bushes.

'I have a plan to get rid of Sarju and free myself of the master, too, but I am going to need your help,' Vottie said. 'I need the Indians to complain about him, in writing, to Protector Tatham. Lots of them must complain.'

'Most of these people can't read or write, you know that,' Lutchmee said.

'I can.'

'What do you need me for, then?' Lutchmee asked.

'They trust you. They will tell you their complaints. Then you can tell them to me, and I'll write them down. I'll find a way to get them to the Protector. I'll think of an excuse to go to Durban and Henry … Mr Rouillard will give me a pass.'

Vottie was right: Lutchmee was well liked in the coolie lines, and she was a welcome face when she went over to talk to anyone who had a story to tell about what Sirdar Sarju had done to them.

Over the next few weeks Lutchmee followed Vottie's instructions, listening carefully to the labourers' grievances, then later relating the details to Vottie, who would write up each complaint. Lutchmee would then take the document back to the complainant, who would sign it with their thumbprint.

The complaints ranged from the merely indignant to the criminally serious. All were true.

A worker called Surga said that when he and some other Indians were sitting in his house and passing time by singing songs, Sirdar Sarju had come in and taken the tabla from him and stamped on it, breaking it into pieces.

Another worker called Bhagoo accused Sarju of locking him up in the chicken run for three days and two nights without food, for the infraction of not going to work because he had a bad stomach.

One Rathinam said that Sarju had forced her to go back to work after three days of confinement, and that her baby had died as a result of being in the heat.

Married couple Pungan and Salamma complained that they were working more than thirteen hours a day but had not been paid and as a result had nothing to eat. Pungan had complained of a pain in his knee and wanted to see the doctor but had received a beating for asking Sirdar Sarju.

Kaulesari, a young widow, tearfully told Lutchmee that her husband, Shivcharan, had hanged himself after he had been whipped into unconsciousness on Sarju's orders.

Sasamah, a married woman, complained that a junior overseer had repeatedly asked her to lie with him and she had refused. She was finally put to work alone, apart from other women, in a cane field. The overseer had trapped her there, stuffing a cloth in her mouth so that she couldn't scream, and raped her. She'd reported this to Sirdar Sarju, who had told her it was none of his business what rice-cookers did in the fields.

20
Sezela Sugar Estate
March 1910

Henry Rouillard looked at the letter on his desk. Since opening the envelope it had come in, he'd developed a throbbing headache. Massaging his temples, he reread it.

It was from Protector Tatham, and stated that the Protector was in receipt of written statements detailing ill treatment of the workers by Sirdar Sarju Singh on Sezela Sugar Estate. The Protector was doubly unhappy, as copies of all the complaints had been sent to Gandhi's newspaper. It was all there in the *Indian Opinion*, on the front page, with Sezela Sugar Estate coming off very badly, and the journalist who'd penned it calling for Henry Rouillard's head and insisting that other planters who were guilty of abusing their workers be dragged to court. The Indian Immigration Trust Board was baying for blood.

Protector Tatham's letter finished curtly, accusing Rouillard of allowing a litany of cruel acts to be committed on his plantation, and swearing to see to it that justice was served.

Rouillard called for a servant and instructed Sirdar Sarju be summoned immediately.

Sarju arrived on a wagon and casually walked up the hill to the master, where he was waiting on the veranda. He smiled and bowed. 'Master, you wanted to see me? Good things, I hope?'

Sarju was actually glad for the opportunity to speak with Rouillard, as he'd not seen his wife in weeks, and he regarded this as a chance to assert his right to Vottie. The master could find another domestic servant.

He noticed that Rouillard was holding a sheaf of papers in one hand and his sjambok in the other.

The first lash was lightning quick and landed partly across Sarju's back as he tried to twist away to avoid it. 'Master, what have I done?' the sirdar cried out in bewilderment, cowering in anticipation of the next blow.

'The Indians, you coolie bastard!' Rouillard shouted, throwing the papers at him. They fluttered down around Sarju, malignant butterflies. 'They have made complaints! It's in the bloody newspaper, and now Protector Tatham is going to instigate an enquiry. You useless coolie! I told you to lay off the workers!'

Sarju was on the floor, on his knees, his palms pressed together. 'Master, they do not want to work. What else could I do?' he whined. 'I told them to keep their mouths shut. I told them that you do not like complaints, Master. It should be them that you are giving lashes to!' He reached out a trembling hand and picked up one of the sheets of paper. 'What are those pariah bastards saying about me?' he muttered, casting an eye over the complaint headed 'Imprisoned and starved' and dated two weeks previously.

Then his breath caught in his throat. The hand that had penned this complaint: he knew it as well as he knew his own. Vottie!

The white-hot agony of betrayal shot through him and he raised his stricken eyes to his master. 'This …' he began. 'You … My wife …'

His face instantly suffused with fury, Rouillard roared, 'This has nothing to do with your wife, you bloody coolie!' as he delivered two more lashes across Sarju's legs, and a third one that caught him across the face, opening up a cut on his cheek.

Sarju lay trembling and crying in a widening pool of blood.

'Get up,' the master said in disgust. 'And get off my plantation. I never want to see you again.'

Sarju struggled to his feet and stared at Henry, ignoring the blood that was running down his face. Henry whistled and a massive African man appeared, carrying a sjambok.

With nothing to lose, Sarju blurted, 'Where is my wife? She must come too.'

'Vottie will stay here,' Rouillard said. 'She is needed in the house. But you – you have to go.'

Sarju reached out to grab Rouillard in desperation, leaving his bloody prints on the master's trousers. Rouillard flicked his sjambok, catching Sarju on his outstretched arm. 'Get off,' he spat and he raised the sjambok in the air again.

Sarju pleaded. 'Please, Master, let me see Vottie.'

Rouillard raised the sjambok threateningly again, and Sarju knew he had lost.

The huge African turned the little Indian man around and pointed him down the hill towards the wagon he'd come in. 'Hamba,' he said, his voice a growl, poking Sarju hard in his back with the handle of his sjambok.

As Sarju stumbled down the hill, the African turned back to his master, awaiting instructions.

'Make it look like an accident,' Henry said, and the big man nodded his understanding.

Rouillard watched the wagon leave and felt a frisson of triumph. Tomorrow he would go and see Protector Tatham and explain that there had been, alas, one more tragic death on the estate – but that it had been, by a happy coincidence, the demise of the overseer who had caused so many problems for everyone. He would assure Tatham that the labour problems on the estate would be resolved, and that now that the rogue sirdar was dead, he would have no more complaints from Sezela.

Anyway, Rouillard thought, walking into his study, towards the sideboard where he kept his brandy, he'd never met a public official who couldn't be persuaded to look the other way. John Tatham may think he was different, that he didn't have a price. But he did. They all did.

Before she knocked on the study door, Vottie put the tray holding the master's evening meal down on the floor and loosened her plait, allowing her hair to cascade over her shoulders. Rouillard loved burying his face in her hair.

Henry was reading the newspaper when she entered and didn't look up. She placed the tray on the desk and, without invitation, went and sat down on the sofa. He closed his paper, then looked over at her, smiling, his eyes flickering with desire.

Her body was becoming so familiar that he could feel her firm breasts beneath his fingers without even touching her. But what he felt for Vottie was about more than just physical gratification. She was such a tonic for him. She demanded nothing, and he loved it when he looked into her eyes and saw what he thought was worship and adoration for him.

When he lay his head on her lap in the evenings, the world melted away. In the study, on the plush leather sofa, she would caress his face and listen keenly while he spoke about what his day had been like. Sometimes she would offer a remark but mostly she was just present, and exuded care and affection for him. It was a world where only the two of them existed.

Vottie, despite herself, felt safe with the master. Although she understood full well that she'd merely exchanged the slavery she'd experienced with Sarju for servitude of a different sort with Rouillard, and she knew that he too was a monster, just another kind, at least, with Henry she was fairly sure that there would be no beatings.

During the day, they went back to their roles. She would make the master's breakfast and take the tray to his study. She wouldn't so much as look at him, and that made their affair all the more exciting and tantalising for Henry, but also filled him with a longing that he'd never known before.

And in the mornings, when Vottie appeared from his bedroom, she no longer let the stares of the servants upset her. Things were going exactly as she'd planned.

The money Henry gave her, as cash gifts on top of her wages for working in the house, went to good use. With it, she'd paid the thirteen workers who'd brought grievances against her husband. And she was putting the rest of it away in savings, for a day would come when Angel would need to go to school. Vottie thought often of Mrs Naidoo and her educated daughter, and she wanted the same for the little girl who'd had such a difficult start to life.

And, finally, when she went into Durban to do shopping, Vottie always made sure she came back with the ingredients for her special remedy so that her womb would remain uninhabited.

21
Sezela Sugar Estate
April 1910

Elise was due back any day now. She'd written to her husband to tell him that the long break in a civilised country, in the company of civilised people, had entirely restored her to her old self, and that she was ready to come home. The children, too, were longing for their father, and apparently Ella had never stopped complaining about missing her friends.

The servants were deep-cleaning, dusting, scrubbing and washing everything in the big house in preparation for the return of the madam – but, much more to the point, they were curious about what would happen to Vottie.

Henry was uneasy, and as the day of his wife's return grew closer, he became ever more unpredictable in his moods, sometimes even shouting at Vottie for real or imagined transgressions.

Now, he was reading the *Indian Opinion* and occasionally sipping the coffee that Vottie had brought him. Breaking with her usual routine, she hadn't left the study, and was standing on the other side of the big desk, watching Henry.

'I knew this Satyagraha nonsense wouldn't last,' he said, banging the newspaper with the back of one hand. 'You can't feed your family if you're in prison. It goes to show that a coolie in a suit is still a coolie. Gandhi thinks he can put a stop to the annual tax and let the Indians roam freely, as if this is their country.' He let out a grunt of indignation.

'People are saying that indenture will end,' Vottie offered.

'Claptrap!' Henry roared at her, his ears turning red. 'How will the Indians cope without a master? You think they can think for themselves? Really, Vottie, sometimes I forget how silly you are …'

'I'm not as silly as you think,' Vottie said, her voice icy enough to catch Henry's attention. He looked up. 'Do you remember all those complaints? It was me. I wrote them.'

Henry, who'd never seen Vottie write before, and hadn't even thought to ask her if she was capable of it, stared at her in confusion.

'And now you are going to do a bit of writing for me,' Vottie said, suddenly businesslike. With that, she went to the chest of drawers in the corner of the study, took out the key that was hidden underneath it, and opened the top drawer. She removed a single sheet of paper, then walked back across the room and placed it in front of Henry. It was a Certificate of Freedom, given to Indians once their term of indenture was served.

Rouillard laughed uneasily. 'You still have four years to serve, Vottie,' he said. 'And if you're not careful, you're going to start all over again at five, and on someone else's estate.'

Vottie ignored him. 'I have written to the Protector and the letter is safe for now, but I have given instructions for it to be delivered if …' Vottie motioned with her head at the blank certificate.

Rouillard stared at her, astonished. It was slowly dawning on him that he'd seriously underestimated this woman. 'What does the letter say?' he asked, swallowing hard.

'Everything, Henry,' Vottie replied, stressing the name 'Henry' with unmistaken sarcasm – she'd never called him by his first name before, and the sound of it in her mouth sent an unexpected chill down Rouillard's spine. 'It tells the Protector where the bodies are buried, where Sarju's is—'

'Vottie, you're not thinking clearly. This is ridiculous!' he spluttered, standing up.

'There is also a letter to Madam,' Vottie said, and watched in some satisfaction as Rouillard slumped back down into his seat. 'That letter, too, is safe, unless you decide not to sign this certificate and give me my freedom. I don't think you want that, do you?'

Rouillard, beginning to fully realise the extent of the checkmate, glared at Vottie. 'You're a bitch,' he said. 'A useless coolie bitch.'

Vottie's expression remained unchanged. 'Well, all you have to do is sign here, and you will never see this useless coolie bitch again.'

Rouillard picked up his pen.

22
Sezela Sugar Estate
July 1910

'This is good work here, bhai,' Sappani said to Kuppen as they admired the freshly varnished benches they'd made for the new school.

Sappani was pleased to have had both wisdom and woodwork lessons from Kuppen in the last few months. The greying retiree had had to return to his position as head sirdar after Sarju had been found dead in a far cane field, the victim of the fatally venomous bite of a black mamba.

'Education, that is what we must give the children. Then, when we die, we have no worries: they can take care of themselves.' Sappani had heard these words from Kuppen many times before but, with the school almost ready, it made an education for the children real.

Sappani pressed his hands together and bowed as he would have done to his own father, then watched Kuppen walking slowly to his home, where his wife, Devi, stood on the front step, holding a lantern above her head, peering out for him.

As Sappani approached his own home, he could hear his family's laughter before he could see them. Sappani felt closer to the dream now. He was working in the mill and had learnt how to operate the cane-crushing machine.

The family's vegetable garden was thriving; Sappani was meticulous about tending it, adding compost from the stables when he could lay his hands on some, and making several trips to the dam, each day if necessary, to ensure that the plants had all the water they needed.

Seyan was thriving every bit as well as the plants themselves, while little Angel was a delightful, sunny toddler, taking her first tentative steps.

They all looked up as Sappani approached. Lutchmee was sitting heavily on the dark-wood chair he'd made for her, with her initials engraved into it in loops and curls. Angel was on her lap. Seyan was attempting to catch insects.

'You're home,' Lutchmee said, happily, shifting the toddler onto her hip and cupping her very pregnant belly while trying to heave herself into a standing position.

Sappani moved quickly to help her up, and together the family went inside to get the evening meal ready.

Lutchmee had become a regular at the market bazaar in Durban town, where she sold her homegrown produce to mostly white ladies. In fact, so popular were the Mottais' delicious fruit and vegetables, and so successful was Lutchmee at selling them, that she now paid a few women to help her in the market, as she found the days long and tiring as the pregnancy developed.

Lutchmee was known not only for her fresh wares – green beans that snapped with firmness, plump orange carrots, and pumpkins and squashes in varying shapes and colours – but also for her ease with English, and the fact that she always settled on a fair price. As was the case with so many of the Indian women's names, the white ladies struggled to pronounce Lutchmee's, and thoughtlessly called her and others 'Coolie Mary'.

The white madams were picky but Lutchmee had a few customers who sought her out without fail. She put aside the best produce for them and remembered their names. She even went as far as making a fuss of their bonneted babies as they sat up in their prams, giving them a mango to hold or a fresh strawberry.

The women sought Lutchmee's advice on various ways to prepare vegetables – aside from the ubiquitous boiling for which the whites were so well known, of course – and as their faith in her recipes grew, so Lutchmee began buying spices from Mrs Naidoo and selling those alongside her fresh produce.

The extra money Lutchmee's business brought in made it possible for the growing family to eat well, their evening meals often containing fatty mutton and fresh fish. They even saved a little every month.

This Saturday, it was early afternoon and all her produce had been sold. She tucked the money into the folds of her petticoat and took the tram into the centre of town.

Her first stop was the bakery. Lutchmee stared at the cakes, while flies buzzed drowsily above them. She chose one with pink icing – Angel loved sweet things and this would be perfect.

Mrs Naidoo's shop was next; she needed to replenish her stock of spices and see if there was any news.

The bell above the door tinkled merrily as she walked in.

'I have been waiting to see you!' Mrs Naidoo hugged her and pointed, as usual, to one of the upturned crates. 'Sit, sit.' She offered Lutchmee a glass of water, then repeated her order for spices to the barefoot African boy with the bright eyes. He scampered off, reciting, 'Cardamom, star anise, garam masala, mirchi …'

The two women chatted, with Mrs Naidoo as usual flitting off mid-sentence once or twice to serve customers.

Finally, when the shop was empty, Mrs Naidoo pulled a sealed envelope out from under the counter. 'This is for you,' she said.

Lutchmee recognised Vottie's neat writing on the envelope.

Lutchmee hadn't heard from her friend in months, since she'd slipped away one night. Vottie hadn't told Lutchmee any of her plans. 'It's better that way, safer for you,' she'd said. But she'd reassured Lutchmee that she had arranged everything so that she would be safe, and would have enough money to start a new life on her own. 'I will write to you when I can, care of Mrs Naidoo,' had been her final promise.

The next day, a Sunday, the family decided to spend the afternoon at the beach. Seyan skipped in front of them, while Angel dawdled behind, picking wild flowers and clutching them tightly in her sweaty little hands.

'Those are pretty. Who are they for?' Lutchmee asked.

'Chinmah Mummy,' the little girl replied – one of the few phrases in her small but ever-growing vocabulary.

First, the four of them made their way to the coolie cemetery over the rise. Even though Chinmah wasn't buried there, this is where they came to remember her. One day, when she could understand, Lutchmee would tell Angel all she knew about her mother.

The flowers lovingly laid under a tree, the little family crossed the railway line and walked down to the beach. Above them, on the hill, the big house looked forlorn and desolate. The rich curtains were gone and the green lawn was overrun with weeds and wild flowers. Although the Rouillards had tried to keep it quiet, the servants knew everything, and the news had spread shortly after the madam had returned: she had found out – nobody knew how – that the master had been sleeping with one of the coolies, and all hell had broken loose.

With no reason to stay, Elise Rouillard had turned tail at once, arranging almost overnight to have the entire house packed up and shipped back to England, and taking not only the children but Ella too. It turned out that the money that had paid for the plantation had been hers, given to her by her wealthy family when she married. Elise had left instructions for the house and farm to be sold immediately.

Nobody had seen Henry Rouillard leave, and it was assumed he'd crept away in the middle of the night. There were rumours that he'd returned to France.

While the workers had some trepidation about who would own the farm next, the Indian lawyer Mahatma Gandhi had been making huge strides in drawing worldwide attention to not only the unacceptable conditions on the estates, but also the humiliating prejudice suffered by him and his fellow Indians in their adopted country. The rumours that indenture would be ended once and for all were steadily growing.

Once on the beach, Lutchmee settled herself with her feet extended into a shallow pool, easing her swollen ankles. The children splashed into the shallow water, fully clothed. Sappani lowered himself onto the sand next to Lutchmee. He neatly rolled up the bottoms of his trousers and unbuttoned a few buttons of his shirt.

'You look very handsome,' Lutchmee said teasingly.

He leant over and rubbed the protruding bump beneath her dress. 'Right now, I have everything I need.'

Lutchmee inhaled deeply and let the warmth of the sun and the refreshing coolness of the sea lapping at her feet fill her to the very brim of happiness. 'Please read me the letter from Vottie,' she said, pulling it from a pocket in her dress and handing it to her husband.

My dear Lutchmee

I am sorry that it has taken me this long to write but I had to be sure that I could give you good news. I am fine and I have found work in the Transvaal. Although there are no sugar-cane fields here, conditions for immigrant Indians are not good. I have met some women who are resisting the rules and working for change, and I have joined them to do what I can.

I hope that you and Sappani will stay on in South Africa. After all we have endured, it seems only right that our children get to reap some of the rewards.

I miss you. I have written my address below, so that you can tell me what is happening in your life. One day soon I hope we will be able to see each other again.

Your kapal karahi

Glossary

Aap khubsoorat hain: you are beautiful
Aap-ka naam kya hai: what is your name?
Aboot: about
Aiyoo: phrase used to show disbelief
Agarbatti: incense
Akka: sister
Aloo gobi: curry cooked with potato and cauliflower
Amma: mother
Apna khayal rakhna: take care
Arkati: recruiter paid to sign up Indians to indenture; also known as kanjani
Arre ram: Oh God
Atchadhai: 'sacred rice'; rice mixed with turmeric, scattered on a wedding couple
Ayah: nursemaid; grandmother
Babalaas: hangover
Bahan: sister
Bairn: baby
Beedi: rolled cigarette
Behinchod: sisterfucker
Bheti: daughter; term of affection for young girl
Bhagavad Gita: Hindu scripture
Bhai: brother
Bhajan: spiritual song

Bharatanatyam: Indian classical dance
Blootered: drunk
Boondi: fried snack made from chickpea flour
Bottu: dot worn on forehead of married women
Brahmin: highest caste, traditionally priests, teachers and physicians
Braw: beautiful
Burfi: milk-based dessert
Cannae: can't
Chai: tea
Chai wallah: tea seller
Challo: let's go
Chappals: leather sandals
Chapati: flatbread
Chellam: my dear
Chowk: open-air market
Chutia: idiot
Chut marike: imbecile
Cohosh: flowering perennial plant
Daaru: homemade alcohol
Dhaba: stainless-steel tin that holds spices
Dhanyavad: thank you
Dhoti: piece of cloth worn around the waist
Dholak: drum
Dinnae: don't
Diwali: Festival of Light
Diya: clay lamp
Dom: Indian of low caste, working as a cremator of the dead; 'untouchable'
Dreich: dreary
Dunderheid: idiot
Eejit: idiot
Enakku pasi: I am hungry
En anpe: my darling
Erse: arse

Funeral ghat: place dedicated to cremation rituals
Gaandu: offspring of an ass
Ganja: marijuana
Gulab jamun: sweet made of deep-fried dough coated in syrup
Hamba: go
Haraami: forbidden/unclean; bastard
Haud yer wheesht: shut up
Hawan: ritual fire
Heid: head
Hijra: transgender; third gender (neither male nor female)
Hingy: ill
Hoor: whore
I dinnae ken: I don't know
It's a sair fecht for hauf a loaf: it's a lot of work for not much return
Jahaji: 'ship friends'
Jalebi: popular sweet snack
Jeera: cumin
Jharu: broom
Jhimkis: earrings
Kanchipuram: region in Tamil Nadu
Kallu: palm wine
Kapal karahi: boat friend
Karahi: pot similar to a wok but with steeper sides
Kathak: classical dance
Kena punda: arsehole
Khassas and bandannas: printed cotton cloth
Khoodhi: pussy (vagina)
Khurta: tunic-like top
Kumkum: mixture of turmeric and lime used for religious occasions
Kushti: wrestling
Ladoo: sweet made with flour and syrup
Lascar: Indian seaman
Lassi: flavoured milkshake

Lassie: girl
Lavvy: lavatory
Lota: round water pot, usually brass
Lungi: type of sarong worn by men
Maadher chod: motherfucker
Madhiya vanakkam: good afternoon
Mair: more
Mamiyar: mother-in-law
Mandap: temporary covered structured used for weddings
Mangulsutra: necklace worn by bride
Methi: fenugreek
Miga nandri: thank you so much
Mika alakana: very beautiful
Mirchi: hot; sometimes used to refer to small red chillies
Mithai: desserts made to celebrate Diwali
Moksha: enlightenment/release
Moollamaari: stupid person, without standards
Muharram: Muslim festival marking the start of reflection
Muttaa koodhi: stupid cunt
Naimittika: rituals
Nandri: thank you
Nelengu: cleansing ceremony for bride
Nimbu pani: sweet lemon-lime water
Nowt: nobody, nothing
Odissi: ancient classical dance
Om shreem maha Lakshmiyei namaha: my salutations to the great Lakshmi
Paan: adult snack made with sweet masala and tobacco
Pagal: crazy (usually said playfully)
Pallu: hem of a sari
Pandit: man with specialised knowledge in any field of Hinduism
Pariah: southern Indian of low caste, working as labourer or servant; 'untouchable'
Pish: piss

Poli: biscuit filled with fried coconut
Pottu: a red powder that is applied to the bride's hair parting as a symbol of marriage
Pox: venereal disease, usually syphilis
Pugla: crazy person
Puja: Hindu prayer, ritually performed
Pumped: fucked
Rangoli: artform of patterns on floor
Roaster: person making a fool of themselves
Saag bhaji: curry made with spinach and potatoes
Saala kutta: bloody dog
Saari: I'm sorry
Sadhu: holy man
Sahib: master
Sambar: spicy stew
Sarangi: stringed instrument
Sati: Hindu custom in which a widow is burnt on her husband's funeral pyre
Satyagraha: policy of passive political resistance advocated by Gandhi against British rule
Scran: food
Scunnert: fed up
Sepoy: Indian soldier
Sirdar: overseer/manager
Sjambok: heavy leather whip
Skelp: slap or smack
Sukra hai: thank God
Tabla: Indian drum
Tadger: penis
Tattie: potato
Thaali: 'sacred thread'; yellow string that represents the marriage of a woman
Thatuvani munda: prostitute
Thawa: griddle or pan

Thunee: card game
Tiffin: metal lunch box that holds curry
Valayal: bracelet, usually made from gold
Veda: religious teachings
Wallah: vendor
Walloper: dick
Wind blaws lang and sairly: inclement weather
Wummin: women, woman
Yaar: yes
Yethava: bastard

Acknowledgements

This book would not be in your hands without the good people at Penguin Random House South Africa. Thank you for helping me to realise a dream.

To my editor, Tracey Hawthorne, who just got me and what I was trying to do in writing this novel: you have no idea what your optimism, straight talk and editing genius mean to me. Every writer should have an editor like you in their corner: invested and enthusiastic!

This endeavour would not have been possible without the research that I had to undertake. Thank you to the University of KwaZulu-Natal, Special Collections, Gandhi-Luthuli Documentation Centre: you have preserved the heritage of millions and, in doing that, kept our legacy alive.

To the writing groups – especially Roddy Phillips and fellow writers in Bourne to Write. Thank you for accepting me and always being free with your praise and feedback when I just needed to believe this was possible. You not only cleared a space for me but encouraged me and forced me to produce the next instalment, giving me the impetus I needed.

To my family, friends and neighbours and ex-students in the UK and South Africa. I am humbled and grateful for your faith in me, and thank you for being relentless with your questions about the novel, encouraging me to get it out there and promising to buy a copy!

To my friends at Ratton School – especially everyone in the English Department. Thank you for the motivation and the interest you've shown in my novel. I have only awe for all teachers – doing all you do to keep stories alive – every day.

Teachers really do shape the future and I am forever indebted to the late Mr JK Naidoo and Mrs Rennie Behari. My English teachers in South Africa, who saw something in me as a girl and used their magic to tease it out. The only way I know how to repay the debt is to keep doing the work you started with me – to share our love of literature with others even if they are reluctant …

To my childhood friend, Nadine Pillay, who was not with us long enough. Not only did you introduce me to so many great books, but you also showed me love and true friendship. I will carry you with me – always.

To Marlin Webster, there cannot be a truer (or more critical) friend and I love you for it. Not only did you understand this dream but you helped me to bring this to fruition, by being unyielding until I got there. Thank you Ian Fenton for your boundless optimism, you are truly the best of humanity. Thiru Pillay and Donavan Dirks, my friends who are always so happy for me – so much so that I feel happy all over again.

To Kershnee Thambu and Dhereshni Moodley, my Beastly Besties. You have always just let me be me. I appreciate you both for the harsh truths, the hysterical laughter and being constant through all the highs and lows.

To my lifetime family: Doris Mottai, Mumzy, your tenacity and work ethic have got me to this place. 'I fell and got up' – how many times have you used yourself as an example to encourage me to keep going? You started me on this road with the stories of your childhood and growing up in Nottingham Road. Be proud, knowing that your wilful youngest daughter did sometimes listen and took your advice to heart.

My sisters, Heather Moyce, Nichola Pather and Joslyn Bianchi, you have been my fierce protectors and supported me beyond my own memories. I am thankful to be your 'Shevy'. The physical distance between us doesn't matter a jot. I know I am loved, always have been by you three. Much like the women in this novel, you inspire me and our bond knows no limits.

Sherazade, Zahirah, Aneeqa, Tariq, Leah, Japheth, Riyaadh, Nadia, and the grandbabies, Skyler and Jayden. I am blessed to be called your 'Mamma'. Take our family onwards.

To Kesh Byroo, my husband of twenty-five years (yikes!). Thank you for keeping the show on the road during my sabbatical, when I wrote this novel. You believed in me from the outset and you were a source of encouragement and a shoulder for me to wipe my snotty nose on when I was really tired and frustrated because I was failing to reach my word count or didn't know how to resolve an issue in the novel.

Thank you for offering unsolicited advice recurrently. With you by my side there could be no other outcome – this novel was going to get out there.

I so appreciate you creating the space (at the bottom of the garden) where I do more napping, reading and daydreaming than writing. I still maintain this is all a part of my creative process. Tess, Izzy and I love hanging out in my 'writer's cabin'. Thank you for also giving in when I insisted that a second 'writing/Covid pup' was essential as she would help my creative process.

To Khevane Byroo and Taegan Byroo, my darling sons: I almost combust withpride as you become the men that this world needs. Young men (who drive me to distraction) but also value hard work and dedication, constantly trying to better themselves. Being holed away while writing this novel meant that I did not always give you the time and attention you needed. Thank you for your understanding and support – it means so much to me. I love the way you believe in me, even when I am doubtful myself. Being your mother is a privilege and I do appreciate how much you accept me – warts and all.

This novel is your legacy, one that I hope will stretch into the generations to come. I know it will be in good hands. I love you both endlessly and (I hasten to add) equally.

Lastly – when I started my research I did not expect that I would be plagued by the stories and people that I encountered in the documents I sifted through. I made a connection with real people, people who were often just reduced to an indenture number and I could not get away from that. I never met them and they certainly never knew me. The women, specifically, got under my skin. I saw you – the women of indenture – and while I cannot thank you in person, I hope that my telling of your stories goes some way to show my gratitude for your daring and resolve.